He's Making A List

PAUL BULLIMORE

ACKNOWLEDGMENTS

After I completed my first book I said that there would never be another, but one day on a treadmill a lurking idea erupted. For that I would like to thank the little girl from across the road, who happens to share some characteristics with the main character of this book. I will let anyone who knows her decide which ones.

Once more I have to thank my wonderful wife and children for their patience whilst I was writing this book. Much of it was written during strange times and I hope that the times in which it is read are kinder.

Characters in works of fiction come from experience and observation. I have been lucky enough to meet a lot of wonderful people along my particular journey and I hope that none of you mind if I took a little part of you and put it on a page somewhere.

CHAPTER 1

Saturday 19th December, Evening

Droplets of water dripped slowly down Wendy's cheeks, passing through the false beard that had been so carefully gummed to her chin that afternoon before finally settling on the red coat that was doing its best to keep her warm. Around her head snowflakes swirled in the wind, just visible in the darkness of the covering trees and the wall that surrounded the house, and it was those same snowflakes that Wendy hoped were responsible for the water that made her face cold and wet, because if that wasn't the case then she must be crying. The heavy object in her hand was like a deadweight, swaying gently besides her red trousers and black riding boots, her arm seemingly numb and useless by her side. Her eyes blinked rapidly as she tried to force herself forwards one more time, to take the final steps that would allow her to bring the day, and her suffering, to its conclusion.

The wave of fatigue from moments before was back again, surely the result of the large quantity of wine that she had drunk that day and the physical efforts that she had taken in preparing for her quest. There were other feelings around now though, ones that she hadn't experienced for a long time, and despite their destabilising effects she welcomed them like the long-lost friends that they were. She had stopped performing in operatic shows following her break up with Gavin over thirty years before but she would never forget how she had felt just before she used to take the stage. The time when the technical work of practice and perfection would come up against the anxiety and nerves that a public performance always brought out in her, the moment where her movement and voice would be pitted against the expectations of three hundred and fifty anonymous spectators, the detail of their faces hidden by the shadows of the stage lights behind them. That feeling was called fear, a feeling that caused sweat to line her clothes, that caused her stomach to gurgle and growl and that heightened the sensitivity of her eyesight and hearing. It was the same fear that she felt now, made worse by the wine and her aching limbs, and it was this that kept her fixed to the spot, unable to move forward and take the next steps that she had planned. It would come though, she knew, it always did. She would breathe deliberately through pursed lips and the music for the opening number would build in her head. Her arms would free up first with her shoulders rolling and her fingers stretching in time with the music. Her abdomen would then relax and finally her legs would tremble as her hips swayed gently from side to side. Just at the right moment all of these movements would align and her brain would click into place as she took the first, decisive step forward. It was always the same. For the moment she breathed deeply, but the music was not there.

Wendy filled the silence reflecting on the incredible week where she had received the unexpected, yet flattering, contact from her old friend, Sharon. She had shown Wendy how she had wasted so many years moping around, a victim of the actions of others, when all of the time she should have been acting herself and taking things in her own hands. From that moment Wendy had changed, day by day and step by step, and it was these changes that had put her there that night, drunkenly disguised as Father Christmas and ready to carry out the most horrendous of crimes possible. On the other side of the wall was the person that had been responsible for ruining her life and tonight it was payback time.

The steady beat of a bass built in her head as the accompaniment of strings joined in. Her shoulders started to slowly roll as an unseen chorus started singing about Another Opening, Another Show. All other thoughts disappeared as Wendy raised a gloved hand in order to move the branches out of the way before taking a steady, determined step forwards towards her destiny.

CHAPTER 2

Sunday 13th December, Afternoon

There were many variables that could impact the quality of writing on a flipchart. Stability of the chart itself was pretty random, but could be improved to some degree by adjusting the settings on the legs. Height of heels was a choice, and bust size was just something you were forced to accept and live with. The marker pens themselves though were the tools of the trade. You could either pay attention to the detail or you could accept mediocrity, and given the choice between detail and mediocrity Wendy would never falter.

The first clue is in the name. With a flipchart, or as it used to be known a paperboard, you are writing on some form of paper. Whiteboard markers just don't work the same, giving you about six letters maximum before the paper starts drying out the tip, leaving you with nothing but a fading mess. So many places never learned though, leaving their visiting presenters to struggle on by with whiteboard markers due to nothing but a lack of knowledge and preparation. Next it was crucial to have the correct nib size. Wendy had once been presented with a nib so thick that it had been impossible to fit words of more than ten letters on a sixty five centimetre chart. Admittedly she didn't often need words that long, but you had to be prepared for all eventualities. Other markers had nibs so fine that people further away than the front row had no idea as to what had actually been written. Any trainer worth their salt knew that the wisdom that they left on that paperboard was the most important part of any session, the spontaneous nuggets of experience that were pulled out of them as an unplanned reaction to the ebb and flow of the group. Finally, there was the variety of colours, a distinguishing factor that allowed for highlighting of particular words, but where the red pen was often taken up by angry people with nothing but a point to prove. The psychologists all agreed that red was an aggressive colour for a reason, because it was, and to avoid encouraging people to rage there were no red pens in Wendy's own selection, with violet, orange and other fruity colours being preferred for contrast against the dull blues, blacks and greens.

The markers were there in front of her, each one tested that afternoon and neatly packed into their leather case. Powerpoint presentations had replaced acetates, just as acetates had replaced chalkboards, but that was a story that Wendy didn't want to tell. All that she knew was that her ability to write on the flipchart was the skill that ensured her success, and when it came to that it wasn't Wendy's style to leave anything to chance.

Next to the markers were the post-its, another item that required loving care and attention. The top post-it was almost always curled up, drying out the glue and making it more likely to drift to the floor. Crawling around on the floor searching for lost post-its was to be avoided at all costs, a further consequence of high heels and a large bust. A bit of pruning and an elastic band worked wonders though, and the three sizes of notes in multiple colours were themselves stacked neatly together and placed snugly besides the markers. Completing her kit were rolls of assorted tape, clips, pins and blutack. The other side of the case contained a collection of games and exercises, there for the times when Wendy might need to stray from the main agenda in order to raise the energy level of the group, calm it down or just to fill in any spare time that circumstances might throw at her. In short, she had everything a girl needed in order to run a week of training.

The leather case was now packed and Wendy rounded the bed and placed it tidily inside the matching suitcase. Her bedroom was neat and practical with a handful of small tables around the room providing space for trinkets and make up whilst three large sliding doors kept her clothes out of sight. It was the middle of a bright, Sunday afternoon in late December and the sun shone through the large windows, lighting up the pale, pastel colours that she preferred. She moved to the bed's end where her clothes for the week were neatly laid out, taking advantage of the purity of the daylight in order to check them over. She would never forget the time in Preston where a red cardigan and orange blouse, that had looked so great together under electric lighting the night before, had turned into a crashing, kaleidoscopic disaster. She chuckled out loud as she carried out the final checks, her normal pre session routine now almost complete. The constant threat of food stains meant that she needed at least two of everything, plus a jacket or cardigan that could be used as a cover of last resort. She gave a small nod, certain that she was now all colour coordinated and stain resistant and ready for another week away in the classroom.

***

Steam rose from her cup of tea, defying the cold

outside, and she placed it on the small coffee table before sitting down in her favourite armchair. The living room was similar to her bedroom with light, neutral shades all around and a sprinkling of furniture that spoke more of neat efficiency than luxury. She leaned forward, taking her agenda and class list in her hand.

PERSONAL DEVELOPMENT FOR LEADERS

It was a bit like 'gardening for gnomes' or 'yoga for elephants' as she was certain that the eight people due to attend would never find a use within their desperately empty worlds for any of their newly developed skills. Her days of running programmes for young, eager management trainees were long behind her and Wendy now inhabited a different world, one of local authority funded courses where the words 'young' and 'eager' had long been forgotten. She looked again at the programme, the rustle of the pages a welcome distraction from the silence of the quiet afternoon, taking in one by one the list of subjects that she would yet again be going through. The people who would be participating didn't need any of the management speak and fancy ideas that were planned, simply learning how to live again would be enough. Leading had always been just an extension of living properly, a fact that even evaded the best. The people on the list were fortunate though, because Wendy had no shortage of things to share with them, her real lessons of life being a perfect accompaniment to the subjects that were planned. If they invested in her as much as she would invest in them then anything was possible, and there might even be one or two of them who she could really help out after all. Or not. Her eyes closed and she started running one last time through her ideas for the week.

Wendy had often wondered if everyone talked to themselves in their heads with their own voice. She was convinced that it sounded like her anyway, though the lack of any real noise made her uncertain. To be fair, she wasn't even sure now how she actually sounded in any case, as every time she had heard recordings of herself she was always taken aback by the high pitched, snooty sounds that seemed to be coming from her mouth. She'd once tried to imagine her thoughts with different voices but soon gave up as it became too difficult, with the unnatural effort getting in the way of the actual thinking. In any case there was certainly no replacement for real conversation. She gave a knowing smile as she tidied up the papers before placing them in a leather document holder which was then itself slipped into the suitcase which was waiting faithfully by the door, her ritual now complete. The sun was making its last movements downwards leaving vivid red streaks of newly arrived cloud shining out in the darkening sky. With a heavy sigh Wendy got up from her chair, walked over to close the curtains and put on the light before finally going into the kitchen. From the inside of her fridge a bottle of Graves was calling out to her, all chilled to perfection and promising the rich taste of the Sauvignon grape. The week to come would no doubt offer nothing but over cooled Chardonnay, with some New World vineyard owner happy to tell you which grape had been used but nothing about the earth where it had grown or the place where it had been bottled. It was too easy for them, like everything else these days. Perhaps a glass would be in order after all, but just the one.

One final tour of the house took her a few more minutes and finally Wendy sat down in the second armchair, a glass in her hand and her feet tucked under her thighs, before for the first time that day she spoke.

"Musico, play some musicals."

Drum rolls and a trumpet fanfare rang out and a flush of warmth came over her.

"Musico, stop!" The command was almost shouted.

She crossed the room quickly, opened her laptop and expertly moved around the offending files. It was a simple error really, Gilbert and Sullivan needed to be classed as operetta and not musicals. With everything once more as it should be, she sat down again and repeated her initial command.

A female voice sang of impossible love, joined by a male voice as together they told how tonight would be the night. That was better, West Side Story. She closed her eyes as the music wrapped warmly around her, taking her back to another time and place.

CHAPTER 3

Sunday 13th December, Evening

Visitors to the house, and there hadn't been many in recent years, would remember it as being the storeroom. It was full of rubbish she would say before quickly moving them along. Only Wendy knew what was really inside.

The instant that the switch was flicked her eyes struggled to adapt as a series of bright spotlights attached to the ceiling sparked into life. Gone was the soft lighting of the rest of the house, as too were the delicate pastel colours and discrete furniture. In front of her the wall had been painted black, though not much of the base colour was still visible beneath the many things attached to it. The remaining walls were plain, broken by just one solitary window, itself covered by a black screen that prevented the room from ever being disturbed by anything that may be happening outside. The only pieces of furniture were to be found in the centre of the room, where a plastic topped table with metal legs was accompanied by a single plastic chair, two lonely visitors in a room made for one. On the floor was a dark plastic sheet, placed there years before to protect the carpet whilst the walls had been painted but never removed since. Yes, it was a storeroom, but little that was stored there was physical.

Wendy slumped into the chair, its creaking sound accompanied by the clank of a full glass and an almost empty bottle. The six standard glasses of wine that fit into a bottle was a stupid limit, being just enough to tempt you in to opening another bottle that you knew that you shouldn't. She leaned back and sighed, her eyes finally adjusting to the lighting as she began to focus on the display in front of her.

"Musico, random music." It was the sound of her voice again.

She leaned forward, her eyes moving around the wall as the glass in her hand swayed from side to side.

A smile flashed over her lips for the briefest of moments as she heard Billy Bragg singing his only number one single. A love song, of sorts, stolen from the Beatles and then returned with a nasal cockney accent. Everything was possible.

She called it her crime room. The once black wall was an evidence board inspired by the cop shows that she sometimes found herself watching in lonely hotel rooms on her travels. Who did it? It was filled with photos and notes, copies of documents and neatly pinned pieces of coloured string, all linking the suspects and their movements to the most terrible crime. She drained her glass and tried in vain to get another drop out of the now empty bottle, then finally accepted that she'd just have to face it all again sober. There were nine suspects before her, well ten really as two of them came as an inseparable pair, and amongst them was the person who had done it. Their details were spread out over the wall in front of her, and all she needed to do, all that she had needed to do for the years that she had been working on it, was to identify who that guilty person was. What had been their crime? One of them had ruined her life, knocking her off her righteous path and leaving her in a desperate struggle with the unhappiness that she felt every single day. Many would say, 'so what? We all have struggles love,' but that didn't cut it with Wendy. It was her life and it wasn't supposed to have turned out how it had, and there in front of her on the wall were the main suspects.

It was Wendy herself who took pride of place in the centre of the wall, with a series of photographs that started with an early Sunday School anniversary and ended with her fiftieth birthday so called celebrations. She knew the face so well in all of its versions, the one that looked back at her every morning and every night as she brushed her teeth. The bosom got bigger and the smile got weaker as the fashions came and went, but it was unmistakeably her. Somewhere along the way though the damage had been done.

Also in the middle, but above the rest, were the pair that couldn't be separated, her parents. Her breathing deepened as she searched again for the memories that just had to be hidden away somewhere. She'd never read any books on the subject, they were far too long, but she'd googled it and read a few articles. Freud and the others all said the same, that it was always the parents' fault. It was their neglect, their abuse, their lack of everything that caused the underlying damage that would wait until the most fragile periods before rearing its ugly head. She breathed again, gently now, as her tiring eyes tried even harder to focus on the photo. She had spent hours and hours combing over every memory she ever had of Roger and Pam, but had found nothing at all. The articles said it wouldn't be that easy, that the dark memories were locked away in hidden compartments in the brain just waiting for the wrong moment to be released. The wine glass was still empty as she tried again to focus on the faces staring back at her. No, it couldn't be them. They had never given her anything but love, a 1970s love maybe, but love none the less. They had protected her, they had guided her, the most important things that parents could do. A half smile raised the corners of her mouth as she saw her dress in the Sunday School photo. There could have been no bigger abuse than those clothes she was wearing, as out of context as it was. Of course, in the 70s everyone dressed like that, it was even coming back into fashion now. What wonderful memories she had, there in her head not hidden or locked away. Holidays every year together, songs sung along to the radio and day trips to all corners of the country. Everything told her it couldn't have been them but Freud would surely disagree, and until she could be certain of the matter they had to stay there, taking pride of place on her wall amongst the others.

CHAPTER 4

Monday 14th December, Morning

People often offered to help ladies put their cases on the shelf, but Wendy was used to doing hers on her own. The last-minute high heel dash from the station entrance to the platform had forced her into taking large gulps of air, but her breathing had eventually become more normal as she had found a place and sat down. It was not a bad result at all, a window seat on her own in a carriage that appeared quite respectable, there being no lingering smells coming from hot food, no bags or feet on any seats and just one or two conversations being shouted out to unseen partners far away. When she'd been young anyone talking to themselves would have been considered a nutter, but nowadays everyone did it. Marco was probably going to be looking for a new job if the contract wasn't signed that day and Ellie wasn't planning on a second date with the guy from the dating app, and a problem shared in that carriage was a problem divided in eight. The rest of her co-voyagers seemed oblivious to the news though, with a combination of headphones and social networks reducing Marco and Ellie's news to a background interference that could be easily ignored.

Now that she was seated she felt her stomach settle quickly. She had never known what caused it, always putting it down to either some strange sort of middle-aged nerves or more likely the wine. No matter how close to her departure she made her last trip to the bathroom the following casual walk to her destination nearly always ended up as a last-minute dash. She'd always assumed that lots of other people must suffer in the same way but looking around at the people in the carriage, as she often did, she never saw anyone else who was as clearly relieved to be sitting down comfortably as she was. Perhaps she didn't let it show either.

Harshton was about fifty miles away from Webledon, just too far to make travelling home each night worthwhile. A couple of smaller stations that Beeching had somehow missed would slow the journey down just enough to give it a leisurely, rustic feel. She looked out through the window beside her, all dirty from the dried-out splashes of the recent rain, happy that she was still able to make out the rolling countryside as it drew its first warmth from the slowly rising sun. Here they were too far south to have known the dark satanic mills, and mine shafts had been few and far between, but in the valleys it was still possible to make out the smaller towns now completely reliant on their farmers and their weekly markets. Each one had its own monument to the past, a derelict old engineering works or an abandoned town hospital, their own personal reminders of better days gone by. She had known them all in different times, in happier times when she had worked in them developing groups of eager graduates in preparation for careers that had all ended too soon, just like her own. A smile settled on her lips, one with no warmth behind it but one that allowed her to carry on staring without fear of having her sentimental thoughts discovered. Rocking gently to the rhythm of the train she continued to look around, Wendy had no need for headphones or something to read to keep her occupied, just her eyes to take in the sights of the surrounding countryside. A beautiful sunshine and the green, green grass of the rolling valleys, all wrapped around a story of neglect and decay.

***

The short trip from the train station to the Grand Hotel took Wendy through streets filled with opticians, sausage rolls and whitewashed windows and peeling nameboards, her heels clicking on the paving stones like a slow, steady typewriter, accompanied by the rhythmic rattle and roll of the wheels on her suitcase. The hotel lived up to its Grand name in both stature and in size, being one of the handful of buildings that still gave Harshton a reminder of the better days gone by. The Edwardian façade would have looked much better if it had been cleaned during the previous twenty years, but despite the dirt it still stood out like a shining beacon amongst the bland Sixties buildings all around it. The roll of the suitcase disappeared and the heels slowed as she took the five steps up to the double doors, past where once upon a time a top hatted footman would have stood, and made her way inside.

Five minutes of questions at reception later and the sound of heels and suitcase wheels were muffled by a newly laid but inexpensive deep blue carpet. The Brunel room was on the first floor of the hotel, its windows looking out over the hotel kitchen. As ever Wendy's first job was to locate the emergency exits and the toilets, one that she knew for certain would be needed and the other that she hoped would not. With well-rehearsed ease her coat was taken off, her leather cases removed from her suitcase and there she stood, shoulders back and head shaking, mistress of her destiny and ready to go.

"Well this won't do at all."

Nobody heard her, and nobody saw. The room was at least twice as big as she'd need for eight people and someone had set it out like a bloody classroom. She glided around, moving tables out of the way and placing the chairs into some sort of tribal semicircle at the front of the room. The two flipcharts were manoeuvred into more advantageous positions and her computer was placed on a small side table and connected to the projector. The handouts were neatly placed to one side and the lady bringing the coffee and biscuits was welcomed with a warm smile and a quick 'good morning'. All that was needed then was a quick trip to the toilet before the final act, the ceremonial changing of the marker pens.

The hotel markers were quickly moved out of the way as Wendy lovingly took out her own set, each one being double checked by marking a quick line in the top corner of the flipcharts. Her look was detailed and serious, scanning the room in search of any fault that she might have missed. There were none and she breathed out a half-hearted sigh of relief as a glance at the clock showed that she had again timed things to perfection before the arrival of her guests.

"Fuck me. Is this Alcoholics Anonymous, love? I'm looking for the development class, me."

CHAPTER 5

Monday 14th December, Morning

A fraction of a second was all that was needed for the scowl to turn into a radiant smile.

"Well it looks like you've found it then. Hi, I'm Wendy, welcome."

She had him at mid-forties with hair that was requiring less attention as each year passed. Black trousers and white shirt, with some sort of tee-shirt underneath and all topped off by a well-worn leather jacket. Wendy stifled a snigger as she wondered what he had done with his blazer, though to be fair to him he could probably still fit in it, which made him either sporty or undernourished.

"Just me and you then is it, Wendy Welcome?"

He gave his own version of a smile, but there was no underlying sense of menace. He was fifteen minutes early and dressed for school, he should be no trouble at all.

"No, there should be some others. There are drinks and some biscuits at the back, make yourself at home."

With uncertain steps her visitor made his way towards the refreshments. He hadn't offered a name but then the twenty first century wasn't well known for its politeness. She swallowed hard as she played with the chairs one more time, happy that her first encounter was over.

"The name's Brian, by the way."

She took the firmly offered hand as she joined him by the drinks. Swearing and dunking Custard Creams, the man had everything.

The sound of voices from behind them announced that others were starting to arrive and a cool dribble of sweat ran slowly down Wendy's spine as she turned towards the noise. A young couple, though obviously not a couple in that sense, had the door blocked like a cork. They were like chalk and cheese and both late twenties, and between them were confirmation that the organisers would let anyone come along these days. The male was just normal, put him on any bus in town and you would almost certainly not even notice him. The female? There wasn't time to take half of it in and the pressure of the other people trying to get in fortunately unblocked the door, giving Wendy less challenging things to look at.

"There's drinks and stuff here, everyone. Come and get stuck in." Brian's voice boomed out across the room in a sign that he might actually come in handy after all.

Wendy hoped that nobody would be too upset when they realised that all of the Custard Creams had gone already.

Her movement became more rigid as she almost marched along to the music building in her head. Kiss me Kate had been one of her first musicals, and the rousing opening number as the on stage cast prepared for the opening night always reminded her of the nervous thrill that she still felt on the first day. It was time again, another opening to another show. Her heartbeat became louder, to her at least, and her breathing became deeper as she sensed it was time. Her shoulders pushed back in anticipation of her first announcement to the whole group.

"Oh, excuse me, are you Wendy, the one in charge?"

Once again, her scowl transformed into a smile as she span round. The voice had been deep but clearly feminine, from the local area but without the edges. Late forties and oh so neatly dressed, with the cut of everything from hair to shoe leather impeccable. Twenty years earlier she would have been a right looker.

"Yes, that's me, how can I help?"

Her assailant leaned forwards, her words barely whispered.

"Listen, I'm Maria, Maria Stephens, and look, to be honest I've done all of this stuff a hundred times already. I'm a company director, you must have heard of some of my companies. Stephens Services, Stephens Security, Alpha Decorators? I really just need to not be here this week because I've got so many other things that I need to get done." The words continued, but Wendy had stopped listening.

"So, which of these companies needs your direction at the moment?"

The question was dry, as was Wendy's look, and Maria Stephens got it straight away. Everyone was there for a reason and everyone would stay until the end of the week. The look on the company director's face was worth a couple of hundred words at least as she moved uncertainly towards the others, and free once more Wendy started to work again on her breathing. It had been too many years to count since her first session and she had always believed that things would get easier. Her stomach told her that they didn't. Right then, shoulders back, tits out, lights, camera, action.

She turned and smiled, looking towards the lighting box at the back of the theatre just as she'd been taught. In the absence of an actual lighting box to focus on a picture of Brunel would have to do. That smile, perfected over many nights in hotel rooms, took its shape and she was ready to start.

HE'S MAKING A LIST

"Yes, you bastards! Yes, yes, yes!"

It wasn't her voice and she looked around urgently, identifying the source as a scruffily dressed man clutching at a Rich Tea.

"Fuck you lot of losers, I'm out of here."

"Calm down mate, what's up?" Brian asked the question that Wendy was thinking.

"I got the job. Stevie boy here got the fucking job! They want me to start tomorrow, team leader for the bike distributors. Yes!" He clenched his fist and punched the air in front of him. "No need to waste my time with you losers on this shitty course, I'm off."

Stevie boy pushed his way through the others, heading towards the door with an assortment of fist pumps and fucks. Not the start that she'd planned for, or wanted, but that was life. Now they were seven.

***

"Fuck sake Dorothy, I bet you don't buy many lottery tickets." Brian was just a despicable human being, but not even he could prevent Wendy's smile arriving on demand.

"Come on now Brian, we're not here to make judgements on each other. Dot has a past, just like the rest of us, and this is just time for us all to introduce ourselves."

Dot gave a half smile as she shuffled back into her seat. She was as quiet as a mouse and dressed in clothes that Wendy's mum might have worn. Brian did have a point mind. She'd spent over thirty years with Harpers Bikes, lasting until the last racer had sort of rolled off the line. Her Payroll job had been replaced by wages going directly into peoples' bank accounts, then cash collection and allocation had been outsourced to India, followed by Travel and Living processing going to Romania. Accounts payable had been replaced by electronic invoicing, and the lack of projects meant that project financing had no longer been needed. Dot had a story like hundreds of others.

"You don't mind us calling you Dot, do you? Good. Right then, who's next?"

She looked around the assembled faces and chose the one that had spent most of the morning looking firmly at the floor. The introductions were very important for Wendy. Yes, they would all learn a bit about each other, but Wendy would learn much more about them and how she could use them during the week. She would decide who she could use as a stooge when she wanted to ask questions, and who she would need to keep quiet. Brian was already on the latter list just as Dot was on the list of people who'd need encouragement. They were all there for a reason and it was Wendy's job to make sure they all made the most of their opportunity.

"How about you, Desmond?"

***

It had already been fifteen minutes but seemed much longer. Nodding her head and keeping the smile fixed were becoming painful, just as the comments that Brian kept muttering under his breath were becoming annoying. Desmond was a stutterer, and a ginger one at that. Fortunately, he'd found that being a whiz with figures didn't require him to speak much, but unfortunately he'd found himself another victim of austerity and seemingly stuck on the scrapheap at thirty five years old. On the bright side, at this rate it was possible that they would get to the lunch break without her having to actually do any work, and she nodded again as he explained the end of his time at the transport department, whilst dearly hoping that this was the last episode he had to tell. Post-its, that's what she would need later, an ideal tool for loudmouths like Brian, stutterers like Desmond and shy old ladies like Dot. Providing that Brian knew how to, making them write down their ideas would give them all a level playing field.

The young female from earlier was apparently called Flash, though Wendy didn't dare to ask if the name was real or made up. Despite having more than an hour to get used to her appearance, Wendy still found the sight before her uncomfortable. Flash's eyes were beautiful, a blue that was even clearer than Wendy's. They moved slowly around the room as she spoke, flicking every now again into an intense stare as they appeared to lock onto some invisible thing that they had been searching for. Her earrings were sophisticated, if more numerous than Wendy was used to seeing, and even the nose rings and studs on her upper lip were tasteful. It was the tattoos that did it, making Wendy so uneasy as she looked in front of her. Despite the room not being the warmest the girl was wearing just a low-cut tee-shirt, showing the brightly coloured swirls of some pagan pattern that started at the top of her chest and went right to the top of her neck, just beneath her chin. Had Wendy been able to focus she would have probably found the detail magnificent but she just couldn't manage to look at the girl with the necessary level of concentration. Each arm was also adorned with coloured ink, as were the ankles that were just visible beneath a long skirt. Why anyone would ever want to advertise themselves in such a way, Wendy didn't know, and wasn't particularly interested in finding out.

"What, like Flash Gordon." Brian was his normal, understanding self.

"No, just Flash, Bri." The blue eyes shone defiantly. "And it is my real name, so don't go thinking otherwise." Her local accent was rich and her tone combative.

"And so how did you end up here?" Wendy intervened, trying to keep Brian out of the discussion and hoping to keep the agenda on track after Desmond the stutterer had blown them off course.

Flash took a breath and her eyes shone again around the room, almost daring the others to interrupt her.

"I'm like the rest of you, I've had a bit of bad luck and I'm looking for a chance to have another go at things." Six heads nodded along in agreement. "I'm only thirty and I worked as a social care officer, for the council."

"Bloody do gooder were you, helping all of the spongers." Flash took a step forward but Brian showed no sign of backing down. Wendy stood; a jest that was enough to tell Flash to just carry on.

"Spongers to you perhaps, and listening to you it doesn't surprise me that you think like that. For me every one of them was a person who needed help, help that they couldn't get from anywhere else. Old people, young people, people with mental health problems and each one needing more support than their family or the people around them were capable of giving." There was real passion in her voice and the blue eyes became even more intense as she continued. "And then the banking crash came and the Tories decided that the poor and helpless should pay for it." Brian sniggered as the rest of the group remained silent. "So I'm here hoping to learn new skills, while my old charges are struggling by on their own." She sat down, her speech in the end nowhere near as flamboyant as the decorations on her body.

"Okay then, let's have a quick break, and then we can start getting stuck into the interesting stuff."

The race for the best biscuits had already begun.

CHAPTER 6

Monday 14th December, Late Morning

Wendy selected a bright orange marker from the neatly lined collection in front of her and approached the flipchart as closely as her assets would allow. The letters were well shaped, evenly spaced and would have stood up to any straightness test that they could have been subjected to.

GROUNDRULES

She had often wondered if it should be one word or two, but keeping it as a single chain of letters avoided an extra space and allowed her to fit in the eleven letters without having to worry about over running. Nobody had ever questioned her on the subject anyway.

"Okay, so let's start off with some basic rules, to get an agreement on the way that we are going to interact with each other this week."

From around the room there was at least one 'tut' and a definite sharp exhaling of breath.

"You've used these before, surely, to make sure that meetings and things like that pass without problems?"

The additional phrase only rewarded her with a selection of blank faces.

"Come on Maria, you must have an example, something we can agree on to make our brief time together even more productive than it already promises to be?" If you don't get any answers from the group ask someone directly, preferably making sure that it isn't a ginger stutterer.

Wendy smiled, eyes large and inviting an answer.

"Well I'm sure you've got a good list already prepared Wendy, why don't you just write them up on the board and let us get on with the fun stuff?"

The reply was so dripping in sarcasm you could almost drink it. Or was it irony? Either way, it wasn't the answer Wendy had been hoping for.

"Me giving out rules makes me a dictator, Maria, and I'm not here for that. The idea is that we all work together this week, with me being here simply to help things go smoothly. Setting the groundrules is all about us agreeing together what we're going to do. Come on we'll do it differently. I'll give you all two post-its each and you can write one proposed rule per note. Here you are, take five minutes to write down the rules that you think we should use. I know you've done this before, you're just being shy with me." A Wendy wink showed them all that she was being light hearted.

She distributed the post-its and sat on the desk looking them up and down as they wrote.

"Right then, who's going first?"

***

It had been twenty minutes since they had started, and it wasn't going as smoothly as it should.

"But of course some ideas are stupid. Have you seen some of the shit that people spout out on the internet?" It was difficult to tell if Brian was a deliberate provocateur or

HE'S MAKING A LIST

just stupid.

"Well sometimes you have to look behind the words Brian and sense the meaning of the phrase." Brian looked towards her with big puppy dog eyes. "I'm sure that what Jack means is that we should listen to all ideas, because we never know when we might be positively surprised. That doesn't mean that we can say stupid things, it means that we should look for the good parts in what people say. Anyway Brian, let's have one of your rules."

Brian passed forward a bright orange square of paper. Reading the rules out herself had avoided the need to sit through five minutes of Desmond stuttering and Wendy read this one out slowly, trying desperately to prevent a look of surprise from taking over her face.

"Only the strongest will survive." She stared momentarily at Brian before quickly moving her look to the rest of the group.

"Well, we did just say that no ideas were stupid, so I suppose we need to build on this one a little bit?" It was Flash who spoke, her look as philosophical as someone with so many tattoos could have.

Sensing that someone else was trying to take the lead Brian butted in quickly.

"It's the first law of the jungle isn't it, though? If you want to get by, you have to be strong. You don't see any weak lions, do you."

"So how should we apply this one amongst ourselves for this week of training? Do you really mean the strongest, or could the clever and the quick and the adaptable survive too?" Wendy had many years of practice. The best way to fool an idiot was to ask them a question.

Brian gave her the look of a fool and she turned to write on the board.

"Let's say that I will write 'Everyone should participate to the best of their strengths', and that can mean any strength. Is that okay?" Of course, it was. "And now you, Maria?"

"Well, would you believe it, my two are already on the board." Maria's smile was sensational.

It was accompanied by her crumpling her two pieces of green paper in her hands and dropping them onto the floor. Wendy silently acknowledged the challenge and moved on.

"Okay, so that wasn't too difficult, was it? Here are our groundrules for the rest of the week, all agreed between us and ready to help us perform more efficiently. If ever we see people not following them, feel free to remind them." Stepping away from the board the rules were clear to see.

1. No smartphones – concentrate!!
2. Think before speaking
3. Ask questions, and respect the questions of others
4. Listen with an open mind
5. All ideas should be considered
6. Everyone should participate to the best of their strengths

Wendy carefully detached the piece of paper from the board and started to tape it to the wall where it would remain in view for the rest of the week.

"But that's the whole problem nowadays isn't it." Brian was a talker, that was for sure. "We lock ourselves in our little bubbles here, with groundrules and stuff to keep us all safe, and then bam! We're out in the real bastard world where there's no one to look after us and protect us, and the rules that the people out there play by aren't the same as our own. Just another fucking way to make us all softer and easier to pick off." Brian's comment was half muttered, half spoken, and didn't sound like it required an answer or any discussion.

He was probably right too, the world was a different place, but these rules were all about making life in Wendy's safe little bubble go as smoothly as possible. Wendy gave a 'yes, you're probably right, but we're doing it this way anyway' smile and then pushed her hands into a small prayer like shape in front of her chest.

"Well that's the morning finished, so let's have some lunch before we get stuck into the really interesting stuff. The food is in the small room next door and we'll start again at one thirty?" Her bright, breezy tones cleared out any doubt that was left in the room and the first morning was over.

CHAPTER 7

1979

He stood there before her, nervous and sweating like a gunfighter in a spaghetti western. He was still beautiful though, the school uniform that everyone was forced to wear in order to make them all look the same simply served to make beautiful people like Stuart stick out even more. Wendy looked into his eyes, willing him to put them both out of their misery by spitting out whatever it was that he wanted to say. She didn't have long to wait.

"I don't want to go out with you anymore."

She carried on staring, her eyes blinking rapidly and her lips pulled together. Her stomach tightened so much that she couldn't breathe and her hand clasped around the end of the tie that was sticking out below her jumper. Whilst everyone else took part in a competition to have the largest Windsor knot possible, Stuart and Wendy had thin knots that left the tie long, it was the thing that linked them together. Her mind was working overtime as it tried to process the nine words that it had just heard.

"I'm going out with Kate instead."

With his two statements delivered he gave a flick of his wonderful hair, turned and set off towards the other side of the field, dribbling his football as he went. Wendy could see them now, the group of girls in the background who were looking in her direction and giggling. Kate must be one of them, though who she was Wendy had no idea. Still unable to move she stood there silent, concentrating on the muscles around her mouth as she fought back the tears. Stuart had been the first person outside of her family that she could ever remember meeting, one day long ago as they had played together in the park. He'd been her boyfriend for over five years now, for as long as it had been normal to have a relationship with a person of the opposite sex, and he'd dumped her and it wasn't even the end of term. Just two sentences and off he'd run, him and his football going off into the sunset to kiss a girl called Kate.

"Are you sure you don't want to talk about it?"

She asked the question to nobody, in a vain attempt to give herself courage. The tears were still in danger of bursting out from her overworked eyes and her cheek muscles risked freezing and leaving her with a permanent grimace. Through the whirl of people running around her she could see that Stuart had arrived at the group of girls and had put his foot on top of his ball. One of them, with a hideous tie knot that filled the whole of the V in her jumper, had placed her hands around his back and was about to kiss him. Wendy felt dizzy.

"But don't decide straight away, you can come back if you change your mind."

Her mumbled words tailed off as she looked again and saw the two of them snogging away on their own, the other girls now moving away to give them some privacy. Wendy forced herself to look away, finding that focussing on the rugby posts made her feel better. She breathed deeply now, from her diaphragm, just as her old trombone teacher had taught her. It had been a short-lived experiment but at that moment she found it comforting and effective. With each breath the threat of tears reduced and her face muscles gradually retook control. She would have more than enough time for tears that night.

"Wendy. There you are, I've been looking all over for you. Has he done it then?"

Wendy turned to see Susan coming rapidly to a halt behind her, all freckles and toothy grin. She was a typical farmers daughter, nice but forever cursed by red cheeks and the smell of cow shit.

"Done what, Susan?"

"Dumped you. He was telling everyone this morning that he was going to do it. He's a fool if you ask me, I think you're lovely."

Wendy hadn't been planning on asking Susan, but found herself once again fighting back tears as the other girl stood before her, both of them making hesitant movements around one another whilst being careful not to touch. It appeared that she had been the last to find out.

"Do you want to come and join us?" Susan indicated a group of girls huddled together around the cricket square. "Fiona's just telling us what Martin Edwards tried to do to her last night, and it's just horrendous." The last words were screeched in mock horror.

Susan's way with words had given Wendy renewed stability. She wiped her damp eyes as she gave an approving nod and the two girls started to walk slowly across the grass.

"And this afternoon we've got music and we can sing that new song again. Have you managed to learn all of the words yet?"

Susan talked energetically as she walked in front whilst Wendy followed behind, glad for the privacy, glad for the opportunity to move and glad that Susan had come to her aid. Unseen behind her Stuart had been put down by Kate and was dribbling the ball as a large group of other boys tried to get it off him. They would never succeed.

"Yes, I learned them at the weekend. It's a great song, isn't it?"

Wendy talked with an enthusiasm that she didn't feel. She was strong though and with the help of music and double English she would survive the afternoon, before she would finally creep home and cry her heart out.

CHAPTER 8

Monday 14th December, Early Afternoon

The statement 'Lunch Included' was never a guarantee, even in somewhere as nice as the Grand Hotel. It ensured that everyone would stay together, as the type of people who ended up on one of these sessions were rarely in the position to turn down a free lunch, but the budget ensured that the only certainty was uncertainty. As she had feared it had been a typical village hall christening but without the beer, with a depressing collection of mini pizza and quiche. In addition she had, as usual on the first day, been forced to lead the conversation, taking her place in their little circle like an aged aunt joining in with the Okey Cokey, as the first attempts at social cohesion were attempted. Now she looked at her watch, it was one forty, and she slowly and deliberately turned to the list of groundrules, took a marker and then wrote on the paper whilst speaking at the same time.

"7. Respect the timing – if we start on time, we finish on time." The disappointment of the late start didn't stop her voice from sparkling as it always did

She looked up, ignoring the imaginary spotlights behind their heads and drilling into their eyes.

"Right then, now the hard work really starts." she turned towards the board, again writing as she spoke, the perfect way to emphasise the key words. "Development is all about you, and it all starts with you. This afternoon we are going to look at two absolutely key subjects. Confidence in YOU and confidence in those around YOU."

She took a small step backwards, a horrified look coming across her face as she saw the board in front of her. She had started off too quickly and the 'CONFI' had been too spread out. Fitting the 'DENCE' in had forced her to close the letters up too much and the writing curved gently downwards. She could hear Brian already, saying 'But that's all wonky, Wendy!'. Hoping that she hadn't gone red she turned guiltily to face them, the tight ball in her stomach disappearing in a flash as she saw nothing at all in their faces, no spark of interest and certainly no puzzled looks at the quality of her writing. All she saw were seven people taking a sudden shared interest in the carpet. Profiting from their apathy towards the quality of her writing she quickly moved on.

"So, to start we're all going to take some post-its and write on them the behaviours we expect to see in ourselves when our confidence is at its maximum. All okay?"

***

They were five minutes into the exercise and it was just like she'd asked them to write a story in Greek, the only sound being Brian screwing up unwanted pieces of paper as he changed his mind yet again. Fortunately, Wendy was expecting it as the groups were always the same at the start of the week. Given some time they would all get used to the way she worked.

"Are you sure you've got the right course, Wendy Welcome?"

She gave Brian a smile as she set off on a tour of the

room. As she suspected her presence was enough to get the scribbling started, and in any case she was paid just as much for silence as she was for talking.

Twenty minutes later and they had all done a good job. Well, a decent one at least. Making a vision board was hardly ground breaking but she had been asked to include it in the agenda and so she had done. Even Maria, the most unsuccessful business woman in Harshton, had come up with some interesting subjects that would help her focus on her confidence. Jack was having more difficulty.

"So, I thought that, like, I could behave more naturally when I explain my ideas to older people." His voice was quiet, no real drive behind it but with perhaps a hint of hidden life.

"Can you explain more?" If in doubt, ask a question.

The others were all ready for their mid-afternoon tea, a hard-earned reward for their writing and talking, and Wendy was with them all the way.

Jack was by far the youngest of the group, just twenty eight years old, but seemed to have lived far more than them all. His accent was local and broad, one of the many gifts that the large estate that made up the southern end of town had bestowed upon him. Some families often talked fondly of the first of their line to go to university, but Wendy suspected that for Jack's family they probably looked on him as being the first to finish school. Wendy smiled at him, encouraging him to carry on speaking.

"Well it's just that in my last job I kept looking at how we did things and seeing that it was obviously not the best way." An interest came into his voice, the hidden life that she had suspected was starting to shine through. "So, I kept thinking of easier ways to do things, and then I'd tell the boss about it, so that we could be better."

"Well that already sounds very interesting and good. So, what happened next?" Wendy encouraged him to go on.

HE'S MAKING A LIST

"What do you think happened next?" It was Brian, jumping in to take over. "Nobody likes a smart arse, especially when it's a snivelling little kid. They'd have ignored him the first few times, and then given him the sack." Brian's laugh annoyed her and Jack's face confirmed that it was true. Flash started to stand and Wendy quickly announced the start of the afternoon break.

***

There was nothing like a cup of tea to calm everyone down, and nothing like the clock striking four to announce the last part of the day. Everyone had the basis for their vision boards and even if they never got any use out of them at least they would have something concrete to take back home.

"So then, how do we give others confidence in ourselves, and make sure that we have confidence in others?" The silence was shorter this time and Wendy was soon drawing her figure of eight model on the board.

At the top was the accountable loop, where everyone owned their behaviour and worked towards delivering on their commitments. On the bottom, the victim loop where denial and blame reigned and nothing ever improved. Surely they would see the importance of accountable behaviour.

"So, what you're saying is, we should stop being a victim, and stick up for ourselves?" Brian was wrestling with an idea.

"Not quite that, no. It's not about sticking up for yourself, it's about taking ownership for the situations we find ourselves in." The speaker surprised her.

Up until that moment he had sat there quietly at the back, sweating into his lumberjack shirt and doing the minimum to survive.

"That's right Sachin, it's having a situation where we do what we say we'll do, and if we don't, we learn from it and try and get it right the next time. This gives others confidence in us, and we encourage everyone on the team to do the same."

"Well that won't fucking work much. Not with most of the arseholes I've had to work with round here." Brian was starting off on a speech and Sachin seemed happy to just leave him to get on with it.

Sachin must have been around the same age as Wendy and from the look of him was just as physically active, though he clearly didn't benefit from her genes. From his introduction that morning he had been one of the dying breed of shopkeepers for which the country was so famous. Surprisingly there were still brave people around who were undaunted by the frequency of the 'To Let' signs being put up, and Sachin was often the man they would call on to organise the running of their shop. He must have worked in at least half of the shops in town collecting more and more redundancy notices as he went on.

Brian finished his monologue and together Wendy and Sachin outlined a plan that could be used for helping those around you to change. After all, no-one said it would be easy. For the first time that day her smile didn't feel forced and after a quick wrap up she was twenty percent towards the end of the week.

"Right then, has anyone got any comments before we finish for the day?" The offer of finishing always made sure that comments were few and far between. Going once, going twice…

"Well to be honest Wendy, it was all a load of bollocks really." A last-minute reflex stopped her smile from dropping.

She started breathing through her mouth and gave Brian a nodded invitation to carry on.

"Vision boards and accounting loops and all of that is probably good in the text books, and with your normal types, but how are we supposed to learn anything from that? I haven't even got room for a board in my kitchen." Every aspect of the laugh that followed repulsed her, and the blank and bored looks from the rest of the room confirmed that the others weren't too interested either.

Wendy needed something a bit more down to earth, quick and clear and perfect for bringing the day to a close.

"Look, in a way you're right. This afternoon has given us some good long-term actions, but life is all about simple things, things that we won't forget and we can use every day." For the first time that afternoon the majority of the room actually looked interested. "Right, not everyone can have the confidence of Flash, that's for sure."

"Confidence, me?" Flash's denials would get her nowhere and Wendy needed an example.

"Yes, confidence. To walk around like you do every day speaks of nothing but confidence, but here are two things for the rest of you to always remember. So, number one, thinking about something is worse than actually doing it. Stop worrying about what might happen, and just get on and do it. Look at you all here. How many of you were worried last night about coming here today?"

Two or three hands were half raised and Wendy carried on.

"And was it worth the worry, in the end? No, of course it wasn't, you've all been great. Never worry about things until it's actually time to do them." Her stare rested momentarily on every face and she was sure that she had struck home. "Encourage those around you to do the same, and life will become better for everyone. And number two, smile." The pause that followed gave them all a chance to try, even Maria whose lips appeared to have curled at least a millimetre or two. "Smile at strangers, smile when you are on your own, just smile. What may just look like confidence will end up becoming confidence, for you and for everyone around you. Look at Desmond and see his smile from where I'm standing, just breathing confidence to anyone who's looking at him." There she was pushing the boat out perhaps a little bit too far, but every example needed a person behind it.

Desmond, like Flash before him, looked surprised whilst Brian was clearly getting ready to add some of his own wisdom.

"Okay then, thank you all for a great first day, and I'll see you all tomorrow." She walked to her bag, a clear visual sign that they were finished.

Around her the chatter and movement of seven people getting up covered the sound of the relieved whistle coming out through her rolled up lips. Day one was over.

CHAPTER 9

Monday 14th December, Evening

The still full suitcase had been opened and now lay on the bed, but the real packing away would wait until later. Wendy was ready to hit the bar, a just reward for a long day in the training room, and she was soon walking back along the corridor and going down the central flight of stairs. The bar was next to the main entrance and at this time of day was giving forth a bright, shining light and the sound of music.

A series of barely felt vibrations as she approached were enough for her to identify the song that she had heard so many times before. The unmistakeable voice of Noddy Holder that greeted her as she entered the bar simply confirmed it all, as he sang to her yet again about rock and rolling grannies and old songs being the best. Yes, it was that time of year. Music had always been important to her and there was nothing quite like Christmas songs for evoking memories from the past. She swanned up to the bar, quickly taking hold of an over cold glass of New World Chardonnay, and then used the large mirror below the row of spirits as a means of eying up the situation without the inconvenience of having to turn around.

An expert in observation might just have noticed but to the unsuspecting the smile on her face held its shape as she made out the small group of people in the far corner. Wendy had a reason to be in the bar, being all on her own, miles away from home, but why would people who lived in Harshton have stayed behind after the course for a drink? There were three of them, huddled together around seldom seen half pint glasses, one for economic reasons, one for health reasons and the last one simply because it was expected no doubt. Worse than that they had obviously seen her, with their conversation seemingly turning to her arrival in the bar. There was nothing else she could do so she turned with a flamboyant swish of hair and her heels took her as fast as they could across the floor.

"Well then, fancy seeing you lot here. You don't mind if I join you, do you?"

They didn't and so she did, giving her if not the best evening of her life at least one with something to pass the time. Three had become two, eventually leaving just the one and a somewhat uncomfortable last fifteen minutes until Wendy had finally been left alone.

***

Opening the door to her room had seemed more complicated than it should have but she was finally back inside, unsure of exactly how many she had drunk but certain that it was too many for a Monday evening. She had even ended up signing her bar bill using her computer password, which was worth a little snigger all in itself for the look on the face of the poor lad who had struggled to understand what 'V@gina1966!' really meant. At least it wasn't going to be guessed by too many people. She shook her head again as she completed her unpacking, neatly placing all of her toiletries and then wrapping herself up in the warm cardigan that had been brought along just for times like these. Once everything was tidied away she sat in an old wooden framed chair in the corner of the now dark room and closed her eyes.

Inside her head the memories span round, the crime room, the young friends playing all day in the sunshine and the way that Stuart Palmer, her first love and the person beside her in the picture that she could see, had brought her world crashing down around her. Wendy had googled it once just to be sure, to see if there really had been more sunshine in the seventies. Nothing she'd found seemed to confirm it, but deep down she was certain. The youngsters of today must surely curse it, the sun that forced them to close curtains to avoid shadows on computer and television screens, but back then it had been different. As her thoughts came into focus she shivered, despite her cardigan, the warmth of the hotel room and those fond memories of sunshine.

People often talked of something being their earliest memory, but this was a throw away phrase that never told the listener exactly how hard fought those memories were to come by. Through screwed up eyelids Wendy could just about go back the nearly fifty years necessary to gather the one that she was searching for. There was no fine detail, the memory seemingly played back in an out of focus black and white slide show, but with added effort she could sharpen up the images, seeing them, hearing them and feeling the same excitement now as she had at the time. She had been out in the park and there had been another person, the same size as her, who also wanted to play. The adults stood by watching and encouraging as the two children, Wendy and Stuart, gradually introduced themselves and created those first unspoken rules. They laughed and played and over the next ten years grew that first romance. They had talked of love and shared simple dreams of marriage, children and a happy ever after life together. Scott and Charlene had never been heard of, let alone Becks and Posh, so the yearnings for fame and celebrity that children seemed to dream of nowadays had never cast a shadow over them.

The end was inevitable, and the day that he had feebly mumbled to her that it was over would never leave her. Wendy had grown up, and out, but never turned into a swan, being more a bit of an old goose. Stuart had become the main man, the captain of the team, and with that came the horde of adoring girls. A gush of warmth came over Wendy's body as she recalled again the day that he'd destroyed her dreams and what remained of her teenage confidence in an emotionless, two minute conversation.

He was the first real person on her list, her parents only being there to please Freud. She took quick steps now to her bathroom, needing one last glass of water before she slept. She knew that it had been first love but she still felt even now that hammer blow on her poor, shattered heart. With hindsight it had all been a lucky escape. It had turned out that he wasn't that good at football after all, and after being turned down by Doncaster he'd given up. Married at twenty and divorced with three kids at twenty five he was now delivering parcels from the back of a dirty white van. She slammed her plastic cup onto the bathroom surface as she risked a quick glance at herself in the mirror.

Her hurt was old but still as powerful as ever. She didn't know if she had ever really recovered or not, and that was why the photos with Stuart remained pinned to the wall in her crime room.

CHAPTER 10

Saturday 19th December, Evening

It was already getting late by the time the computer was switched on, providing the only light in the otherwise dark room. It had been a long day, firstly stuck in a training room at the Grand Hotel and then holed up in the hotel bar, but now that was all over and it was time to experience some of the real world. The fingers expertly tapped away at the login screen and seconds later a photograph of a beautiful blond woman was displayed next to the user handle 'ITK1690'.

ITK1690 was a good handle, well known and respected amongst the online community. Just as using a real picture of yourself wasn't cool neither was using a proper name, so the photograph of some little known eastern European model was used to attract the knuckle dragging class and the user name was a code that would tell both everything and nothing about the person behind it.

ITK was "In The Know", something that you had to be, or at least be believed to be, in order to have any impact in the dog eat dog world of fake news. Who would be interested in what you had to say if you knew nothing more than the hundreds of others who also tried to create the news?

1690 was the date of the Battle of the Boyne. There had been a time when it was useful for winding up the anti-British crowd, but in the years since the Brexit referendum, the new age of disinformation, such fancy additions were no longer required. Winding people up was easy and ITK1690 was one of the best.

It had taken a while for ITK to get the right balance. Several months had been spent trying out various online identities before the importance of the false name and the fake picture had been fully understood. Then there was the need for a good location, with ITK finally choosing Manchester, not out of any affiliation but because it was a much cooler place than some little town in the middle of nowhere. Once the correct identity had been chosen it was just a matter of slowly filling up your follower base and then, boom, you were popular. By day you could be some no name nobody attending useless training courses, but by night you were ITK1690, the master of what was really going on.

One by one the full array of tools came to life and finally everything was in place for influencing the stupid and insecure. Computer screens and laptops had been as easy as apples to get hold of when all of the local businesses had been closing down, and ITK had enough good contacts to get hold of the four good sized screens and the old laptop that were now impersonating the flight deck from the Starship Enterprise. A connection to the neighbours wifi and a few hours of help from the young kid on the ground floor had done the rest.

It had been a revelation that first time that ITK had

discovered the real world. Not the made up one where development courses with a bunch of losers were order of the day, but a world where people of a like mind could exchange between themselves on the subjects of the day that really mattered. ITK scrolled through some of the current threads, rapidly typing in some quickfire comments.

'Snowflake'

'Get over it, Buttercup'

'Share your sources, loser'

'That looks lovely!!'

It hadn't always been that easy. At the start ITK had spent hours exploring the internet looking for the news reports that would confirm what was really happening in the world. Searching the BBC, ITV and Sky websites had taken an age, and the real stories that mattered were hardly ever reported on truthfully. The Main Stream Media, or MSM as people now called them, were just puppets of the rich and the liberal left and couldn't be trusted at all. Then one day ITK had discovered the true media, the alternative sites that reported on the real news stories. There was no need to search anymore as you could just look at story after story that confirmed what you knew was really happening all over the world. Traitorous politicians, immigrants committing all sorts of disgusting crimes and a theological struggle that appeared to have left almost every church in France on fire. The poor people of Dover must almost be able to see the smoke from their windows. All of this though was being hidden from the people by the MSM, with just the real patriots managing to make the truth known. Dave Pance and the alternative news channels never let the people down and ITK had soon realised what needed to be done to help spread this news as widely as possible. The non-believers needed mocking and the believers needed to be wound up into a fervour, all the time knowing that any comment, no matter how negative, still helped to spread the word. A few pictures of empty parliaments and thronging crowds alongside some provocative words could give rise not only to hours of fun but also to the continued distribution of the real truth. Of course, sometimes things had to be made up, but that was not so much lying as making the truth easier to understand for the people who might need some extra help. Madonna may not have actually said the quote in question, or the photo of London might actually have a picture of the Liverpool team coach in it, but it didn't really change the truth in the message, did it? Again, the fingers typed.

'All traitors must hang'

'Snowflake'

'Our forefathers fought the Boers to give us freedom'

'Did you, really?'

The night ahead promised to be long and full of entertainment, but first ITK had other things to attend to.

Wendy was a stupid bitch, all tits and heels. ITK had seen lots like her before and would certainly see many more in the future. A bottle of wine and she hadn't stopped talking, pouring out all of her sorrows to anyone able to hear her above the sound of the Christmas music. The two others had seemed more interested in Shaking Stevens but ITK had been all ears, noting every word and identifying every weakness, knowing full well that Wendy would never suspect anything in the morning, even if she remembered what she'd said. It had been happening for years, people looking through ITK and dismissing any possibility of danger, but perhaps now the time had come. Getting a verbal reaction from people was always much easier than getting them to actually do something, especially for ITK and others who thought the same way. The environmental kids had managed to almost shut down London, or at least that was what the BBC had said, just by being a load of idiots, yet seventeen point four million Brexit supporters had never managed to organise anything half as disruptive. Obviously, they all had jobs to go to, and most of them lived in the North and had family commitments and all that, but in the end it was pointless if the words didn't drive any action. The stupid bitch was almost a gift, ripe and ready, if only ITK could pull it all together. It would need to be a random action, not really linked with the cause, but it would send a message and prove that ITK was up there with the best. You could almost consider it as an experiment.

Trotsky had identified it in his model of subversion, something that ITK had found one day somewhere on the internet, and even with him being a liberal lefty it didn't necessarily mean that some of his ideas weren't useful. He'd said that all it took were small numbers of well-trained individuals, successfully carrying out small acts of sabotage, in order to make the revolution grow. It was all so simple and hardly worth an ice pick in the head. For ITK, Wobbly Wendy would be an excellent test case, the perfect opportunity to show how to convert simmering hatred into action.

The next steps were easy and ones that ITK had done many times before when confronted with an obstinate opponent, but it was amazing what you could do with a hunch and a few pieces of vital information such as email addresses and dates of birth. There was no Snap or Insta for Wendy, she was much too old for those, and so ITK focussed on the old people's networks, where it shouldn't be too hard to find a way in to Wendy's past through a simple misplaced post that anyone could access. The fingers tapped away, the flutter of the key strokes a calming sound that was preferable to a Shaking Stevens Christmas melody any day of the week. Unsurprisingly, Wendy herself was far too boring to leave anything of use but others had identified her several years ago, and a web of relationships soon began to develop. There were picture matches, old newspaper cuttings, long since forgotten class lists, all things that some unsuspecting moron thought it would be a good idea to share with the billions of other people who also had access to the internet. Despite the late hour ITK worked with a sense of urgency and intrigue, with each discovery bringing new energy to the search.

Finally, it was done, all of the pieces were in place and the contact was identified. As had been done many times before, ITK set up a brand-new email address, smiling at the knowledge that Wendy would wake up to an impressive hangover and a new message from a long-lost friend. Depending on the response to this message, ITK would decide exactly how far Wendy could be taken towards the mayhem that was planned. The message was carefully constructed and the send key pressed.

Leaning back in the chair the screens flicked back one after the other as the few, insignificant moments from the life of a stupid bitch of a trainer were replaced by the real-life struggles of all right-thinking people in the West. The patriots in the US, struggling to Keep America Great Again, were once more being victimised by the liberal fucktards who wanted to stop them taking their guns to the supermarket. Could they really not see how much better the UK would be if people could carry weapons too?

'Snowflake'

'Don't believe anything you read in the MSM, dimwit'

'Carry on sister, without A2 we're all going to get it'

'Wow, that's cute'

'Suck it up buttercup!'

Back now in the rhythm that made ITK feel so comfortable the end of the night would pass without problem. The next day would hopefully be filled with Wendy Welcome's haughty screech, a medicine to keep the sleep away long enough to get through another eight hours of purgatory at the Grand Hotel.

CHAPTER 11

Tuesday 15th December, Morning

Wendy sang quietly under her breath as she quickly passed around the room checking that everything was in place, the words just audible above the sound of her movement. If you mentioned Irving Berlin few people would come up with Call Me Madam, but Wendy had performed in the show many years before and the song had stayed with her ever since. As she completed her preparations there was no doubting the feeling that it was indeed a lovely day.

There were a lot of criticisms that you could level at Wendy, and a lot of people did, but recovery after a night on the booze was one of her strong points. Okay, she might not remember a lot of what she'd said, but Wendy the morning after was always like a breath of fresh air. Added to that the fact that she was one day closer to the end of the course, and the fact that she'd received an unexpected message, and the loveliness was easy to understand. She selected a bright purple marker and wrote on the flipchart, stepping back to admire her work and giving a nod of the head and a satisfying smile. The sad memories of the mis-matched CONFIDENCE from the day before were in the past as her new ten letter word shone like a beacon, with each one the same height and not the slightest hint of anything off centre. Things were good.

***

One hour later, and things were not quite so rosy.

"But that wasn't what they said when I did this at the end of the last century. The 'R' is for Reachable." Brian had started where he had left off the day before.

His black shoes, black trousers and white shirt were exactly the same as the previous day, and the t-shirt hidden beneath was either a new one of a different colour or the same but dirtier. Wendy delved into her matronly reserves.

"But that wouldn't work at all would it, Brian. Achievable and Reachable both mean the same thing, don't they?" Her response was clear, reasoned and explained with a smile.

"So perhaps the 'A' is Attainable, not Achievable then?" Brian was not backing down.

Wendy's sigh was loud in her head, but unnoticeable on the outside.

"They're both the same too. Look, it's as I told you. SMART objectives are essential for all leaders to make sure that what we do is well defined, and above all to make sure that what we expect of others is too. All our objectives need to be SMART!" Her voice rose as if she was doing a voiceover in an advert for some seedy carpet shop. "Specific, Measurable, Achievable, Relevant and Timebound. SMART."

"Timebound? Are you sure that's not Timely? I sometimes get the idea that you're making this up as you go along Wendy." The half flirting look on Brian's face made her inwardly cringe, but at least he was passing the time and saving the others from hearing her voice.

"Timebound Brian, we give it an end date. Timely

would mean that it needs doing now, and that we cover with the Relevant part. 'T' is for Timebound."

"If you say so, Wendy Welcome, if you fucking say so."

The swearing was met with yet another smile, he was obviously doing it just to be annoying. Anyway, it would soon be time for the mid-morning break and despite it looking like they would have the same biscuit collection as the day before it would be a break none the less.

"Well, whose example shall we work through then?" She scanned the room and settled on the safe option. "Sachin, what have you got for us as an objective based on our future, confident state. Come up here and let's work through it on the board."

Sachin stood and moved obediently towards the front of the room as Wendy prepared yet another empty sheet of paper on the flipchart.

***

"Well, well, well. Weight loss eh? That's not a surprise, to be honest, though you do realise that you'll have to buy lots of new clobber, which will be difficult on the basis that you've managed to shut down half of the shops in town yourself and are skint as a result." There were a few accompanying sniggers to go with Brian's own laughter.

She would have to find a way to sort him out, but for the moment the smile stayed in place as she switched from Brian's idiocy to Sachin's example.

"Thank you, Brian, I'm sure Sachin will be eager to come to you for fashion advice once he needs to go shopping." She was subtle, but effective. "So, Sachin, how do we make the objective SMART?"

Sachin turned to the flipchart like a pro. He'd taken the blue marker, which was a surprise as it had started squeaking a bit, but he set out the five letters vertically on the page all ready to explain.

"So, the objective is to lose some weight, and more

specifically to lose ten kilos. Obviously, that is measurable because I've got a balance at home and I think that it's achievable as well."

"Achievable, I reckon from here you could lose at least twenty." Why did some people have to be seen to be funny all of the time? She gave Brian a 'please stop being an idiot' look and nodded at Sachin to continue.

"Losing ten kilos is the objective, and that is achievable also when I tie it to the timebound part, because I want to do this before Easter. Every objective has to also be linked to the timing." Sachin had nods of support from most of the others.

"And the relevant part?" Flash asked the question on everyone's lips.

"Relevant because from a health point of view I need to do it. Not working seems to pile the weight on me for some reason, and it's also relevant because it's for my daughter. It will be the school sports day again in May, and last year I came last in the Dads' one hundred metres dash. That's something that no young girl should have to go through, especially as I don't get to see her all of the time, so I promised her that this year I'd do better."

The appreciative 'aahs' were still dying down as Brian dunked his first Custard Cream.

***

Since the break they had worked well, redefining their own personal objectives. For the first time that day Wendy felt that the smile was almost real and the lunch break was fast approaching. Things were too good to be true.

"But it's a bit like yesterday, isn't it? I might not remember what all of the letters are supposed to mean, but fuck me this is all from the last century." Muscles around the lower part of Wendy's face were secretly assigned the task of keeping the smile in place.

It must have been Maria who added the 'Amen' under

her breath, sat there silently behind all of the others. Whilst Brian had stubbornly stuck with his clothes from the day before, Maria had undergone a full overhaul from top to toe. All of those failed businesses had obviously not hurt her pocket too much.

"These days it's all about agility and innovation. Staying one step ahead of the rest." Brian was not letting things go, so it was time to discuss.

"So, Maria," Wendy turned to face her, "is that what you found with your businesses? Was there no room for SMART objectives, just the cut and thrust of innovation and agility?" Wendy was pleased, her theatrical delivery of questions always managed to put her victims off guard. The response was a surprise though as Maria lost immediately the cool exterior that she normally displayed as she answered in a dull monotone.

"It was just strange, in the end." The low volume mumbling was almost inaudible. Maria's hands moved from ruffling her hair to straightening her clothes and then back again. Her voice finally gained a bit more confidence. "One day we had great products and loyal customers and the next it was all gone. By the time we tried to do something different it was too late." She finished her phrase and then her head dropped as she looked towards her bright red shoes. In an act of kindness Flash broke the sudden silence.

"It isn't the strongest species that survive, nor the most intelligent, but the ones most responsive to change. Isn't that what it's all about?"

"Ee e e e e e einstein w w w wasn't it?" Even Desmond was joining in.

"No, Darwin I read." Jack offered another source, but Wendy was sure that some trainer had invented it themselves, many years before.

For any quote to be believed it had to have a famous name next to it. Nobody cared what Brian from Bradgate, or even Wendy the trainer from Webledon, might have to say about something, but if Madonna said something it must be right. A bit of Wendy wisdom was needed to close the session.

"Listen. Objectives, agility, innovation, all of the things that we talk about have one main aim, to force us to take action. Thinking about things doesn't get them done, we only progress when we act. For us, our barrier is often fear and uncertainty, but just because you've never done something, doesn't mean that you can't do it, and especially that you shouldn't try. And it's never too late to start trying, for anything at all. So, when you have your goals, work towards them. Being agile just means doing things quicker, and innovation is just daring to try. An innovative idea isn't magic, it's just something that you tried that worked. Do you see that?" The nods were genuine and the smell from the next room suggested that the food was ready.

"Right then, let's break for lunch. Oh, wait. Has anyone got any questions?" It never failed.

Nobody had questions just after they'd been offered food.

CHAPTER 12

1980

"Well come on then, is it a sine or a cosine? The question is quite straightforward."

It was the third time that Mr Denzil had asked, and each time his tone had become sterner and the question harder. Not that the tone had been light the first time he asked it, as Mr Denzil was old school, nothing like the younger teachers who taught most classes. They said that he had only stopped wearing his cape the year that Wendy had started at the school. A chair leg scraped against the hard floor and a new bout of giggling came from the desk behind. Wendy focused as hard as she could on the page in front of her, but despite all of her efforts it still made as little sense as it had done five minutes before.

"Come on, you're holding the whole class up!" A wooden ruler was brought down violently against the desk bringing an immediate silence to the room.

Wendy's eyes moved from the book to the desk to the pencil case to the book. Her heartbeat raced and she squeezed her eyes shut in an attempt to keep out the sweat that was beading on her forehead. She sensed movement as Keith in the seat next to her edged further away, desperately trying to avoid catching her stupidity. She started to look up, hoping to find some hidden clue in the white scribble on the board in front of her.

There was more surprise than pain in the contact, as the soft side of a chalkboard rubber struck her on the ear, greeted by a series of muffled sniggers from the rest of the class. It was easier to be brave when you knew that there was no object to hand. It had been unexpected in that she had heard no noise, but it was Mr Denzil's favourite trick and in that case there was nothing new. Wendy simply looked back at her book, no longer searching for the answer to a question but instead searching for a secret passageway to somewhere else. Keith beside her brushed the sleeve of his blazer.

"Stand up girl, come on. Let us all see wonderful Wendy before us, unable to answer the simplest of questions in trigonometry, and at this moment resembling Hecate, the hag from the Scottish play."

The severity in his voice was momentarily disguised, replaced by what seemed like a perverse happiness as he destroyed the young girl. Wendy pushed back on her chair, alarmed by the screeching of the legs on the hard floor. Fine particles of chalk dust fell from her hair, covering the book on her desk as though a storm of powdery snow had somehow passed overhead. As she reached her full height the board rubber itself finally fell from her lap, landing on the floor with a dull thud. The concentration behind her movement had given her a welcome, if momentary, respite from her anguish. As she started to look upwards her terror started to return. Her head was raised slowly, allowing her to take in the chalk stains that covered the left-hand side of her red blazer. Now that she was finally standing she gave an instinctive shake of her head, being rewarded with nothing more than another downpour of dust on to her desk, a strange sight considering the blue sky that was visible through the classroom windows.

Breathing as deeply as she could, Wendy finally raised her eyes and turned slightly to the side, regretting immediately the stare that she was now exchanging with her teacher. Denzil screwed a piece of paper into a ball and moved towards the blackboard, using the paper to clear it as he spoke.

"You are in a good form here girl and from what I understand your other results are good. You just seem to lose concentration when it comes to studying the proper subjects." He took up a piece of chalk and started to write on the board. "And so, perhaps tonight you can do a little bit less playing and a little more studying. Come back tomorrow and tell us all how to do exercise two on page one hundred and one."

He smiled as he finished writing. There was no homework for the class that night as Wendy would be doing it for them. His eyes penetrated Wendy's one last time, the look appearing to be a mixture of uncertainty, pity and loathing. Before anything else could be said the bell rang and the room erupted into its normal end of class mayhem. All around Wendy was noise as bags were filled, chairs pushed back and conversations exchanged. Amongst it all she stood still, once more trying to master her breathing and prevent the tears from flowing. Her legs shook as she focused on the writing on the board in an attempt to stay straight and not fall over. One by one the class left the room, leaving Wendy there alone, none of her classmates having the desire to shorten their breaktime in order to see if she was okay.

Finally she slumped back down into her chair, relieved to at last be out of danger. She patted her sleeve vigorously until most of the chalk had gone whilst doing her best to find something to laugh about as her senses finally started to return to normal. She remembered how ridiculous others had looked when it had been their turn, but despite her best efforts no laughter would come. Tidily she packed her books and pencil case into her bag and then left, carefully placing the board rubber in its proper place on the desk on her way out.

CHAPTER 13

Tuesday 15th December, Afternoon

With her eye firmly on the clock, Wendy fidgeted around at the front of the room as everyone slowly took their seats again after their feast of baked potatoes and various exotic fillings. The poor man's food had made her think of Dickens, with his Christmas books attacking the baddies of his age, reminding her that even though the holders of the roles of baddy and goody had changed, the victims were all still poor.

Situational role playing would be perfect for a Tuesday afternoon, with very little introduction needed from Wendy before the group could just be left to get on with things whilst the potatoes were fully digested. The sound of McCartney and Lennon warbling on about Christmas in the bar that evening almost sounded real already.

"Right then, this afternoon is all about feedback. How to give it in a way that is constructive and how to receive it in a way that helps us to improve. In a while we'll be splitting into pairs, but first let's take a look at what's really going on when we are in a feedback situation." Brian had a gleam in his eye, Desmond looked despondent and all of the others just looked bored.

HE'S MAKING A LIST

Perhaps the afternoon would be longer than she'd thought after all.

***

On any other day she would have offered to make the numbers up but today she just couldn't be bothered. They had discussed the theory part in some sort of detail, the need for the feedback to be immediate, constructive, fact based, blah blah blah, and they had now split into two pairs and a group of three in order to practice. They would soon be working together, giving Wendy the time to think through the messages that she had received overnight and at lunch. There was something strangely exciting about being contacted out of the blue by someone from your past.

"But this isn't ever going to work, he's a ginger and she looks like someone's grandma. How am I supposed to do a role play where I'm giving some young bird a bit of feedback?" Wendy looked up, of course it had to be Brian.

"You'll just have to try your best, Brian. It should make the exercise even more of a challenge for you, and we don't get anywhere without a challenge do we."

It was hardly the dream team but two into seven didn't go, and the other teams had formed quickly leaving Brian, Dot and Desmond as the trio. It was definitely a crowd, but Brian might actually help the other two get something useful from the exercise. She left them huffing and puffing along, hoping that Brian would quickly blow himself out before finally just getting on with it. The moaners were always the same, defiant in their desperation for five minutes of infamy but then as eager as children to join in with the games once they had something practical to get on with.

In the far corner were Sachin and Maria, who after her little wobble that morning seemed to be dropping her defences under Sachin's obvious charm. There was even perhaps a hint of a smile on her face as she received some feedback on her way of giving feedback. Brunel looked down with an approving glance anyway, one of the lucky people to see his exploits survive the recasting of history that inevitably happened when times changed. There had been no slaves or tobacco in his portfolio of achievements.

The centre of the room contained the young ones, Flash and Jack. In an ideal world she would have kept them apart and forced them to mix with the older generation, but their chairs had been turned to face each other before she had even finished the instructions. Breaking them apart at that point was too much like hard work and she could see Jack's eyes drilling into those of Flash with his normal intensity. Wendy's would have been drilling too, anything to save her from having to look at those awful tattoos and piercings.

With everything seemingly in order, Wendy took a seat and looked on with glazed eyes as her thoughts wandered once more. Eventually she became aware of a noise building in the room and looking up she could see Jack becoming more and more animated. Finally her senses focussed just as he reached his crescendo.

"Well if you realised that I was only a child, then perhaps you might know how to treat me properly." The phrase had been half-shouted with an unnatural mixture of understated anguish.

Wendy was quick to her feet, relieved to see that Flash had already moved towards him, thus relieving her of any need to understand the cause of his outburst or to provide any psychiatric support.

"Well it looks like it's time for the afternoon break then." Her escape was complete.

***

After the earlier hysterics, the rest of the afternoon ended without further incident, leaving nothing more to complete but the end of day round table.

"If you really are interested in feedback though, we could do with a change in biscuits tomorrow Wends. That's four times already we've had that same selection box. Can you have a word please?" Her nod was polite and her smile radiant as Brian had his ritual last word.

"Anyway, before we go just another way of looking at things." There was just a little more Wendy wizardry to fit in before the day ended, and she could then check and see if she had received any more messages that afternoon. "Feedback is hard. It's hard to give and even harder to take, and that is all because we confuse feedback with criticism. Never forget that what other people think of you should be none of your business. It shouldn't bother you at all. You will irritate some people just by being you, just as other people will irritate you just by being them. Isn't that right Brian?"

Brian almost looked hurt, just for an instant, but he was big enough to be used as the stooge for this one, and making it personal for him would stop it being personal for the others.

"That irritation is life, but telling people about it isn't feedback. Feedback is based on the behaviours that we observe, and that is what allows us all to become better at whatever it is we are trying to do. Alright?" There were nods all round. "Good, so I'll see you all again tomorrow, bright and ready to go." The smile gave its last big push, and another one bought the dust.

CHAPTER 14

Tuesday 15th December, Late Evening

ITK was back home at last in the bright, modulating lights of the computer room, feeling elated to be in the real world again after another day spent first in a training room and then with the dross in the hotel bar. Perhaps it hadn't quite been wasted as the project with Wendy was gathering pace, but for now there was a whole day of events from the real world to catch up on and literally thousands of people to wind up and piss off. After a few clicks and keystrokes ITK was logged back in and ready for action.

They were traitors each and every one and nobody with a right mind could deny it. All over the screens ITK could follow the latest deadly developments. All of them had been elected on a pledge to protect, to look after the fellow residents of their great island nation. The NHS had been the pride of the world and the model on which every other country had built health systems of their own, well most of them anyway. But what had the people elected to oversee it done? They'd bled it dry of funds, making the waiting lists longer and longer. Then they'd let every Eastern European who was fit enough to be wheeled up to reception deplete it even further. After that they'd sold it off to the money men, weakening it to breaking point, and leaving people to die on benches in the corridors. Now the final humiliation was afoot, as it was being sold off piece by piece to the Americans, making private insurance an essential that the working Briton could never afford. And the politicians, traitors every last one, were just letting them get away with it. ITK scanned the threads, drinking in the hate and stupidity of the people who saw it as a good thing. Moving expertly between screens and applications ITK pasted the links and pictures for all to see, knowing that some were old, or unrelated, but certain that they told the real, underlying story, the one that people needed to be aware of.

'Are you afraid of the facts, read this!'

'Suck it up'

'If only you'd done what you should have when you had the chance'

'You'll pay the price in the end, just like we all will'

'So funny!!!'

The problem with most of the people leaving their opinions was that they were just a bunch of fuckwits. How had they ever survived as long as they had, believing all of the shit that they were fed on a daily basis?

One last blow across the cup and the tea that had been so sadly missed all evening in the hotel bar was ready to drink. Beer had once been a pleasure, but now even the half pint glasses were hardly worth the discomfort in the morning. The bitch had been on form again though, with her hair a bit more of a mess and another inch or two of cleavage revealed as a further button was left undone. Wendy's stupid mouth had done its job however, revealing yet more of the fool that she was and making ITK's plan seem even more perfect.

Fortunately, Wendy liked talking about herself, so there was no shortage of information. ITK was sure that even though the others were also asking questions, there was only one person noting the answers. What had at first seemed like a bloody stupid idea was now something that ITK believed could really be pulled off. The concept was simple, convincing a person to do something evil just by preying on their uncertainties, but for ITK it was a perfect project, a project that was born from actually being next to a real adversary and not just doing battle with them on-line.

'We never fell for it the last time, so why should we now?'

'You and your type are responsible for this mess. You'll never have forgiveness, you scum'

'Brilliant photo!'

The daft cow had been taken in by the messages from her long-lost friend hook, line and sinker, proving beyond reasonable doubt that she was all tits and heels and generally clueless. ITK had seen her during every break that day and every five minutes in the bar that night checking her phone for new messages and then smiling like a fool whenever ITK sent a reply. The situation was like the perfect storm, with an unstable bitch uncomfortably revealing all of her worries to a bunch of strangers in a bar, just as she receives an unexpected contact from a long, lost friend. Bitter, sentimental and stupid.

ITK had chosen well and it hadn't taken long to gain Wendy's confidence. It had been a gentle reintroduction into the life of a long-lost friend, nothing too complicated, with a neat mixture of probing questions and soothing affirmations. Combining this with the outpourings of failure that were being drunkenly revealed in the bar each night, it had been easy to put Wendy at ease and keep her talking. What a fucking self-centred idiot she was, believing that her problems were in any way comparable to the injustice that the privileged elite enforced on the working people on a daily basis. But she was there and ready, primed to become a tool that ITK could use by converting the anger into action. ITK read carefully through the messages one more time, desperate to make sure that nothing had been missed. What a day it had been. Wonderful Wendy was hooked and ITK was just opening the door and settling into the driving seat.

In celebration, it was time to start up a new story designed to fuel the fires of discord. An old photo of an empty House of Commons was posted alongside an obviously false claim that it was one of MPs debating child abuse grooming gangs. That should get them howling both for and against. It helped being 'In The Know'.

CHAPTER 15

Tuesday 15th December, Late Evening

It was difficult to stop humming when you got a tune in your head, especially when they were as catchy as I Wish It Could be Christmas Everyday and Merry Christmas Everybody. Everyone had their favourite, but how could you choose one over the other when they were both so clearly classic? After the success of the first night in the bar it had seemed only natural that they should all stay behind again, and even though the conversation had hardly been electrifying the evening as a whole hadn't been bad. The second day of training with Wendy had seemed even longer than the first one, with the subjects becoming more interesting but more difficult to take on board, so winding down with a half pint or two was well earned and definitely preferable to spending an evening all alone. A single light in the centre of the ceiling sprang into life and the sound of an arse hitting a sofa accompanied the whir of an old laptop starting up.

There would probably be nobody left on-line but it was always worth a try, and after the initial slowness as the old machine warmed up it took no time at all to log in. The profile picture was real, there being nothing to hide from a small group of contacts who were all proper friends in the real world. The user name was different though and the search for something which was unique and at the same time described the true person had given the world Smiler2468. The internet was a haven for anyone who wanted to remain anonymous, hurling abuse whilst hiding behind fake photos, but it had been a great way for Smiler to stay in touch, as friends and family had moved around in a world which became smaller and more mobile every day. Wobbly Wendy might not get everything right but her tip about smiling was not new in this household, though most of the people who knew about Smiler's real life might ask what there really was to smile about.

Scrolling through the timeline revealed picture after picture flashing by. There were lots of places on the internet which focussed on words, but that didn't interest Smiler at all as talking generally meant arguing, and there was nothing worse than the bipartisan arguments that passed for debate these days. Half of the people were always for and the other half against, and no-one was really interested in converting the preachers, being simply content to relentlessly hammer home their own point of view. On the few occasions that Smiler had taken the time to read through a full thread it had just made it even more obvious that the world was in trouble. No, Smiler was a picture person, loving all of the images that were posted every day. Yes, you could find pictures of everything on the internet, but seeing famous iconic images with people that you knew in front of them was where the real magic came from, the unexpectedness, the awkwardness, the pure joy in the faces was where the real pleasure could be found. It had been a quiet day photo wise with just a few shots of faraway nephews to raise a smile, and as suspected none of Smiler's contacts were still on line so it was time to call it a day. The next day of training promised to be another long one, and the short walk to the bedroom was accompanied by a computer whining to a halt and some softly murmured words, as Smiler joined in with Roy Wood and the rest of Wizard with a song of snowmen and great, big, smiling faces.

CHAPTER 16

Tuesday 15th December, Late Evening

She was stupid, stupid and drunk. Well, perhaps not drunk, but definitely talking more than she should. Wendy was still coming to terms with the totally unexpected messages that she had received from Sharon, and this had opened her up even more than the Chardonnay normally did.

It was illogical really, Wendy hadn't seen the girl for over thirty years, yet still the opportunity to renew their connection had been strong and exciting. The years hadn't made Sharon any more talkative than she had been in the sixth form, she still replied with short sentences and questions, but she had actually spent some time trying to make contact with Wendy which was actually quite touching. Wendy poured another glass from the minibar as she bounced off the bed and sat once more in the armchair in the corner of her room.

Outside the town centre was quiet with just a dull orange glow entering the room, the light from a nearby streetlight forcing its way between an imperfect match in the thick curtains. Her eyes closed slowly, encouraged by her gently nodding head, and she found herself once again staring towards the black painted wall in the crime room.

The memories had visited her already at lunchtime, and the picture that accompanied them was one of a late middle-aged man dressed in an old-fashioned suit and tie, his eerie smile forcing itself out of the yellowing paper. It was almost like the eyes of the Mona Lisa, with the smile following Wendy wherever she moved in the room. Next to the photo there were additional documents pinned to the wall, school reports, each one telling the same story. Wendy was bright, intuitive, hardworking, a pleasure to have in the class, a great role model and just plain stupid. Yes, he'd said stupid. In her hotel room she clung hard to her empty glass, her eyes squeezed so close together that none of the light sneaking between the curtains had a chance of making it through to her retina. Back in the crime room her bottom lip stuck out as she breathed rapidly and stared once more at that main photograph.

Mr Denzil was his name, and he had been one of the last of the old school Masters, clinging on desperately in the period before teachers became trendy disciples of left-wing politics. There was no 'call me Dave' about Denzil, just a strict stubbornness to the principles that had clearly made the Empire great. She had always seen him as near retirement age when he taught her, but from what she had learned since he would only have been mid to late forties making him even worse, just a throwback to an earlier age, an imposter playing a role that wasn't even his to play. Where he had got his extraordinary skill from nobody knew, though they said that he'd played cricket and it was whispered that he regularly took advantage of the dartboard that hung in the staffroom. What was certain though was that he was lethal with a board rubber in his hands, a fact that he proved time after time.

HE'S MAKING A LIST

The Wendy in her hotel room squirmed as she heard the words again, uncomfortable for the pain her younger self had been put through, and even more so because Denzil had been right. How could she have been so useless at maths when she excelled in almost every other subject? She was reasonable at sports and she sang like a lark in the choir, but maths she just didn't get. It was her weakness, and Denzil knew it and was rightfully embarrassed by it himself. He had failed to make her understand, and she had surely deserved each and every one of the board rubbers that had come her way. She must have been stupid.

A new flush of heat passed and her eyes opened defiantly. Had she ever needed trigonometry in the last forty years? Of course she hadn't, but it had oh so hurt her at the time. Clever girls were supposed to be clever at everything, and thick girls were supposed to be good at drawing. She had failed at maths and couldn't draw for toffee, and Denzil had reminded her of that fact every single day. She knew that he was still alive and living with his younger wife, though surely now just waiting for his end to come.

She was finished with the past and was up and walking briskly around the room, tidying away the empty glasses and bottles and then sitting down again to check her messages. At last, a smile came back to her face. Wherever Sharon was she was still awake and was still happy to stay in touch, and she would surely remember old Denzil. Thank the Lord for old friends.

CHAPTER 17

Wednesday 16th December, Morning

That morning Wendy's breathing was more forced than usual and her heels had taken on an unnatural wobble. Back in the day some nerd had told her that her heels would be exerting a pressure of about 1 500 pounds per square inch, slightly more than a mid-sized elephant. Therein was a lesson in itself, a real-life example of the benefit there was to be had from being good at maths. No, it was Woden's day which was always the same, with the risk of a midweek slip in confidence being forever present. It was certainly nothing to do with the extra glasses of wine the evening before.

Had Woden been looking down that morning, with his all-seeing eye or whatever it was that he had, he would have been wetting himself with laughter. Replying to her new messages had been one distraction too many for Wendy and had resulted in a sizeable tea stain on her left breast and a good dollop of natural yoghurt on her crutch, both guaranteed to encourage more questions than they answered. Fortunately, she had come well equipped with a cardigan that was large enough to cover both stains, but it would be a long, warm day if the heating was set at the same level as it had been the day before. The smooth sound of her markers died down and the morning's title was written clearly on the board. 'Come on Wendy' she thought, giving herself a bit of final encouragement as her smile slipped effortlessly in to place just in time to meet the first arrivals.

If her ramblings in the bar the night before had given her new friends anything to hide from her, she was certain that she would see it in their eyes. Hers were blue and beautiful, theirs would be shifty and suspicious. It wasn't ideal not being able to remember what you had said, but if anyone was secretly laughing at her, or looking on at her in disgust, their eyes wouldn't be able to hide it from her. She walked amongst them, the delicate smell of weak filter coffee calming her nerves as she exchanged pleasantries and tried to search the souls of her three so-called drinking buddies.

The first set were pale green, almost grey, and had never seen anything interesting in their life. The next dark brown, with the hint of a glint of something that could have once been mischief. The last were bright blue, almost like Wendy's, but out of place on a face that was so bland. There were no secrets or intrigue being hidden there. Her smile took on a hint of warmth as she moved towards her flipchart and the front of the class, content in the knowledge that she was still being a good girl and keeping her secrets to herself. One by one the participants sat down, all ready for day three of their personal development journey.
"Right then, this morning will all be about our path to personal change, and the absolutely wonderful impact it can have on us, those around us and those who work with and for us." Boy, when she was good, she was very, very good. Her smile hit maximum upcurve and off they went.

***

She glanced yet again at the clock, dismayed that the thirty minutes to break time that she had been looking at previously still had twenty eight minutes left to go. She had to raise her hands, guilty as charged, she had got it all wrong. Dot had at least brought silence to the room, you couldn't even ruffle in your chair without drowning her out. 'Trying to talk a bit louder and clearer' should have been her obvious choice for a small personal change to make, but instead she had gone round and round the houses, finally ending up on 'being more impatient'. More impatient? Wendy couldn't even believe she had anyone to be impatient with. But that had been just a minor blip, as passing from her to Desmond had sounded the death knell. She had to give him an opportunity to speak in front of the group, but putting him on after Dot had just been one step too far.

"Come on, sp sp spit it out Desy boy." Brian laughed out loud, but not for the first time alone. Desmond's face gave a resigned look, what little confidence he'd built up being quickly washed away.

"Brian, stop it!" Her look carried more sympathy than threat, though to whom the sympathy was directed was unclear. "That was very good Desmond. Change is all about small changes, step changes. All of the studies tell us that healthy workers are good workers, so starting to do regular exercise is a great personal change to make. You know, I once had a friend whose brother stuttered all of the time except when he sang. He used to have all of the lead roles and attracted lots of girls." Her smile was met by a resigned frown. Desmond obviously didn't sing.

"Okay then, let's take fifteen minutes for coffee. We'll start back at ten to." Her phone was out of her bag and in her hand before Maria had even stood up.

Just outside the entrance to the room was a rest area

and Wendy sat down in a large chair of the type that you imagined finding in front of a roaring log fire in the study of a Lord or Minister, but which in the Grand Hotel was no doubt some fake leather imitation knocked out cheaply in the 70s. At least it gave her some cover, and in terms of small personal changes she would be drinking less coffee. There were two messages from earlier, Sharon was upping the speed, with one a reply to Wendy's message from the morning that confirmed their shared memories of Denzil and the other from much earlier that morning that Wendy needed to read twice. Thinking back, Sharon had always had a bit of character about her, even if she had sometimes been quieter than the other girls. It was good to see that at least on that front she clearly hadn't changed.

***

It was now almost lunchtime and Wendy should have been feeling happy at being half way through the week, but her favourite participant was still on form.

"But for fuck's sake, if you want me to stop swearing how would it be a punishment for me if I just stopped doing it in one go?"

Perhaps Brian wasn't so easy to read after all. He surely couldn't be that thick and must be taking the mickey. A glance around the room showed that others agreed with her appraisal of the situation.

"Brian, Brian, Brian have you been paying attention?" Hands on hips, she gave him her best matronly scowl.

She must remember to ask the reception to turn the heating down at lunchtime.

"Jack, where do we start out?" A polite nod invited Jack to help them out.

"At the moment we're in the comfort zone." Wendy wasn't sure, but Jack's confidence seemed to be building as the week went on. "In that zone we do what we want, and nothing changes for us. If we want to make successful changes we need to move out of that zone, in a way that stretches us but keeps us safe." A Wendy nod was all that was needed in order to tell everyone that Jack had done well. Brian didn't seem to care.

"Good, and so Maria, which zone was Brian all confused about just now?"

The irritation on Maria's face was enough to let Wendy know that she was still as uninterested as ever. She did look good though, with her third outfit in three days. A little trouser suit with off colour jacket on top of a great looking blouse and with a pair of trendy trainers to complete the look. The lady had class.

"That would be the punishment zone, Wendy." Sarcasm oozed out of every over-emphasised syllable. "We end up there if we try to change too much, too quickly. Like if you try and go from swearing a thousand times a day to zero Brian. The change will become too much for you and you'd find yourself seeking refuge again in the comfort zone, hence no change." There had been a hint of pride in her voice in the end. She was trying to play the victim, but couldn't help herself.

"But that's what the bloody druggies do, isn't it? They go cold turkey, and just cut it off at once. They shake and shiver for a while and then it's all over, so why should it be any different for us?" God, a couple of them were even nodding along in agreement. Wendy needed to get back on the straight and narrow.

"Of course, you're right with that Brian. But in that case we are talking about separation from something that is addictive and bad for you, whilst here we are talking about development, so choices we make and efforts we put in to try and better ourselves. Flash, where do we need to go in order to make this happen?"

"The change zone, of course." If it wasn't for all of the metal and ink she could almost be quite nice, Flash. "Just far enough away to make a difference, but not so far that we reject the change completely. It has to be a safe zone,

one where we are allowed to make mistakes, so long as we learn from them, and one that changes every day as we make progress towards our goal." Bullseye!

"So, you see Brian, start out with small steps. Don't try and do everything all at once. For example, you could just decide to stop swearing when there are ladies present, or during meetings, something like that."

"Or I could just say bastard instead of fucking. You're bastard mad, that'd be a small step." There was no hope.

The rich aroma of a hearty hotpot wafted into the room announcing that lunch was ready.

CHAPTER 18

1987

"So how do you like your eggs in the morning then, love?"

Wendy didn't even have time to think of an answer before the rest of the table replied in unison.

"Unfertilised."

A large hand slapped the table, causing what was left of the cutlery to jump up and down whilst her seven tormentors howled in laughter. The question had been asked by the one opposite her who she believed was called Berty, but it could have been any of the other dwarves he was named after, except Bashful. A dwarf though he definitely was not. Wendy guessed that standing he would be well over six feet tall and would be pushing on for sixteen stones. His suit was probably the one that had been bought for his university interviews but it was already straining at the seams to keep his body in place. The top button of his shirt would never be fastened up again and the collar was being lightly held in place by what passed for a tie. Below his tightly curled hair was a large, rubbery face and in his large hand was an empty pint pot.

"Do you want one love, I'm just going to the bar?" Now that was an offer that Wendy would never refuse.

HE'S MAKING A LIST

Another burst of laughter exploded from her right and Wendy turned cautiously to see what was happening, surprised to see a condom attached to someone's head that was being inflated as they breathed in through their mouth and out through their nose.

"So how did you end up on a table with the rugby club then?" came the question. It was a good one indeed.

The day had started out well enough. Wendy had long got over the disappointment of not being picked as a bridesmaid, and had even recovered from the shock of not being an usher, or something else important like that. Her mum had treated her to a nice new dress and a lovely matching jacket and she had been one of the first to arrive at church, which had been good for talking to Steve, the groom, but not so good for saying hello to Shanny, who was duty bound to turn up late. They hadn't talked that much since the hen night to be honest, which everyone said that Wendy had organised perfectly, so she would have liked to have a little chat, but there you are. Anyway, she had turned up early, found a seat on the bride's side with a lovely view and marvelled at how wonderful the whole service had been. It was expected that the singing would be good, after all most of them were from the uni operatic society, but even the vicar had been witty and fun. She had even shed a little tear as Shanny had walked past in her wonderful dress.

"Here you are love, I got you a large one." The glass of wine was placed on the table in front of her. She gave a warm smile of thanks and took a sip.

Anyway, after the church they had all set off for the Harbour Hotel and it had sort of gone downhill from there. Bathed in religion and rewarded with a nice glass of white they had taken advantage of the warm weather and were talking on the lawn. Wendy was in deep discussion with the operatics whilst the various members of the two families milled around in small, uncertain groups as long-lost members were identified and rounded up. The rugby boys had stayed inside and were monopolising the bar. Bride and groom arrived, the photos were taken and then it was inside for the reception. A neat little easel had been installed at the main entrance to the dining room and on it was the seating plan, with every one stopping for a little look before moving on to find their table, and it was there that things started to go wrong. Of course, the top table was for family, as were the next ones, and then came two tables for the operatics, plus another two for other various friends from childhood and uni. Steve had wisely decided to put the cricket team next and the rugby team right at the back of the room, far away from the respectable people and right next to the bar. It had taken Wendy fifteen minutes to find her name, letting everyone else pass as she checked the plan again and again.

It had been a walk of shame. Entering through double doors next to the top table, Shanny had given her half a glance as she had walked in, the sky blue of her jacket indicating that she was the last of the guests and not the first of the waitresses. She had looked straight in front of her as she passed the operatics, all of them obviously sniggering as she walked by, and had continued with ever weakening legs until she arrived at the very last table in the corner. The table was already overcrowded just with the seven of them, but after checking the name tag twice she finally sat down, doing all that she could to avoid hyperventilating.

"Hi, I'm Wendy. Pleased to meet you," she had said, hearing nothing of the seven names that were thrown at her as she had looked on in shock.

Shanny had been her best friend, but now she was just another faceless person, barely visible at the other end of the room. The speeches had come and gone and the operatics had serenaded the bride and groom with One

Enchanted Evening from South Pacific, whilst Wendy had mumbled along with the rugby club's Swing Low Sweet Chariot, though at least she had learnt the hand actions.

The loud bang of an exploding condom brought Wendy back to the room. The tables were being cleared away to make space for dancing, and as the rugby guys started to fasten their ties around their heads, Wendy drank the rest of her glass in one large gulp, took her bag and walked quickly through the hall, not looking back once as she went to her bedroom.

CHAPTER 19

Wednesday 16th December, Afternoon

Woden and his all-seeing eye now had even more to laugh about as the fashionable change to eating upright with only a fork for company had added splashes of hotpot to the tea and yoghurt spills from that morning. A full costume overhaul would be needed later, but as Wendy would by then be sixty percent through the week her remaining outfits would manage to see out the last two days without too much fuss. Meanwhile she had other things on her mind.

Looking quickly over her shoulder she could see them, all scattered around the dining area, their cohesion as a group already over. Bless them, they were doing their best, or at least most of them were. Jack had managed a long period with no more little wobbles and the peaceful afternoon that was planned would put a lid on any conflict, which was good because they were going to spend the Thursday morning looking at how best to manage the nasty stuff whenever it came along. Her fingers moved swiftly through the marker pens as she unconsciously lined all of the cap clips with the name of the manufacturer on the side. She glanced at them again, unable to stop herself giving them a mid-term report.

The young ones were doing okay. Wendy hadn't heard them talk about partners at all, and the odds looked better than evens that they might take more from the course than just her pearls of wisdom. It happened quite often, when people thrown together hit it off after a week of high-pressure closeness. She sighed as she placed the yellow marker between the orange and the green. Flash, the half Amazonian, half Maori warrior must have frightened her vulnerable social charges half to death, but was blessed with a sympathetic understanding. Wendy wondered sometimes if the tattoos were preening peacock feathers or chameleon camouflage. Jack was quiet, intelligent and keen to learn, despite his occasional emotional wobbles. His deliberate way of talking was less a sign of stupidity and more of someone frightened to make a mistake in company. He had suffered the same problem as thousands of other kids, having just been born in the wrong place. They were cute working together but were never going to get an invite from Wendy for dinner.

Maria and Sachin were chalk and cheese. Wendy peeled a curled post it from the top of the pile, crunching it in her hand and placing it in the bin as the thought of chalk and the thickness of her cardigan caused fine droplets of sweat to make the back of her blouse even stickier than it already was. Maria was the model failed Director, with her clothing and attitude there to tell everyone that she was better than them and that their presence together on the same course was some sort of accident. On discovering that mistake someone would surely come and rescue her, thus saving everyone's embarrassment at the misunderstanding. Wendy knew that nobody would be coming to the rescue as no mistake had been made, the only difference between them being that Maria had been responsible for her own downfall and therefore had no-one else she could really blame. The time that it took her to accept that would be the time that she needed to start building again, perfectly supported by the lessons that she was receiving from Wendy during the week. Sachin was part of the strangest breed that existed, the shopkeepers that fought the eternal battle against competition. In the beginning they had fought each other, then it was the large out of town stores. Now it was the online sellers with their armies of delivery drivers, making it easier to return an item that you didn't want than it actually was to talk to a person and get the right advice in the first place. Despite these difficulties it seemed that no matter how many fell, there were always others willing to take their place, hoping that their concept would be better than the one that went before and would allow them to succeed. Of course, there were fewer and fewer now, the empty shopfronts the gravestones to long lost traders, but Sachin and his type, members of one of the surviving ancient occupations, would never give up. As one idea faded the next would rise and other people would risk their money and reputation in order to join the nation of shopkeepers.

Unseen to the others she replaced the top sheet on her flipchart, all clean and ready for the next destination that she would take them to. The remaining three, though slightly different in age, were peas in a pod, the people that time forgot. Dot looked over, catching Wendy's eye and receiving a broad smile in return. All three had been born too early to be comfortable with the uncertainty that people such as Flash and Jack took for granted, and none of them had ever known the energy and excitement of taking risks in the same way as Maria and Sachin. A job for life had been promised and then disappeared, leaving them ill-equipped to deal with the fall out. Oh well, at least it gave Wendy some work, preparing them for a next step that was almost certainly never going to come. There were five minutes still to go, just enough time to see if Sharon had replied.

***

"Look love, I see what we're doing, but I don't see the point in it." And not for the first time, she thought, as Brian carried on. "The fact is, I don't want to buy a new computer, so why would I spend half an hour of my valuable time *prioritising the characteristics that I would use later, in order to evaluate the potential choices?*" His memory was better than his impersonation, he had at least remembered fifteen consecutive words from the introduction that Wendy had given over an hour ago.

Maria's inevitable siding with Brian now came more in the form of nods of agreement, a sure sign of a not very dedicated rebel. The others had all seemed to be enjoying the exercise. Wendy's smile didn't falter.

"It's just an exercise Brian, something that should help you become confident in applying the tool. Don't forget how we got here, it's all about better using our time to do positive things, like taking decisions and carrying out actions. When we have more things to do than we have time to do them in, we have to make a choice. We either try to do them all with less detail."

"Which means do them badly." A chorus of support was always welcome, and she held up her hand like a politician mid speech calming some overzealous supporters.

"Exactly, which means doing them badly, or we can prioritise. This matrix is a great way for us to set our priorities."

"But why buying a computer, what has that got to do with priorities at work?"

"He's right you know. It might work well as an example for the tool, but that's a situation where you have a choice." Maria's nodding had quickly turned into fully-fledged verbal support. "If I've got to do things for the tax man, for the council, for the unions, for my accountant and for a hundred other useless people, I can't pick and choose. I have to do them all." Wendy looked on, wanting to point out that the past tense was 'had to do them all', but not daring to do so. "And, as Brian says, in that case your silly little exercise doesn't help us at all."

"Exactly Maria, us working people don't live in Wendy's sanitised little training bubble." Wendy's smile flickered, but didn't drop. She didn't need a clever answer, because she had the right answer.

"Very interesting Maria, and thank you Brian for considering our little bubble to be sanitised." At least the impromptu revolt would see them through to the mid-afternoon break. "As we have already established, doing things quickly doesn't make them any better, so we work on the basis that, in the worst case, everything that we manage to do today, we will still do in the future."

"W w w orst case?"

"Yes Desmond, worst case. In the best case some things we'll end up finally not having to do, as the person who asked us for it will end up finding another way to get it done without us. So, at worst we do all of the same things, it's just that we do them in a different order. By doing that, we manage our time better and everyone benefits." Quod Erat Demonstrandum. "So, after the break we'll take a quick look at the difference between Urgent and Important." She turned to face the paperboard, writing the two words neatly, before underlining them with theatrical swooshes. "That should then see us to the end of the day. Any more questions?" The Jammy Dodgers were much more important than the problems of prioritisation, so of course there weren't.

***

The break had been disappointing with no new

messages from Sharon and all of the Bourbon Creams disappearing whilst she had been checking. Brian must be stuffing them into a pocket or something because no-one else had shown any interest in them at all. The group were all working away quietly on their weekend To-Do lists. This was the best way to get them to understand the difference between something that was urgent and something that was important. It might even help them enjoy their weekend a bit more too.

"Right then Desmond, show us what you've come up with." It was the perfect exercise for Desmond, the tasks that were written down on post-its would be put in the correct column and then ordered from top to bottom, with Wendy reading them out herself thus saving an extra bit of time. A quick tour of the room would allow everyone to read out their own top three priorities for the weekend and then they would already be sixty percent through the week. Who wouldn't want to drink to that?

***

"Christmas shopping? On your important and urgent Maria? Crikey, if only they knew about it, they wouldn't all be harking after that fucking high life of yours, would they?" Wendy's eyes looked towards unseen stars and Maria's response was rapid and brutal.

"Don't you ever give it a rest Brian? Have you looked in a mirror recently and seen yourself? We all have different lives you know, there's no need to judge everyone with every stupid comment you make. How I ever ended up in a group with people like you, I'll never know." The last words were thrown over her shoulder as she walked quickly towards the door, her expensive coat still being pulled over her elegant shoulders.

"Well I guess that's one less Christmas card to worry about." Brian was actually laughing about it. Had the levels of outrage really been set so low? "That's what happens when the mighty fall so low."

Wendy searched rapidly for a way to end the day on some sort of upside.

"Look you guys, don't worry about Maria, she'll be back tomorrow." Her gaze passed to a Brian who was showing no sign of remorse at all.

She didn't like her 'urgent' voice, it was too quick and let her pronunciation down, but sometimes it helped everybody to focus on her words.

"This afternoon has been about many things, but the most important is about decisions, and how you take them for yourselves. There are no right or wrong decisions, there are just decisions, and you will make the most appropriate one for you at the time. If you look at them as a bad decision, you are just judging yourself, and if you see them as being the right decision you miss your blind spots. Just learn from them and move on, knowing that at least you did something no matter how stupid it might have been. Anyway, that's all for today. Tomorrow morning, we will be looking at managing conflict." A bit too late for that afternoon, but necessary all the same.

The thought of putting Brian and Maria as a pair together flashed across her mind, and for the first time that day her smile was real. She quickly packed away once more the tools of her trade, eager to get away and check her messages.

CHAPTER 20

Wednesday 16th December, Late Evening

ITK was tired, with the bright glare of the screens in the darkened room putting extra strain on the eyes, even more so late at night and after another long day. Playing the multiple roles of friendly companion in the hotel bar, long lost friend by e-mail and saviour of the people on the internet was starting to take its toll.

Being somebody else was not new to ITK as the false photo and nameless internet handle confirmed, and there had been other made up identities that had been exploited before that. Sharon was just another person to add to the list, made easier by the fact that the pretence was for Wendy's eyes only. Sharon had been at school with Wendy and her empty-headed notices on the old school message board had suggested that she wasn't the brightest star in the sky, but Wendy had been in her circle of so-called friends and there were several old photos of them together. Wendy was just the type of forgetful sentimentalist to receive an out of the blue message and fall for it, which was all the better for what ITK, or should it be Sharon, had in mind.

Now that Wendy was talking directly with Sharon there was much less need for detective work in the bar during the evening, and as such that night had actually been quite fun. There had been a few snippets of interesting information, Wendy was still a drunken bitch after all, but discussing favourite Christmas songs, Christmas films and Christmas television specials had made the time fly. Too much so, as now it was getting late and there were still things to be sorted out. ITK didn't understand how some people could consider Die Hard as being a Christmas film, not when you had Charles Dickens, or the Nativity franchise to go up against, but each to their own. They had all decided that Jona Lewie was the second-best Christmas song, which in the absence of a common first choice must surely have made him effectively first choice overall, but sometimes things just didn't quite work how you would think they should, so they had ended up calling that one a draw. A small smile formed on ITK's lips, as Jona's song of warfare and Christmas played in the background, and a message box sprang in to life.

The change in Wendy had been remarkable, with her transforming from someone who hardly ever looked at her telephone into a person who checked for messages every two minutes. She was just like all of the other idiots out there, tell them what they wanted to hear and you could get them to agree to anything. All that was needed was the right level of fear, plus a little sprinkling of hatred, and they were yours for the taking. ITK had practiced for years when it came to getting people to speak hatred, and the natural next step was soon to follow. The fingers flashed quickly over the keyboard.

'*Of course, you're right. Yes, it's terrible. You can't let them treat you like that, you'll have to do something about it.*' Sharon had written.

HE'S MAKING A LIST

Would she do it, Wendy? Only time would tell, but all of the signs were there. She was desperate, alcoholic, determined. Yes, she had some steel behind her, a real determination so yes, she'd do it and the coming weekend would be the perfect timing. ITK typed again, just short responses of sympathy, there being nothing better than agreeing with people in order to bring them along with you. Everyone likes confirmation that they are right, and a drunken Wendy was no exception. ITK decided to leave Wendy alone, probably crying tears of white wine, and after having played the long-lost friend it was now time for ITK to play the third and final role, the saviour of the people.

With another few clicks all four screens were now full of feeds, lifting ITKs spirits even further as the fingers stretched out ready to type. Most people didn't even realise it but the internet was the battleground of the twenty first century. There was a whole world full of people out there who needed help in understanding what was really happening. They weren't thick or anything like that, well most of them weren't anyway, they just didn't have the time, energy or skills needed to process all of the information that was available in order to come to their own conclusions. It took people like ITK, with their role as an influencer, to do that for them. It wasn't a role where you were appointed, your place at the top table had to be earned by hacking out a following in a world full of false idols. ITK was one of the best though, a saviour for a modern age. Billy Bragg had described the shopping choices of girls years before, with busy ones looking for beauty, pretty ones searching for style, and simple ones buying what they were told to. That concept didn't just apply to girls though, the world was full of busy and simple people and that was what made it all so easy. That knowing smile engulfed ITKs face as another opportunity to reap havoc appeared.

ITK liked to think of the work that was done as creating news stories. Being able to do that using nothing more than an image and two hundred and eighty characters was where the expertise was required. Seeing the opportunity, ITK searched swiftly for the pictures and links that were safely stored away on the computer's hard drive, all the while wondering how the hell it had come to pass that people nowadays called the lefties liberals, when every English person knew that they weren't Liberals at all. Another Americanism had taken its place in Shakespeare's language, inspired by the new, strong links between patriots on either side of the Atlantic.

In the end it was no more than ten minutes work, and the output was stunning. There was a photo montage of a homeless man beside an old ex-pat photo of some cracker pulling Indians celebrating Christmas. Besides that was a link to a four year old news story that told of an immigration influx putting strain on local services. Nobody would bother to check the date, let alone the accuracy, and in any case even the crustiest of students these days could set up a news website that looked believable. Finally, the text was added, attacking the local Labour council and their inability to support local services during the festive period, as reported in that bastion of the Main Stream Media, the Harshton Times. Who should people really be blaming?

'No room at the inn!' It was the perfect headline to get people angry at yuletide.

There was just time for one final check. Picture montage to attract the eye, withering attack from ITK to discredit the actions of the Mayor and blame the immigrants for the problem and a link to an out of date news story to add legitimacy. It was perfect, and once posted, ITK scrolled through some more screens in search of other subjects that would help to pass the time.

'We are praying with you, don't let them take away your guns'

'And you believe what you read in the MSM? Stupid fool'

'We stand with you Piers, don't let them get at you'

'What, a real donkey?'

'You've just been brainwashed by the liberals. You'll see when it all comes back to bite you'

You had to stay polite, that was for sure, as abuse was always punished by having your account suspended. The main objective was to get the people that disagreed to bite and reply to you, thus making your post visible to all of their contacts. If just some of those new people saw it and agreed with your point of view, then you had a convert. The convert would start by following you and seeing what you had to say, before finally making you visible to all of their friends, and all because some loosely connected Johnny Dogooder had disagreed with you in the first place. It really was like taking sweets off babies.

Wendy had still not replied so ITK read carefully once again the twenty two messages that had been exchanged so far. The first mails had been from a long-lost friend getting back in touch, and the following ones had just repeated contents of the bloody woman's drunken mutterings in order to reinforce the impression of familiarity. From there, Wendy had needed no encouragement to give out more and more information which ITK had expertly used to take control of the conversation, starting with small suggestions and then pushing the boundaries just a little bit further each time.

Wendy was everything that ITK detested, clearly thinking herself better than everyone else, despite the fact that her life was just as empty and desperate as theirs were. A victim of a cosy childhood baking cakes no doubt and the entitlement that people like her always seem to believe they deserve. Well this time she was going to get everything she deserved, and more, as ITK was going to turn her into a weapon like no other. ITK breathed deeply and calmly placed the empty cup back on the table, fingers all white from gripping the handle so tightly, thoughts returning to Wendy and what needed to be done next. She hadn't seen Sharon for over thirty years but they'd clearly been close at some point and their teenage friendship was making teenage talk and the slipping in of stupid ideas and suggestions natural and easy.

'*I think in that case I'd probably want to kill them!*' the imaginary Sharon had typed, struggling to keep a straight face.

Yes, ITK would want to kill them, and now was the time to start turning up the heat to see where the two of them could end up for real.

CHAPTER 21

Wednesday 16th December, Late Evening

Smiler pressed the button and the fan on the old computer sprang into life once more. Staying out late saved the need to switch the heating on and with a bit of extra warmth coming from the computer there would probably be no need to change that situation before the old duvet welcomed Smiler into bed. A randomly selected playlist forced Shakin' Stevens to crackle out through the one speaker that still worked with tales of snow-covered children having fun.

Smiler couldn't help humming along, it really was a wonderful time of year. Love and understanding, that was what it was all about. Peace on Earth and just giving everyone their own bit of space to do whatever they wanted to. How could anyone not like that? The hands closed around a warm cup of tea and Smiler got to work.

It had been a bit of a detour, but when you had a half hour walk to get home already what was an extra ten minutes? Some people thought that the man was a nutter, others that he was a vindictive old git who just wanted to piss off his neighbours. The reality was that old Mister Johns just wanted to share something with the good people of Harshton, and his collection of Christmas lights and inflatable festive fancies was the best display that side of Oxford Street. Smiler's phone connected to the computer and once the photo had been successfully uploaded to the timeline the share button was proudly pressed. The angle for the photo was perfect, managing to fit in the majority of the smaller displays whilst giving the ultimate angle to see the giant reindeer on the roof. Many of Smiler's friends may be in places with a bit more style than Harshton but none would have felt the exhilaration that Smiler had done whilst approaching the house that evening. It was just another great example of ordinary people doing extraordinary things, for no reason other than giving pleasure to those around them. Love and understanding.

A quick glimpse revealed that most of Smiler's friends were also getting in the festive spirit. There were trees, lights and market stalls from Bristol, London, Leicester and even one from Strasbourg in France, all with the same common features of smiles and happiness. Oh, and quite a bit of mulled wine by the look of it. A guilty check showed that there were ten likes for the photo already, plus a comment from Uncle. With the photo shared and the fingers now thoroughly warmed against the mug of tea, Smiler sat back, eyes closed, processing the events from earlier.

The evening in the hotel bar had been really good again, and well worth the price of a couple of half pints for the warmth and company alone. Each one of them had participated in the conversations, and nothing was as good as sharing Christmas memories of songs, films, and the television specials. They weren't real friends, obviously, but it was as close as Smiler got at the moment. Being separated from the family wasn't fun but it was what it was, and there was nothing that could be done about it. The melancholy thoughts lasted an instant until the love and understanding took over again. She was fun Wendy, when she let herself go. A bit mad, and she must surely sleep with a coat hanger in her mouth to maintain that smile all day long, but she was fun. There hadn't been a song where she hadn't known the words, or a film where she didn't know the plot. She also had a way of involving everyone in the conversation, a natural ease that must have been picked up at an early age. It all made the rest of her character even more of a pity.

There were twenty likes for the photo now, plus two invites for social events for the next week. Smiler was on a roll. Two new pictures of recently erected Christmas trees had also appeared. Yes, of course most people had a tree, and there was certainly nothing remarkable about the ones on the screen, but for the people who had shared them they were infinitely special. People didn't set out to be selfish and boring, merely to share some of their own personal joy in one of the few ways that were left to them in this day and age. Love and understanding.

The Christmas music had caused quite a bit of debate and it was still difficult to believe that some people actually classed The Power of Love and Stay Another Day as Christmas songs. Yes, they were catchy and had been released at Christmas time, but Smiler could never put them in the same bracket as Slade, Wizard or Cliff Richard. The old crooners were on a different level still, your Crosbys, Martins and Coles. That was before you even mentioned McCartney, Lennon, Rea and Lake. With all of that to listen too why would you have any need for non-Christmassy Christmas songs? A new series of photos appeared on the screen, nativity scenes of all shapes and sizes, and further childhood memories were released. The birth of the baby Jesus had been forgotten by most people years before, but Christmas still remained one of the few times when everyone had the chance to let themselves go a bit and to feel a little bit more love than they did during the rest of the year. The music wasn't there to remind people of shepherds and kings, or even of snowmen and roasting chestnuts, it was just a time that was simpler and happier than they found themselves in during the other eleven months of the year, and any old music could help them make that change. Smiler cast a vote for the homemade effort from the local primary school, by far the most authentic entry and surely a worthy winner of the crib of the year competition.

Drink had never been something that Smiler had a problem with, finding that socially it gave something for the hands to do as well as quenching the thirst. The small warmth that the alcohol gave was also pleasant, a lubricant to make the engine run just a little bit smoother. Wendy had a problem though, seeming to take no pleasure from something that she bought by the bottle and consumed in great gulps, her only comments being criticisms of its taste and its temperature. It changed her mood too, taking almost no time at all to transform her from gushing in her detailed appreciation for Alastair Sim in his role as Ebenezer Scrooge to whispered disgruntlement about people that Smiler had never even heard of. The whispers were aimed at anyone sat next to her, hushed mutterings of hate and revenge during which her eyes gave no indication that the secrets that she was revealing would probably be best kept hidden. For Smiler it was a definite shame that she couldn't be more careful and more cool, with more love and understanding.

There was just time for one last look through the timeline, the warmth of the mug now gone, whilst the eyes started to sting with tiredness. Weeks like this were always difficult but none the less useful and it would surely only be a matter of time before Smiler would have an opportunity to put all of the newly discovered tools into action. How cute did little dogs look dressed up as reindeer? Smiler added one final like and then turned to the sink to wash the mug. The few steps from the living area to the sleeping area took no time at all, accompanied by the music that existed now only in Smiler's head. Love and understanding.

CHAPTER 22

Wednesday 16th December, Late Evening

Fortunately, the minibar had been well stocked. Wendy slumped once again into her chair in the corner of the room no longer worried about adding extra stains to the clothes that would not be worn again that week. Her stomach reminded her that she should eat as well as drink, but at that hour it was way too late. In a now familiar routine her eyes squeezed shut and she found herself once again transported back home to the crime room.

Her memories from earlier that day had already prepared her for the next person on the list, the old faded colours of the previous days giving way to pictures with bright shades that announced brashly that the eighties had well and truly arrived. There was high hair and make-up and brightly coloured clothing, with everything about the whole period announced by an excited scream.

Wendy had met Shanny Easter in her first days at university and it had been a meeting that had changed her life. Shanny was a city girl of mixed race who seemed to make life ten times bigger than it really was, with cool clothes, new music and a sublime singing voice that Wendy would have killed for. They had both followed their shared passion by joining the Amateur Operatic Society, with Shanny taking most of the main parts while Wendy slowly moved up from the back line of the chorus to the front row. Shanny was Wendy's best friend.

When the fateful wedding came it was announced quickly, the hurry becoming clearer a few months after the happy day. Wendy had revelled in the organisation of the hen party, nothing more than a pub crawl followed by a dodgy club but par for the course before a week in Ibiza became fashionable. It had been just afterwards that the realisation began to hit, as Wendy discovered that she wasn't on the list to be a bridesmaid, and wouldn't even be some sort of female usher. The embarrassment of the reception, being stuck on her own besides the rugby team, was an experience that still marked her now. Wendy wasn't Shanny's best friend.

The silence in the hotel room was broken by a nose blown hard into a paper tissue. Wendy had given everything to that friendship, support during the sad times, laughter during the happy times and company whenever Shanny had been lonely. She had even been to watch a game of rugby for crying out loud and her reward had been the embarrassment of sitting alone with the beer swilling riff raff whilst elsewhere the refined people in the room had celebrated the holy union of Shanny and Steve in style. The lesson had been hard, but useful. Some people were just takers, there to exploit the good ones, choosing whoever served them best at the time in order to extract as much as they could from them, before eventually moving on. Wendy had fought the rugby team off, gone back to her room and cried, knowing that things between them could never be the same again.

The photos before her had once given such happiness, but now gave nothing but pain. They were there together on stage in Iolanthe, sitting in a group studying by the river on a hot summer's day and also in a wedding photo, with Wendy's hair just about visible over the shoulder of some six foot prop forward at the far end of the line. The wedding invitation was there too, inexpensive and faded just like their friendship. By the time the baby came along they no longer even talked, with Wendy deep in rehearsals as an understudy for one of the three little maids, whilst Shanny was changing nappies in some small flat in the city centre, enjoying married life briefly before she was divorced a few weeks after her twenty third birthday. It seemed to be the same all over, good people giving and giving whilst the others just took and gave nothing in return. It had been Wendy's weakness, well one of them at least.

A shake of Wendy's head cleared the memories, an etch-a-sketch mechanism to keep her sane. The small rays of orange from the streetlights outside lit up her path to the minibar and just one final top up to help her sleep. As she sat back down her face lit up in full smartphone afterglow, the sort of face that would have convinced Ebenezer Scrooge that yet another spirit had made their way into his chamber on that fated Christmas Eve. There were ghosts there, but from Wendy's past not Scrooge's, and as she flicked through her latest messages she felt the temperature dropping, her limbs becoming heavier and her face less sensitive as each new sentence that she read took her deeper into her wine glass.

'At some point you need to stop worrying about these things from the past and take some action.'

'They'd deserve it of course. You can't have been the only person that they've done this to. If you don't want to do it for yourself, think

of the others.'

'Imagine the buzz you'll get, the feeling of freedom and release. You never know, it would probably be fun.'

'Of course, we're only talking about it. We're far too old and sensible to think about things like that, aren't we.'

Had Sharon deliberately left off the question mark? Wendy wasn't sure. She readjusted again, back to the crime room and tales of another wedding of woe.

The photograph now was a young handsome man, in costume and performing in the Pajama Game. Hey There, you with the stars in your eyes, he had sung, looking at Wendy who was eagerly watching on from the side of the stage. Gavin had been at Shanny's wedding too and had seen how upset Wendy had been. Their shared love of performing had bound them together and eventually he had professed his love to her, admittedly not in the beautiful way that he sang the songs as the leading man, but as they had fumbled around drunkenly in her living room after a last night party. None the less it was a profession of love, and their couple had grown through The Pajama Game, HMS Pinafore and Follies, leaving a shared future of happiness in front of them. She had even told her parents of their plans. Slowly the scene from 1989 became clear again in her head.

***

"You bastard!"

The glass was thrown with a force that surprised her, but a degree of accuracy that didn't, and a loud crash soon followed as it hit the opposite wall. Had it been in the movies tiny pieces of glass would have rained down onto the floor with a delicate tinkling sound, but this real-world glass from Woolworths simply offered four dull clunks. As with most of Wendy's glasses of wine this one had been empty. Across the room a young man in his mid-twenties was scrabbling to his feet, his dilated eyes searching urgently for any other potential flying objects that might be close to her hands.

"Calm down Wends, we agreed we'd talk about it like adults." Despite the brave look settling over his face there were definite signs of fear in his voice.

"Calm down Gavin, calm down? When I agreed to talk like an adult, I didn't know that you were going to tell me that the last three years of my life had all been wasted, that all of the time that we've spent together has been a sham. You bastard." Wendy's arm again went through a throwing motion but this time released nothing more than fresh air.

"But Wends, I can't help it, it's just the way I feel. I didn't want it to turn out this way. It's just that we love each other." Gavin moved from side to side as he talked, clearly wanting to avoid being seen as a sitting duck should Wendy get her hands on another projectile.

"But we love each other too, Gavin, remember? You tell me all the time, and I tell you back. Anyway, he's a bloody trumpet player, for Christ's sake. If he'd been one of the cast, or a violinist, I could understand it, but not a trumpet player, surely? He must be pretending, playing around with you for fun." Wendy couldn't see herself, but didn't need to in order to know that her eyes were wet and pleading. He couldn't do this to her, not Gavin. They had even set the date for the bloody wedding.

"Look, I'm sorry Wends, but talking about it when you're like this isn't going to help things at all. Planning the wedding and all that just made me realise that I couldn't go on pretending any more. Look, I'll come and collect my stuff sometime when you're out." He stood still and looked gently at her, every inch the leading man in the local amateur operatic society. "I do love you Wendy, I always did and I always will, but in the end, we just weren't meant to spend our lives together." He turned and zig zagged his way out of the kitchen, the door closing gently behind him.

The large cassette player in the corner continued to pump out the music, New Order singing some song about love tearing people apart, a fine sentiment but as out of context as the rest of Wendy's life. Bloody mix tapes never got it right. Wendy walked over to the player, struggled with putting the tape on fast forwards, and finally brought the song to a rapid halt by slamming her hand down on all of the buttons at once.

Looking at yourself in mirrors didn't make things any better they always said, and the one in front of Wendy confirmed just how right they were. The big mop of hair on top of her head stuck out like that of a cartoon horse, whilst beneath it her cheeks were streaked with a mixture of true-life tears and mascara. Her eyes shone out, a deep blue that was somehow out of place in the wreckage of her normally pretty face. Her hair was tufty on top, short at the sides and long at the back, with the curved ends resting on top of the buttoned-up collar of the polka dot shirt that she always saved for special occasions. In the middle of her face her lips quivered uncontrollably, those lips that had until so recently been made for kissing Gavin Bright, the love of her life and the man that she had planned to spend the rest of her life with. He had saved her from one life crisis, only to pick her up and gently carry her on towards the next, which at that moment seemed ten times more painful than the original one. There was never a bottle of Blue Nun around when you needed one.

The door to the flat opened and gentle footsteps moved towards the bathroom.

"Mum, what are you doing here?"

"Gavin came to see me, he said that you might need some company. Oh, come here my love, come here…"

***

Wendy's eyes squeezed so tight that they hurt, as the scene ended. All she had ever wanted was someone to love her and care for her. The tears dried on her face, cold patches on her cheeks and glue to her eyelashes. She walked quickly across the room to the small bathroom, the energy of the movement warming and waking her at the same time. In reality she had been lucky finding out when she did, before they had gone even deeper into the game of happy families. No, she had been lucky to escape. Gavin was still single and still doing the rounds as a singer, now too old to play the lead but still good enough to warble along to his backing tracks at fiftieth birthday parties. She had even seen him a few years ago, the fine voice somehow distracting from the way that life had ravaged his once beautiful face. Andy Trumpet had moved on years before and Gavin still lived on his own, a lonely nobody with nothing but memories of make-up, stage lights and headlines in local newspapers. It served him right. She checked her messages again, but there was nothing new.

'Of course, we're only talking about it. We're far too old and sensible to think about things like that, aren't we.' Sharon's words wouldn't go away.

CHAPTER 23

Thursday 17th December, Morning

Something wasn't quite right, but Wendy couldn't understand exactly what it was. Putting on fresh clothing as she moved into the last two days of the week nearly always gave her an extra boost, as did the knowledge that on Thursday night she would pack her case, but that morning she had felt nothing and had even almost been sick, a suggestion that her remarkable powers of resistance to wine were also seemingly on the wane. First night nerves had plagued her since her very first show, but fourth night wobbles, even in the morning, were unheard of. She walked around rapidly, her heart racing and her blouse already sticking to her back beneath the light top, her heel clicks dampened by the once thick carpet as she prepared markers, post-its and papers, all of the things that would normally take her mind off any problems and focus her back on the job at hand. A vibration on the table startled her and the phone was taken up in a second, revealing a hoped-for message from Sharon. Wendy breathed more easily as she read through her friend's words. Yes, of course it had been a silly exchange the night before, but Sharon wasn't used to drinking and had been at her works party, so no harm had been done with all of those stupid things that they had talked about. She would be in touch again later, once she had got over her hangover.

Wendy sighed, realising that it must have been the memories of their exchanges the night before that had thrown her off course. A chinking cup told her that people were starting to arrive and she turned to see that Maria was already there. Another time Wendy would have perhaps gone over to comfort her, but to be honest at that moment she had nothing to say. She carefully placed the blue marker between green and indigo and straightened up the pile of mid-sized post-its, an empty stare focussing on the day's agenda. Just two more days and then she was free until the New Year. Come on Wendy, you can do it, just two more days.

"Right then, this morning is all about C O N F L I C T." She wrote the letters on the paper board as she said them, pleased with both the dramatic effect of the joint action and the equal sizing and spacing of the letters. "All about conflict and how to manage it. So, Flash, what can you tell us about conflict?" It was a good ploy, ask someone else to answer so that the loudmouth couldn't get in.

She could see the surprise on Brian's face out of the corner of her eye, his brain obviously whirring away in search of some belittling comment that he could throw into the ring later.

For her part, Flash was good. Most people saw conflict as raging arguments, silent sabotage or just plain violence. From the sound of it, Flash had seen all of that and more working with the disadvantaged, helpless and needy of the area. She was clever enough though to really understand that these were extreme cases, what eventually happened when nothing was done in time. Conflict was disagreement, resistance, paths crossing instead of aligning, and the secret came in identifying it early and managing it.

"Yes, excellent Flash. You've hit that many nails on the head there you should be looking for a job as a carpenter." Nobody laughed, but Wendy carried on regardless.

Sometimes you could be open and welcoming and encourage the group to debate and interact, but sometimes you just had to put your head down, turn the pages over and get on with it. That Thursday was a get on with it sort of day.

"So, first we'll look at the reasons for conflict, then we can look at how to recognise them. Before the break it will then be all about the tools that we can use to manage it. Then we'll get into some more role playing, giving you all a chance of doing it for real. Any questions?"

Unsurprisingly he had some questions, Brian always did. Could he be in a different group, because Desmond wasn't very good at role playing? Would the situations be made up or real, because he found it difficult to get into character when they were made up? He was sat there still resplendent in his black and white school uniform, so surely he had more important things to worry about? Poor old Maria seemed to have finally been worn down. Her moody glare still topped off yet another exquisite combination of casual jacket over tailored jeans and tan boots, but her resistance was nothing more than passive. She seemed just like Wendy in a way, resigned to seeing out the last hours before they could all wave goodbye and move on with no worry of ever seeing each other again.

"So then, resistance, decision making and other signs of conflict. Here we go."

***

Looking over the top of her smartphone the group appeared somehow different. They were all far too busy to notice that she was breaking the groundrules, and Wendy gave her head a slow, deliberate shake. Did she genuinely pity them or was she just annoyed that Sharon's hangover was taking longer to clear than she had hoped? It was silly, of course, to think that Sharon would have no work to do and would be free to send and read messages all day, but yearning for things often drove you to silly thoughts.

The morning had gone better than expected and they had even been treated to a change of biscuits. Gingerbread Christmas trees and reindeer, surely broken leftovers from a local church fete, but different all the same. Even Brian had tucked in with no complaints about his 'fucking Jammy Dodgers' not being there. Mixing up the role play pairings had been for everyone's sakes, putting Brian with Flash and Sachin in a group of three, the only two who had a hope of giving back as good as they got without getting annoyed. Desmond was with Maria, who was now seemingly so docile that she would put up with his stuttering without any complaints. In different circumstances Wendy might even have worried about her, but everything that had happened to her seemed to be no-one's fault but her own. Jack was with Dot, a mother and son pairing as low risk as she could imagine. Brian glanced towards her, receiving in return a customary smile from a seemingly concerned trainer, expertly surveying her class.

The sound became a blur, the worn old wallpaper in the room not helping the acoustics, and Wendy's thumb tired of constantly refreshing her message stream. Why was Sharon not replying? Yes, her ideas had been silly, but in every silly idea there was at least an idea of sorts. How had Sharon put it? If you do nothing, nothing happens. It was a full-blown scientific law or something like that, just like Sod's Law. A crescendo in the sound brought her back to the present, and a quick glance showed that it was Jack again, rising to his feet as his voice transformed into an anguished cry.

HE'S MAKING A LIST

"But animals do it, why is it so hard for you?"

Oh no, not that again, had he not got it all out of his system earlier in the week?

"They teach, and they protect. They show their offspring how to hunt, how to hide, how to fight back against anything that tries to attack them. They bring them food, they protect them against predators and the weather and all sorts of other things, and if they can't, they die themselves attempting to do it. Lions do it, deer do it, mice do it, birds do it, they all do it. Why is it that human adults always find something more interesting to do, that they always expect someone else to be better placed to do it for them? Should teachers really be there to teach us right from wrong, to teach us how to respect each other?" Jack's eyes were closed, seeking inspiration for his words from some inner drawer where his feelings had been locked away.

In front of him, Dot looked surprisingly calm. Wendy stood, ready to offer reason before the lunch break, but Jack carried on.

"So, you watched the telly, you went to the pub, you worked and brought home the money, but we never talked. You never gave me advice, or offered me any help? Yes, I'm sure it was hard for you, especially if you'd never had any help yourselves." His rage was subsiding.

His eyes opened and he turned his head slowly around the room, his challenging stare ignored as the others looked away, one by one.

"After all, if animals can do it…" His voice tailed off to silence, as did the rest of the room, with the exception of the sound of Flash once more saving Wendy the horror of a comforting speech as she moved quickly towards him.

"Well, on that note we'll call it quits for this morning. We'll start again at half past."

CHAPTER 24

1998

The click of heels accompanied Wendy's quick march down the long corridor, providing a rhythmic accompaniment to the song that she was humming along to. Well, it wasn't exactly correct to call it a song as she could give it no title and she knew no words, but it had a catchy tune and it had been trapped in her head since she had left the bar the night before with her best friend Liz. They would surely be reunited that morning and the thought made Wendy smile, remembering the fun from not just the night before, but from every time they had been out together during the last ten years. Liz wouldn't be late though, with surely only Wendy having failed to see the curled up post-it that had been stuck on her computer monitor with the time and place of the meeting written on it. Wendy stopped in front of the door, the name plate announcing that it was the office of Mr J Marley, HR Director. She straightened her outfit, put her smile in place and flicked her hair before giving a small knock and pushing her way through.

"Hi everyone, sorry I'm late. Bloody post-its are useless for sticking to plastic." She gave a small friendly giggle, but

HE'S MAKING A LIST

nothing was returned.

As expected, Liz Trout was there with Marley, the two of them having been clearly in deep conversation before Wendy's arrival. Liz was looking fantastic as ever in a white shirt that made the most of her dark skin and a neat pair of trousers. Old Marley was dressed in his normal casual trouser and blazer combination with one of his famously colourful ties underneath his large, equally colourful face.

"No worries Wendy, come on in. We're in no hurry." The reply was friendly, but strangely distant.

Wendy was battling against the music that was still passing round her head and a niggling doubt that not everything was as it seemed. Marley sat down at the head of his small, rectangular table, leaving the two ladies to take their places on either side. Wendy looked across at Liz, her eyes doing all they could to say 'great night last night, what does Marley want?', but failing to do so as Liz was staring determinedly out of the window and across the car park. Marley shuffled a few papers across the table as Wendy was once more consumed by the melody from the night before.

"So anyway, thanks both for coming, I've just got a couple of announcements to make to you, to bring you both up to date."

Hmm, intrigue thought Wendy, again unsuccessfully trying to catch Liz's eye. What was wrong with her that morning?

"Firstly I wanted to let you both know that at Christmas I'll be retiring."

What? Wendy was in a state of shock as the news sank in. Retiring? He was nowhere near old enough.

"Retiring, but you're nowhere near old enough." She said, with a small knowing giggle.

"Flattery will get you nowhere Wendy. Indeed I am a bit young to be going…"

At least he had smiled a little as he'd said it. All sorts of thoughts were going through Wendy's mind now as she imagined how things could play out. With the state that the company was in it was unlikely that they would bring in a new person from outside, they must surely be looking to replace him from within. Once more she looked up eagerly at her friend across the table, but yet again found that Liz was looking elsewhere. What was wrong with her?

"…so anyway I'll be taking advantage of the very fine offer that the company has made and I'll be doing it all a couple of years early." His hands were placed flatly on the table and he looked from one to the other as he made sure that what he had said had sunk in.

So, his first piece of news had been pretty dynamite to Wendy and she wondered what on earth could come next. She leaned forward, put her head on her hands and gave him her friendliest stare in anticipation.

"And the second thing concerns my replacement. I know that you two have been close for quite some time now, so I wanted to be the person to tell you Wendy, that Liz will be taking over from me as of the first of January next year." Marley smiled, Liz looked at her for the first time that morning with a hard stare and Wendy opened her mouth like a goldfish.

Nothing made sense. So everything had been decided behind her back, without her even knowing what was going on. She looked again at Liz, searching for a small acknowledgement of their years of friendship within her dark eyes. The outside of the lips curled a little, transforming the hard stare into a mild stare. Wendy's head started aching as it tried to make sense of everything that had happened. Marley spoke again.

"So she'll be following me around from now until the end of the year, and after that we'll be putting a new name plate on the door." He looked towards his protégé and was rewarded with a warm smile.

"And me?" Wendy looked at him, imploringly.

"There'll be plenty for you to do, Wendy." His lips

hadn't moved and the voice had been Liz's. Wendy turned urgently to face her, praying above all things to find a semblance of warmth in the face she knew so well.

"For a start you can take over the things that I am currently working on, whilst also helping Jason to get up to speed with your role. We think it will be a good time to stretch him a bit and see if he's up to the task. Then from next year you'll be working on special projects."

"Jason. My job. Which projects?" Full sentences were beyond her as she slowly shook her head in disbelief.

"Special ones, Wendy, special ones." Liz stood up and walked into the corner of the room, flicking the switch on a shiny kettle as she picked up a company mug.

Marley gave Wendy one last 'who'd have thought it, eh' shrug and closed the folder in front of him.

"Jason should be waiting for you in your office. Be gentle with him."

CHAPTER 25

Thursday 17th December, Lunchtime

The cricket tea themed spread had been good, honest Anglo-Saxon food, though whatever the Saxons had ever done for us, ITK wasn't sure. The morning had been as much of a disaster as the rest of the week, the stupid woman having no idea of what was going on or how to control it. ITK could see in Wendy's eyes that she was tired. She was tired through lack of sleep, tired of doing what she was doing and really tired of spending all of her life blaming other people for the fact that she was such a dumb cow. Had she really thought that no-one had seen her, miles away in her thoughts looking non-stop at her phone as she waited for another message from Sharon? ITK forced a small giggle, knowing full well that Sharon would be back in touch just as soon as the last tuna and cucumber sandwich was eaten. It was time to be really careful though, as ITK had never taken anyone this far before.

The next hours would be crucial. It was just like pulling a heavy weight with an elastic band, where at first your movement is rewarded with nothing but extra strain, as the object stays still. Finally there comes a moment of truth, when either the object starts to move with you, in which case you have won, or the elastic breaks, leaving the object immobile forever. ITK had started pulling Wendy a few days before but had so far only been rewarded with tension. If things were going to go as planned then now was the time to see how strong that elastic band really was. Making people be verbally violent on-line was not the same as the physical violence that was being planned.

The social distancing that had started within the group on the second day was now complete, and following the initial politeness whilst collecting food the others were all occupied with their own thoughts. Taking advantage, ITK walked over to a seated area at the top of the stairs and took a chair, delighted to see that Wendy was also there, almost invisible seated in a large leather armchair over near the window. The feeling was strange, almost electric, being so close to the target of your contempt, unseen but dangerous. ITK could feel a dampness all over as a flush of heat passed. Wendy the person meant nothing, being just another example of Wendy the species, the entitled who continued to push down on those below. The flush passed, and ITK felt calm again in the knowledge that what would be a never-ending struggle on a general level could ultimately be actioned at an individual level. It was the perfect time to start pulling on that elastic band and to see if Wendy was going to start moving along with her old friend Sharon, or if their bond was going to break.

CHAPTER 26

Thursday 17th December, Afternoon

Wendy carefully drew the triangle on the board, the bright orange colour a stranger amongst the darkness of the room all around it. Turning slowly she saw them all taking their places, a half-smile forming from habit but disappearing quickly as it realised that it would neither be seen nor appreciated. They were a group of losers, to be added to all of the other losers that now passed before her every month of every year. Some people were just destined to be like that, while others were forced into unhappiness by the actions of others. Wendy knew in which group she was to be found.

***

The first part of the afternoon had been quiet and easy. A little bit of theory and explanation was well supported by the fact that no-one really seemed to care about the subject, being more interested in getting the week over with than in actually taking advantage of the many pearls of wisdom that Wendy had to share with them. Flash was at least asking questions, something to break up the monotony of Wendy's voice and move the minute hand along that little bit quicker, but the others did nothing to encourage anything other than Wendy's continued drone.

"Indeed, in this example we are talking about the roles that people decide to take when they interact, not a role that they have in real life at any point in time. We've talked about resistance and conflict and all sorts of other states that people find themselves in, and the model that I've shown you is just there to explain to you how people can react to that with their daily interactions."

"So, you're saying that some people enjoy playing the role of the victim, that it's a choice?" The tone of defence in Flash's voice was evident, but Wendy already had her reply.

"Not at all. What I'm trying to say is that, for various reasons, some people may get picked on during conversations, so becoming a victim. Other times the same person might pick on others, and on and on as they move around the triangle. At this point the conversations stop being productive. When we are a leader, we need to recognise this, and help our people to get out of the triangle and move back to effective communication." It couldn't be clearer.

Brian taking a sharp intake of breath, however, was not a good sign.

"So, basically it means that lover boy over there is happy as Larry being the victim, because it means he can blame someone else." Eyes were raised towards the ceiling all around the room.

"Brian, grow up won't you and leave the boy alone for a while." Sachin beat the others to it, but Brian sensed a bite.

"And there you have it, Sachin. You just couldn't resist playing the fucking game could you. Your act of becoming the unofficial group saviour has in fact turned you into the persecutor, whilst making me the victim, thus changing the dynamics of the triangle. You see Wendy, it's much easier for people to get it with a real-life example. It makes it much more meaningful." God, he was an awful person, but he had at least understood the concept.

"W w w why d don't y y you just g give it a r rest?" Nobody needed to look to identify the latest speaker.

A quick turn of the head showed that Desmond was unusually agitated, probably due to a combination of the long days of silence and having all of those wonderful thoughts trapped inside his head, with no effective way of passing them outside to the rest of the world.

"Oh shit, now we're in for it. The stuttering saviour joins the fray, confirming my new role as victim by rescuing the previous persecutor in Sachin. I must say Wends, this has been the…"

"Look Brian, just shut the fuck up and stop being a knobhead!" Wendy stared in awe.

"That was wonderful." She searched the room for confirmation, but was met by nothing but surprised looks. "Excellent! Where did that come from Desmond?"

Desmond looked at her sheepishly, embarrassed to answer. Brian, for the first time that week, looked unsure of himself whilst the rest maintained their initial looks of surprise.

"I it happens s some t times w w when I g get angry." Wendy couldn't understand why Desmond looked so sad about it.

"So, all we need to do is try and create that anger, in a controlled way, and use it to help you when you need it. Have you thought of ways that you could do that?" For a rare moment her smile was real.

A loser he may be, but this could be a big success for her, with even the possibility of getting a publication out of it if she was lucky. Desmond didn't seem to share her joy.

"The p p problem is th that I s s swear too."

"Ha, ha, ha. The stuttering saviour with Tourette's. You really couldn't fucking make this up, could you."

HE'S MAKING A LIST

Brian was back in the driving seat, while Desmond's anger had clearly been replaced by anguish. The others were eagerly waiting for biscuits and tea. "You might've got away with it on the shop floor my friend, but you accountants aren't supposed to be swearing all the time are you, counting your bastard beans and massaging your fucking figures."

"Okay, that's enough. Let's have a break and then we can round up on what we've worked on today." The brief excitement of a publication was immediately replaced by the desire for a Ginger Nut biscuit, if only she could beat Brian to the tray.

***

Her shoulders slumped as she saw that there were no new messages, despite her feeling during the lunch break that things had started moving along. There was a definite coming together with Sharon, their messages exchanged more often and with a lighter feel, just like the exchanges of love-struck teenage girls. Being surrounded by the group of idiots all day just confirmed that natural selection wasn't cutting it anymore, overruled by technology and a massive dose of Dunning-Kruger. Jack talked about protection and guidance, but how were this lot ever going to do any of that when they had been so badly let down themselves? The more she thought the more she realised that Sharon was right, her life had been screwed up by others and the person who had done it needed to be punished in the severest of ways. All they had to do now was agree on who that person should be, and Wendy was now ninety nine percent sure of the name.

Her hand moved expertly inside her leather bag, and she took out and counted a set of plastic coated cards, each one containing a piece of information that the group would need to use in order to solve a puzzle, so long as they communicated properly and gave each other an opportunity to speak. It was even a game where Desmond could stand up and write on the board so everyone was a winner. The best news? Not only was it something where Wendy could just watch from the sidelines, but it also lasted long enough to take them through to the end of the day. The last night in the Grand Hotel was approaching fast.

***

"Right then you lot, we're getting near the end of the week and so it's time for another lesson that you won't find on the agenda. This one is about humour, and so you, Brian, should listen just a bit closer than the others. We all like to think that we can be funny, and being funny can be an advantage, but at the end of the day, only comedians are paid to make people laugh."

"And clowns Wendy, and clowns." Brian's joke did actually get a laugh for once.

"And clowns, yes Brian. The thing is that we need to understand that humour is subjective. If you find something is funny, share it. Some people will laugh along with you, some people won't, and other people will laugh, but do it on their own so you never knew that you even made them laugh. That is just the way it is, and the positives that it can bring to a group of people are immense. Just don't," her smiling face fixed on Brian, "just don't treat life as one long joke, just don't believe that you are the clown. Take that with you, and all will be okay. So, tomorrow is the last day, and I'll see you all in the morning. Oh, are there any questions before you go?"

Of course there weren't.

CHAPTER 27

Thursday 17th December, Early Evening

It was the last night, pack your bags night as Wendy always called it, when the excitement of going home the next day already started to kick in. Not that going home offered Wendy much more than a calmer colour scheme, some decent lighting and some proper wine. The few hours that she had spent in her room had been mainly shared between the blinding white light of the bathroom and the unlit sleeping area where she had sat, huddled in the imposing armchair whilst reliving her time in the crime room. Now it was time to clear out the drawers and hangers that had been home to her clothes for the week and take a look around.

The usual suspects were all present, the telephone, bible and writing desk, three items that no longer had a use in the twenty first century and would never come back in fashion. Breaking the pattern in the wallpaper was a framed print of smoking cottages and workers gathered around giant haystacks, another image so old now that no living person would ever have seen such a scene in real life, just as in a hundred years people would look back disbelievingly at photos from the beginning of the twenty first century. Her clothes were neatly zipped up in anti-crease bags and placed carefully in the soft leather suitcase, leaving just enough space for her toilet bag to join them in the morning. A silent humming sound came from inside a cheap wooden cabinet, reminding her that the minibar would never go out of fashion and she took out the half empty bottle that was left over from the bar the night before and poured liberally into the clean glass that sat upon the desk. The week had been expensive as well as tiring but redundancy payments had left her with a house that was already paid for, and what was money for anyway, if not for living?

Wendy sat back on her bed, the well stuffed pillows keeping her upright as the first glass went down. She checked yet again for new messages, frustration rising as she saw that none had arrived. It had certainly been a strange week with the finding of Sharon, or more correctly the being found by Sharon, being almost too good to be true. To be honest her memories of Sharon from school were pretty thin, just as they were from the times when they'd done a couple of shows together, with there being only faint recollections that Sharon was neither the best singer or dancer in the world. But despite that Wendy must have really made an impression on the girl, what with all of the effort Sharon must have taken in order to find her again. After all she didn't have her own website or a Wikipedia page, did she? Yes, good old Sharon must have either been much fonder of her than Wendy remembered or she had found herself in one of those melancholy moods where you go searching for your past, hoping to rekindle old relationships in a vain attempt to bring back simpler times.

The wine was far too cold and as characterless as ever. Sharon, on the other hand, had plenty of character, certainly much more than Wendy remembered. It must have been something she had developed after they had left school and gone their separate ways. Her finger tips caressed the expensive material of her blouse, a cardigan no longer necessary to keep her warm, as a strange calmness that she hadn't felt for some time came over her. She looked back again through the latest exchanges, each phrase making more and more sense with every new reading. Suddenly her heart stopped as the small phone in her hand vibrated to announce a new message at last. She quickly changed between screens, her pulse now quickening as fingers and thumbs worked away.

She had smiled a lot that week, some of them had even been sincere, but the one currently rising on her lips was more sneer than smile.

'Well then, have you decided? Dare we do it?'

There was no 'we' about it, Sharon, Wendy would manage this one all on her own. She was going to do it, to clear the air once and for all. The dregs of her glass were downed in one and she rolled off the bed, put her shoes on and ruffled her hair as she left her room.

The journey had already been made three times before, but just as with her room Wendy had never taken the time to look around her. Some would have called the hotel quaint, but to Wendy it was just old and neglected, much like everything else in Harshton. On either side of the corridor were wooden doors, painted smooth and with the metallic room numbers doing their best to shine out in the hotch potch of aging yellow incandescent, warm red compact fluorescent and bright white LED lamps that had at various times been installed in the ceiling. Beneath her feet a bright red carpet did it's best to muffle the sound of her heels, whilst at the same time shifting its shape to adapt to the curving wooden floorboards beneath. Well-worn patches indicated the entrances to the rooms and the path to take towards the breakfast buffet between six and ten every morning. The corridor turned towards the main staircase, passing the corner that contained the now traditional combination of old armchairs standing guard around an even older coffee table. To top it all off there was a shoe shining machine and an ice dispenser, almost looking embarrassed to be included in the scene. The place was stuck in the past, just like Wendy, though unlike Wendy it had no realistic way of freeing itself and moving on.

The sound from the bar area was already loud, much louder than the previous evenings, with the sound of Bing just audible above the noise of excited chattering. Finally, she arrived at the stairs, long and sweeping down towards the hotel entrance, the sort that film stars or Cinderella would have walked down to admiring glances. Well tonight she would have to be the star and she put in place her starriest smile so far that day as she grasped the hand rail, flicking her hair as she looked up to the confirmation of her worst fears. In the large function room opposite the bar could clearly be seen neatly laid tables, and in the air the heavy smell of roast turkey was unmistakeable. There must have been about forty of them, far too many to fit into the hotel bar, and so the reception area was full. On one side were men of all ages, each holding a pint pot and sporting a Christmas themed jumper, whilst on the other were the ladies, all fancy dresses and goldfish sized glasses of G&T, each one topped off with illuminated reindeer antlers. What were the chances of people drunkenly returning to their rooms at all hours, before noisily shagging all night in the next room? She sighed, thankful that they would at least soon be going to eat and taking their noise and poundland Christmas celebrations with them. Reaching the bottom she looked around, pleased to see that a handful of the Christmas jumpers were still staring in her direction. Wendy still had some of that old magic.

Bing had gone, replaced by Kirsty Maccoll and the Pogues who provided a fresh, bobbing jolt of energy to the jumpers and antlers. Wendy searched for something familiar, starting to feel lost in the crowd of revellers, happily noticing a hand waving in her direction. Her posse as she now liked to call them had done well, finding a set of chairs over in the corner of the lobby. They were all there again, though what made them keep showing up she didn't know, but at least it was better than drinking alone. Her head jolted backwards and her smile slid into place as she walked towards them, ready to go out in style on their last night together.

CHAPTER 28

Thursday 17th December, Late Evening

It was only a small glass of whisky, and nothing extraordinary in terms of brand, but ITK savoured every last drop. There would be better to celebrate when Wendy had done the deed but for now it was just fine. Hands expertly flicked on lights, monitors and processing power, with even the small Christmas tree in the corner of the room joining in as its handful of lights lit up. ITK emptied the glass and took a quick walk to the kitchen for a top up, believing that Sharon deserved a celebratory drink too.

The walk was not long, but took ITK from the hub of activity that was the computer room, back into the false, boring world outside. The flat wasn't huge but the difference in style between the high-tech war room and the rest of the place was remarkable all the same. Surely, in the past, ITK had enjoyed an identity, a style or whatever people would call it these days. That had all gone though as the old dreams gave way to mundane reality. The flat had been paid for with a mixture of savings, inheritance and redundancy payments, a fact that at least relieved some of the day to day pressure for survival. It was always a

HE'S MAKING A LIST

comfort to know that the roof over the head couldn't be taken away, even if food, clothing and good whisky did sometimes present a problem. The glass was half filled again, one of a set recovered from aunty Joan when she had passed away. The chairs, table, plates, beds, wardrobes and everything else all had similar origins, as older relatives and other assorted family friends had departed, each one leaving behind their own sad exhibits for an undistinguished antiques roadshow. Auntie Joan had been no loss to ITK, the few birthday cards received as a child being nothing compared with the half decent sideboard and a few old glasses. That glass was filled again, and drink in hand ITK was back inside the computer room and back into the fray.

Wendy was just where ITK wanted her, ready to do the deed but desperate for assurance and help. Their whispered exchanges had been used as best they could, but the coded encouragements of a stranger in a bar were nothing next to the confident urging on of a long-lost friend like Sharon, no matter how pissed Wendy had been. When ITK had left her she had been talking with the three most hideous Christmas jumpers known to man, and knowing her she was probably still there now. Patience was the order of the day and the waiting would help to keep Wendy fragile, whilst preparing her for the challenge to come. In the meantime, ITK had other things to be getting on with.

The false picture of the Indians celebrating Christmas from the day before had been a roaring success, finally achieving over two thousand likes, five hundred retweets and hundreds of comments that were the typical mixture of support and abuse. ITK was apparently a racist, fascist, embarrassment, scum, was stupid, and all sorts of other things, and every time a person took the time to type their insult the initial story became visible to hundreds and then thousands more people. The term liar was another word often used against ITK, but they were stupidly using the old definitions. The truth had changed, transformed from being a combination of facts into the telling of a meaningful story. There were no more truths to discover, they had all been found out long ago, and everyone knew what was really happening in the world nowadays, even if most of them chose to ignore it. The challenge was to find the best way to make everyone aware of the truth, and that involved finding an effective way to tell a story using just a combination of images and two hundred and eighty characters. The ability to do that was what set ITK apart from the others.

Most of the people with big followings didn't need to react. They had thousands and thousands of followers, meaning that they could afford to just put a story out there and move on, safe in the knowledge that all of the snowflakes would complain and all of the sheep would follow. You could say whatever you wanted to them but you'd never get a reply, as all they wanted was coverage for their unconventional views not an intelligent discussion. ITK was still building a following though, so the best way to achieve that was to argue back and attract people that way. Fortunately, a quick-fire wit was available in spades.

'Does your mum know you're out?'

'Have you read article 5.4 of the treaty?'

'And with your lot in charge we'd all be bankrupt by now anyway'

'You all right hun?'

'Er ist wieder da!'

HE'S MAKING A LIST

'Lovely pic'

The whisky was starting to do its job, providing some warmth and loosening the imagination as ITK started searching through the news of the day. ITK had never really been religious but a couple of years attending Sunday school had provided a good understanding of the basics. The initial attacks on Christmas had come from the lefties, with the PC brigade being ready to ignore Christian values in the name of inclusion, and so trees and cards had been banned and Happy Holidays signs appeared everywhere. Now the attacks were coming from other sources, as people were being forced to eat Halal turkeys whether they wanted to or not. It would never have happened in Bernard Mathews' day, that's for certain, but despite all of the evidence there seemed to be no escape, with the government, according to the Prime Minister, seemingly too busy striking trade deals and assuring World peace. It almost made ITK want to cry, the erosion of the values of good old England. Next to that there were the families with loads of children and no way to support them, all able to afford the latest smartphones and forty fags a day but not to provide food for their kids. Why should everyone else pay for them? Christ on a bike there was something wrong with the parents of the twenty first century. ITK laughed, the temptation for another glass of the hard stuff keen, but the self-constraint held firm. The hornets nest was stirred and building nicely, forever generating new followers and more and more discord amongst men, women, and any other gender that people wanted to identify as.

Attention now needed to go back to Wendy and any help that she might need for her Saturday night task. The silly slag appeared to have decided that she was ready to do something, but was no closer to deciding who the target should be. ITK could imagine her now, tears streaming through the mascara as she went yet again through her stupid, non-existent list of evidence. The result would be as it had been for all of the previous years, a reinforced sense of superficial injustice and nothing but more hesitation over who the real person responsible for all of her sadness was. ITK's alter ego Sharon on the other hand no longer had any doubts about who it would be, or that Wendy would be convinced of that decision when necessary. All ITK had to do was to make sure that when that time came all of the necessary information was available, and the flutter of keystrokes announced that the required research was underway.

CHAPTER 29

Thursday 17th December, Late Evening

It had been a mistake to stay behind and try and talk to Wendy, but Smiler was worried about her. Their little tête-à-tête had only confirmed that she was off the rails, her incomplete and incoherent ramblings suggesting that 'IT' was going to happen on Saturday night, though what 'IT' was Smiler didn't know. Wendy was difficult to read, a person who gave off a false confidence all day but who clearly suffered behind the smile, and with people like that some sort of breakdown or even suicide could never be ruled out. How the hell she'd allowed the ghosts from her past to put her into such a situation wasn't clear, but it wasn't a question of trying to understand her but rather finding a way to help her that was the source of Smiler's concern. Some people screamed out for help at every obstacle they found, whilst others preferred to keep their anguish locked inside and hidden, and Wendy was clearly in the second group. Not asking for help didn't diminish the need for it though, and most likely made it even more necessary but harder to find. Smiler gently increased the thermostat on the radiator by the small desk, the cup of tea not providing enough heat on its own, and switched on the computer.

It had been another run of the mill day. The flu epidemic had put a strain on the health service like it had never known before and with the deaths and disorder came the accusations, with the usual suspects targeted for their sins. It was just a rehash of the bad old days of Brexit and the elections that followed, with everyone having their own viewpoint, theory and list of guilty parties. Smiler wouldn't have called the people who shouted loudest racist, xenophobic or even liars, though the majority of them probably were, because for Smiler it was far simpler than that and they were just selfish, interested in nothing other than looking out for themselves. One after another their comments just screamed out that they, and the ones they knew and agreed with, should have priority. It was always a case of me, me, me.

Side by side with this outpouring of discontent and hatred was the next new craze. Rita and Bob weren't sending any cards this year, deciding instead to donate four calling birds and three French hens to the local foodbank, though they did still wish everyone they knew a Happy Christmas all the same. Smiler had never been a great believer in Father Christmas, and had even less time for Jesus Christ, but cards had always been sent wishing the receiver a 'Merry Christmas' or 'Season's Greetings'. The Christmas card had been invented in the age of the written world and the image of Scott of the Antarctic's life being retold through a series of text messages and Insta posts, his thoughts distilled down to a few underexposed photos and a handful of emojis caused a little snigger. Anyway, the Christmas card was just another way of sharing and receiving information whilst reviving shared memories. Giving things to charity was great, and was unfortunately even more necessary than ever, but where did the joy come from now? When reading Rita and Bob's post would people get a warm feeling through imagining the words, however simple, being written out, of the address and stamp being added to the envelope, of their old friends taking the time to think of them? Probably not.

Anyway, in the end none of it really mattered. People would blame who they wanted for the health crisis, and if the twenty first century no longer gave people the desire to write to old friends once a year, so be it. If there was anything that Smiler was proud of it was the ability to be positive, and Wendy was a case in hand. It would be easy to just forget her, to ignore the signs that she was a damsel in distress and to hope never to see headlines in the local newspapers that told a tragic story. Ignoring her was what the others would do, but Smiler had a feeling that was now so certain that it had to be acted on.

Smiler was going to stop 'IT' happening, by hook or by crook, and now was the time to knuckle down and get to work, with a lady's life possibly depending on it.

CHAPTER 30

Thursday 17th December, Late Evening

There would be no skulking about in the dark tonight, of that Wendy was certain as she strode back towards her room full of an invincible confidence and armed with a bottle of wine. There had been three of them, obviously believing that the beer they had drunk had made their pathetic Christmas jumpers invisible at the same time as turning them all into Brad Pitt. It had been a no-lose gamble, going all in on a bluff as she had invited them all back to her room together, only for them to all turn as pale as the snowman on the fat one's jumper and then quickly make their excuses and leave her alone. Thinking about it, it was logical that even without the effect of the beer, ugly people must spend large periods of the day forgetting how ugly they were, just as stupid people probably never even realised that they were stupid in the first place. For some people there was surely no hope.

Back in her room she placed the stolen bottle on the table. It was almost full and of a decent quality, and must have considered itself safe surrounded by such an uneducated group, but Wendy had freed it and would treat it with the respect that its short life merited. Her glass was filled and she stood there, the open curtains allowing an unnecessary light to spill out into the street at the side of the hotel whilst also giving her a perfect view of her own reflection in the window. Once again she found herself staring at more photos back in the crime room.

The two young faces at the centre of the photograph looked happily back out at her, hot, sweating, smiling and full of life and hope. In all of her fifty plus years Wendy had never looked better. She had never been beautiful but she was at least pretty, and from the faded ink in the photo shone out a confidence that, even now, she doubted could ever have truly been there. It had been a celebration evening for winning a big contract with China, and the wine had flowed and they had laughed and danced all evening. She had been a key member of the project team and success gave confidence and that lead to success and then the whole process started again. Her real time reflection in the window reminded her how the same process worked just as effectively in the opposite direction. The girl beside her was beautiful, and any confidence that Wendy was showing was magnified ten-fold in her companion. Around them were other faces, some of which Wendy remembered the names but most of whom she had either never known or had long forgotten. The name of the other girl wasn't a problem though, Elizabeth Trout.

Her memories from lunchtime came back to her again, the embarrassment of working on special projects, before finally leaving Backhams, where they had worked together like sisters for so many years. In the beginning it had been called 'personnel', a formal name for a job which was basically helping people. Helping them out with their problems, helping them to develop in their roles, planning a path for those who wanted to progress and a different path for those who didn't. In short it had been all about making people better. Through time the role had changed, the cold titles and hard words heard when helping people during the 90s transforming into the soft titles and warm words of the new century, where constant delocalisation and headcount reduction had put the focus on different skill sets. It had all been someone's definition of progress.

A blue flashing light outside disturbed Wendy's reflection, and with the breakdown of the image the outside of her lips weakened, passing through neutral to a frown as her reflected face flashed in and out of focus. The cold blue backlight mirrored the cold feelings from her past. The payoff had at least given her the security of owning her own home, and a quick offer to do some training had introduced her to the world of being a consultant, and as they say she had never looked back. Except that she had, and did every time she saw that picture of the two of them together, knowing all the time that Elizabeth Trout had never really been her friend at all. Backhams still survived, in the same way that a tree cut down to the base of its trunk still existed, and Liz was still around town, though Wendy had always managed to avoid her whenever it looked as though their paths might cross.

The next picture was a collective photo, a group one where everyone was happy and smiling despite the fact they were only interested in doing business and not in making friends. In amongst the dinner jackets and ties could be seen an occasional dress, the bright colours in the sea of black making it quick and easy for the wearer to identify themselves. She was at the end of the middle row, almost caught by surprise as the photo had been taken. Five places to her left was the suspect, Hassan Ahmed, dark and assured and with film star looks that had captivated Wendy ever since he had hired her to deliver training classes to the supervisors in his factory. Before her eyes the final scene from 2006 appeared.

HE'S MAKING A LIST

***

"It's never going to happen, is it?"

Wendy had not missed her cue. She had decided that the best time to have the conversation was after their main course. The man before her was incredibly handsome and looked at Wendy with dark brown eyes that had once contained so much passion, but which now held nothing but pity.

"It's okay Hassan, you don't have to say anything, I understand."

She had been stupid to even ask him. She knew what he was going to say and had no desire to hear him say it. It had been a silly, selfish question and one that wasn't necessary as all she had to do was drink her wine and leave. Hassan neatly placed his knife and fork on his plate to show that he was finished.

"Wendy, you knew that it would never be straight forward, didn't you?"

His voice was calm and gentle, and oh so sexy. Wendy stared at him once more, determined that her look would remain defiant. Around them the other diners carried on, oblivious to the heartache that Wendy was feeling. She had chosen the restaurant for their anniversary, the place where they had first been together. Not that it was special at all, it was simply attached to the hotel where the Business Club meeting had been held, where Hassan had booked a room that night to which they had sneaked off when everyone else had gone home in order to make love for that first time. It had never been a relationship full of romance.

"Yes, I knew that, but sometimes it's easy to forget reality when we're so caught up in emotions."

Hassan leaned forward and took her hands in his. She knew that she should pull away but somehow couldn't resist feeling his touch one last time. No doubt he had reserved a room yet again, but tonight Wendy would be taking a taxi home and he would have to sleep on his own.

"It has been three years now, you know, three years that we've been together."

There were many different definitions for being together. This one involved nothing more than a monthly night away whenever Hassan had a meeting or another business trip that was close enough for them to meet. The exhilarating excitement of adventure had weakened though, and now was the time when something like commitment was needed in order to keep the relationship going. They both knew that, just as they both knew that it wouldn't be forthcoming from both sides.

"Your children have left school, your mother in law is in better health. Every barrier that you put between us has come and gone, but still you won't be with me…"

Wendy's voice tailed off as she fought once more against unexpected tears. She pulled her hands back towards her and took another large gulp of wine, understanding perfectly why Stuart Palmer had preferred to dump her with two short phrases. Hassan leaned back, a sympathetic smile coming across his face.

"And what is it now? Business problems? Somebody else needing your attention?"

The look didn't falter. His choice had been made from the start, and nothing that had passed between them had a hope of changing his mind. Wendy took the bottle from the silver ice bucket and emptied it into her glass.

"I'm sorry Wendy, I really am."

Wendy breathed quickly and deeply, her eyes fighting against a surge of tears that were rising in her. Being sorry wasn't something she wanted to hear. Once more she drank.

"Was everything okay for you?" the waitress had arrived unannounced.

Wendy gave her a tight-lipped nod as she forced herself to smile once more. The girl was young and pretty, with a carefree look that Wendy recognised from long ago. Perhaps she'd be lucky in life, perhaps she wouldn't, but

HE'S MAKING A LIST

Wendy really envied the girl the fact that she neither knew or cared what the future held for her. At Wendy's age it was becoming too late for her to find out.

"Shall I bring you a menu for the dessert?"

Wendy had to get out of there. The shake of her head was unseen as she grabbed her handbag and stood. She took one last look at the man before her before turning sharply.

"Not for me, thank you."

Her voice trembled, just as it had done the first time she had spoken on stage. She had eventually learned to hide her nerves when she performed, but the techniques didn't seem to work in real life. She accelerated towards the cloakroom as the curtain closed on yet another show.

***

In the end his business had gone bust, sending Hassan back to where he came from and leaving Wendy to recover alone once again. Her contacts in Leicester told her that he was back on his feet again, and that he was making the most of markets that had long since picked up, but he had never come looking for her and she knew that he never would.

Her back ached, as did her legs and neck and most of all her heart. Leaning against the desk and staring blankly at the window she could just make out her own features looking back at her, but the tears were too small to see and the pain and regrets invisible in the ether around her. She moved away, unsteady on her feet as the blood and alcohol were released to circulate freely once again. The time was near, the time when she would have to make her decision, to choose the name of the person who she was going to punish. Sharon was expecting it, and Wendy now knew above all else that she had to do it. Without action now her purgatory would continue, and that she couldn't afford to let happen.

CHAPTER 31

Friday 18th December, Morning

It was her last day of training and Wendy pushed gently on her bedroom door, the lock giving a surprisingly smooth and efficient click as it was closed for the last time. It was often a stressful moment, knowing that once the key was handed back you had lost the last refuge available for you to retreat to in order to brush your hair, or lie down for a rest, or take advantage of the minibar or use the toilet in peace, but for Wendy that day it was a relief, knowing that it brought her one step closer to the end of the course and her meeting with her destiny.

Wendy had been forced to work hard that morning, the first look in the mirror confirming that her eternal youthfulness wouldn't be quite enough on its own to repair the damage from the night before. She had expertly applied make-up that added a hint of colour to her pale, hollowed cheeks, providing a more solid background from which her eyes could shine out once more. Whethers Engineering had thankfully not had a good enough year to pay for everyone to sleep over, so there had been no Christmas jumpers or flashing antlers lurking noisily in the corridor or the adjoining rooms. An over active mind, plus the bottle of wine liberated from the dining room, had however been far from conducive to a good night's sleep. Years of performing in amateur operatic shows had taught her how to paper over much bigger cracks than the one she had woken up with though, so she had no doubt that everything would stay in place until the four sixteen train back to Webledon left the station that afternoon. She had made a final sweep for lost toiletries and underwear and the fine leather case was at that moment rolling quietly across the worn carpet, accompanied by the soft pattering of a pair of leather loafers. When necessary, Wendy was always willing to sacrifice a bit of style in return for the ability to run for that early train home.

The now familiar training room was empty and calm, almost accepting that at the end of that day it would no longer be required. It had been a good home for the week but there was no time for sentiment, as now it was just a case of getting the last day over and done with. It was strange how rooms got smaller the more time you spent in them. It had gone from a first day where she had struggled to imagine how she would get everyone close enough to the front of the room to participate into a cosy, comfortable front room at an after-pub party.

Her hands worked expertly with the markers, aligning them all neatly at the bottom whilst ensuring that the clip on each cap was facing directly upwards. The post-its, no longer needed, were packed away in a case along with the assortment of tricks and games that had so often been used to buy her peace and quiet whenever it was needed. In their place she installed a toy bingo machine and two sets of cards. Continuing with the agenda that had been planned would be far too dangerous, the exercises associated with 'effective listening' being a sure-fire way to have Jack in tears again, Brian antagonising whoever was unfortunate enough to find themselves as his partner and Desmond stammering through yet another pointless role play. Plan B in such cases was always to do a recap of the entire week, with the bingo balls being used to randomly select both a question and a participant. Well, that was what the others would think anyway. A young girl entered with the coffee and Wendy's empty stomach announced that it might be a good idea for her to take some.

One by one they arrived, somehow all sensing that the end of their time together was fast approaching. Gone was the chatter from the beginning of the week replaced now by the serious looks of people who would soon be going back to their normal weekly routine, the pointless search for an employment opportunity that they knew full well didn't exist in spite of their newly acquired skills. At least there was only one more week for them to survive before the Christmas break. She did her usual routine, passing from face to face and checking the eyes, searching for either a spark of interest that might suggest that their luck was about to change, or in certain cases a spark of intrigue that might suggest that she had said too much the night before. There was nothing to see there, the only hint of life coming from the overlooking gaze of Mr Brunel in his pride of place above the biscuits. No, there was just time to check and see if Sharon had replied to her latest message, and then she would get the show on the road, as together they faced the final curtain.

***

"Right then, number forty seven is Dot, and number twelve is the question. 'In our approach to making small step changes, which zone do we find between the comfort zone and the punishment zone?' Come on, quieten down a bit so we can hear the answer. Dot?"

Wendy had never really understood the concept of a lead balloon. Obviously, she got the science bit, that the lead would make it too heavy to float and all that, but why anyone would decide to link something that was poorly received with a non-floating, heavy object escaped her. That aside, the little quiz session was going down like a lead balloon. Dot was still deep in thought on the subject in hand, her pouted lips surely not helping her ability to speak. Sachin was looking on with some degree of interest and Desmond was just looking on. Flash and Jack were exchanging furtive glances, raising Wendy's heartbeat just a little. Perhaps getting the fierce, tattooed lady and the handsome basket case together could be considered a small success for her efforts that week? Brian seemed more interested in the quality of his school uniform, though after a week of wearing the same clothes he surely couldn't expect it to be anything other than shoddy. Maria was just staring blankly out of the window, today smartly dressed yet again in a combination of her best clothes from during the week, just like the finale of a good old operetta where snippets of all of the best songs were brought together for one last hurrah. In any case it was burning up valuable time and getting them all closer to the end of the week. A small cough roused Wendy and it appeared that Dot now had something to share with them. Wendy's best smile invited the answer.

"I'm sorry Wendy, I can't remember."

Brian couldn't prevent the violent snort coming out and Maria still looked bored. Only Sachin seemed to have any sympathy for poor old Dot.

"Are you sure you can't remember, Dot? Can't the wheel of fortune be vicious, eh?"

"It's not a wheel of fortune Wendy, it's a fucking kiddies bingo set. You're making it all up anyway, with your 'number six is Flash, number thirty two is a question about goldfish' shit. Isn't it dinner time yet? Most of this stuff was deadly boring the first time you did it, so second time around and without the smiles it's killing me." It would have hurt her earlier in the week, but she was past caring.

Brian was probably right anyway, everything she did was useless, but after all she was still in control so he could just get lost.

"Still no ideas, Dot?" she continued as if Brian had said nothing, "Is there anyone here who can help Dot out?"

"Is it the Change zone?" Jack wouldn't let her down.

"Almost right, Jack, yes. It's the zone where real change happens, but we call it the Safety zone of Discomfort. If we stay in our Comfort zone we don't change. If we stretch too far we get to the Punishment zone, and again there is no change. We have to remember that it's all a question of small step changes, and that means we have to create a Safety zone. And that applies to both ourselves when we try to change, and to anyone who works with us who we are helping to change."

Her words had been energetic and vibrant, her face serious but smiling. It happened from time to time, when some long-lost love for the subject caused her to forget the fact that nobody really cared. It made her sad.

"Anyway, that's us all done for this morning. I hope you all enjoyed that little reminder of all of the excellent work that we've done together this week, but unfortunately we're running out of time. As it'll soon be Christmas, and as we've made such great progress, I propose that we take an extra-long lunch and so we'll start again at two o'clock. Oh, are there any questions?"

What a silly question.

CHAPTER 32

Friday 18th December, Lunchtime

It would be easy to think that the Grand Hotel had made a grand effort in the catering department for their last day. A Boxing Day feast was in front of them, cuts of cold turkey besides hot vegetables, a wonderful assortment of pickles and an equally impressive cheeseboard. Wendy's lingering memories of the engineers' fingers on the hands of the lads from the previous night convinced her to choose wisely, going for as light an option as possible. She placed her plate on one of the high tables in the dining area and waited patiently to see if any of the others would join her.

With her back to the group she noticed immediately that there was noise. The previous days had been relatively quiet, the initial excitement of discovering new people being rapidly replaced by the routine of the course and the breakdown of the artificial community. Now it appeared that the last weekend before Christmas was bringing a childlike excitement along with it. She could hear that families were arriving, parties were being attended and hosted, that the places to be seen in and to be avoided were being exchanged. There was even talk of the

HE'S MAKING A LIST

Webledon Santa Fancy Dress Festival that would take place in Wendy's home town the following evening. Wendy combined a relatively fresh-looking piece of Stilton with a crisp looking savoury biscuit, checked that she wouldn't be missed and left.

Surprisingly for a Friday the bar was almost empty, and Wendy sat down with a decent looking mince pie and her final glass of the wonderful hotel Chardonnay that she had been drinking all week. From her position in one of the booths the entrance to the bar was visible in the reflection provided by the mirrored surface of a painting on the wall. It was a typical scene, with moustachioed men with high collars accompanying ladies with parasols and pleated dresses. Horses and carriages were in the mid ground with smoke spewing chimneys behind. It was a scene used to evoke the days gone by, when the industrial might of the region was part of the green and pleasant land of the songs of that age. The name of some long-lost local beer, another victim of progress no doubt, completed the scene. Wendy was sure of one thing, that the pioneers of that age would be left speechless if they knew where their dreams had ended up. She raised her glass and drank to that, happy that none of the others had decided to visit the bar and join her.

Her finger slid silently across the screen of her smartphone, the mixture of sugar and grease from the mince pie creating a smear line from left to right. Adapting to the new technology had not been a problem for her intellectually, though it did give the muscles around her fingers and thumbs a bit of a problem during the colder, wetter months. She opened her messages, disappointed to find nothing new. Sharon had warned her that she wouldn't be around that day but she had still hoped to receive some sort of news. Their frequent exchanges had quickly become part of her basic needs, a distraction from the grind of the day, and she knew that this Friday would be special.

'Take the whole day to think about it, you need to be certain, you can tell me tonight. Will you do it, and who will it be? Then we can plan everything together. Won't it be exciting, to finally take back control?'

Sharon had written the message that morning, demonstrating yet again how much she really understood the situation that Wendy was in. And yes it would be exciting.

That excitement was building, something Wendy hadn't felt in a long time. Not even the sound of carols announcing the virgin birth could dampen the surge of adrenaline that she felt. The dear Christ was entering in wherever the meek souls would let him.

In this world of sin.

CHAPTER 33

Friday 18th December, Lunchtime

The small area just outside the training room was empty when ITK sat in the large leather armchair that directly faced the main door, a position from which anyone leaving or entering could be seen. The stupid cow had slipped out earlier and could be anywhere, most likely in the bar or even the pub over the road knowing Wendy. The conversations that lunchtime with the others had been worrying, with some of the questions that were being asked appearing a little less innocent than their owner made out, and ITK was eager to find out if the secret plans between Sharon and Wendy had somehow been discovered. There was a strange lightness to the body, a tingling feeling, a freshness that ITK hadn't felt for a long time, with the sounds around seeming louder and clearer and a sensation that all of the lights in the hotel had been turned up to maximum brightness. It was difficult to believe it could be true but ITK may even be suffering from nerves. Not that it should be considered a suffering, as all of the studies said that nerves were necessary in order to obtain excellence, it simply being a case of how you controlled those nerves and used them to your advantage that was important, and that was exactly what ITK was planning to do.

The sound of the music escaped from two small, tinny speakers fastened to the wall in the corner. The weak and helpless little Jesus was growing up, crying and smiling like everyone else. It was the strange time when the razzamatazz of dancing snowmen and jingling bells had to resist against the tedium of religion, the carols seeming to be the last bastion of tradition holding out. People with no recollection of the gospel of Luke could still belt out a 'Hosanna in excelsis' when called upon, giving the son of God one last ray of hope against the multinationals. ITK doubted that Jesus had really ever known the same tears though, and in an instant the smartphone was lit up and running.

When Wendy finally said yes, as she obviously would, the real work would start. Spending months to plan a murder was obviously preferable, but in the end the details just got in the way and twenty four hours should be more than enough, with the unsuspecting nature of a crime with no real motive surely providing them enough cover to get away with it. Well, it should provide Wendy with enough cover anyway, as linking poor old Sharon to the event, or linking ITK to Sharon even, would end up in a hellish labyrinth of transferred routers and shadow IP addresses. Indeed, ITK was nervous as hell but loving every minute of the new found excitement. Wendy had been made aware of the radio silence for the day and the pressure of that silence would surely take her even closer to the edge. The good old internet of things was still needed though to make sure that whichever way the cookie crumbled, ITK would be ready with the necessary details to make it all happen. It was going to take more than tidings of comfort and joy to save certain people from Satan's power.

CHAPTER 34

Friday 18th December, Lunchtime

Bloody sacred songs, Smiler had never really understood them with their stories of angels and shepherds, their troubled minds seized by mighty dread. The fear was real though, for it was clear that the suspicions about Wendy were correct. Smiler must have been the only one amongst them who had actually read the planned agenda and for almost a day now Wendy had been nowhere near it, which along with her sudden change in behaviour was a sure-fire sign that something was going on. Alone, next to what remained of the mince pies and coffee, Smiler tried to piece it all together.

From the start she'd clearly been a drinker, and the loosened tongue hadn't needed much encouragement to show her unhappiness. Drunks all over the world regularly spilt their souls to anyone willing to offer sympathy and another glass and at first the stories she told hadn't seemed out of the ordinary at all, but the tone had soon changed. What had first seemed like old memories of a life richly lived had eventually transformed into what Smiler now realised was an outpouring of hatred. The pieces had come together during the few hours of sleep the night before, and the pointless bingo session from that morning had just confirmed that Wendy was out of control and possibly ready to do something drastic. The only thing that Smiler couldn't figure out was what had caused the change? During the week something, or someone, had transformed Wendy from merry and morose into drunk and dangerous.

At the start of the lunch break there had still been some missing pieces, but Smiler had moved around the room innocently asking a few questions in order to fill in the blanks. The result was the list of names that had been carefully written down on the piece of paper now on the table, of the people that Wendy so despised. Whilst the others continued to talk about their Christmas plans, Smiler would sit down at the front of the class and try and make sense of it all. Wendy was still not there, surely hiding away somewhere and making plans herself, the plans that Smiler was desperate to discover. The information was scarce, just the list of names plus a few additional scribbled notes from conversations that had taken place earlier in the week, but it would have to do.

Despite the incomplete information the conviction was absolute. Wendy was in danger and, in the absence of any other obvious candidates, it would be Smiler who had to do the saving.

CHAPTER 35

Friday 18th December, Afternoon

The afternoon had been long, long and painful, and everyone had known it. The participants had been there mainly because they had to be, a condition of their unfortunate circumstances. It was a sad state of affairs defined to overcome an even sadder state, but that was how the world worked.

Wendy gave the room one last scan, smile in place and eyes shining as she took in the indifferent faces of the people in front of her. In her earlier days she had loved every minute that she had spent in front of the young, eager trainees, sucking every bit of know-how out of her that they could. Losers like this did nothing but suck the life out of her.

"Right then, that's almost us all finished for the week. I know I've said it before, but thank you so much again for making it my best session of the year." As she talked she tidied the last of her papers and markers in front of her. Those who had never experienced it would never understand the combination of excitement and fear that being on stage gave you, nor how even here in front of nothing more than a group of nobodies it still managed to feel like a stage. All she knew was that she was glad that it did feel that way, and that she would be stepping into the weekend with that adrenaline fuelled high that only the closing number could give her. It was time for her final medley and the smile snapped into place one last time as she got ready for her last scene of the show.

"Well then, hasn't this week been fun?" her voice was deep, quiet, warm and smooth. Yes, she still had it. "You really have all worked extremely hard on the technical stuff, and I'm really proud of you for that, and I am sure that you will all benefit from it with your next challenges." She wouldn't be holding her breath waiting for those challenges to arrive with most of them, though. "What you also need to remember though, is that most of this is about you, and about how you feel and behave." She breathed deeply, the ability to perform to a bad house being the sign of the ultimate performer, and now that she'd started there was no turning back.

"Firstly, you know more than anything that you are all different. Don't ever worry about that, and never try and change it. Some people will think you are ridiculous, some people will love the difference that you bring, and some people will secretly wish that they were different in the same way as you are too. Just never try and hide these differences that you have," her voice had maintained its husky feel and her eyes scanned the room, expertly focussed on the lights at the back of the hall and not the eyes that were possibly looking back at her.

"Secondly, understand your unique strengths. These are sometimes part of your differences and are sometimes separate. They are the things that will make you valuable to others, so know what they are and try and sell them. Desmond you have great organisation, Jack you have a true desire to understand, Flash you are able to show compassion in all circumstances, the rest of you all have

HE'S MAKING A LIST

your own skills that make you unique too." Not even Wendy could invent a super power for each one of them. "Just don't waste your time trying to be good at what you're not good at, find the best way to make the most of what you are good at." It was time now for her to deliver the ultimate wisdom.

"And last, but not least, remember that no matter what the situation is, it will change. Be prepared for that, in each and any direction. At the moment things might not be quite where you want them to be, but there is no point in skulking around feeling sorry for yourselves. When things change, and they will, for better or for worse, be ready. Everyone else will be impacted by the same changes, and it's the ones who are prepared and ready who will end up making the most of the new situation." She increased the volume and tone of the last few words in order to give them emphasis, but also announcing that her little monologue was over.

As her eyes dropped to actually see the people in front of her she was surprised to see that some of them were actually nodding in agreement.

It was time for a quick round table to get all of the feedback before they went their very separate ways. To her left were the stutterer and Brian, to the right Sachin and Maria. The last ones to speak would always just say 'well, I haven't got much more to add that hasn't already been said', so the choice was easy.

"Right then, Maria, let's start with you."

***

With farewells and festive wishes exchanged the last person was just leaving the room as Wendy's smile finally dropped and her face twisted into an evil grimace. The git had done it deliberately. She had seen his eyes calculating the time it would take her and her suitcase to negotiate the cobbles and make it to the station in time for her train. She had seen the delight on his face as the clock ticked down, and he had obviously seen the horror on hers as she contemplated spending an extra hour in Harshton before she could finally get a train home. A simple 'well, the others have already said everything' would have been fine, leaving the stutterer a few minutes to say the same, but not jilted Brian, the bloody moron. She was angry.

The temperature had been wrong, the food not right and the lighting not sufficient. The handouts had been poor quality and it had been difficult to read what was written on the board. Difficult to read? Every letter had been well spaced and at least four centimetres tall, so the guy obviously didn't have a clue. Wendy leaned forwards against the desk, breathing out rapidly.

"But what did you think of the content?" she had asked without thinking, knowing that any answer would be time consuming and irrelevant, but forced into it by a long-lost pride.

"Complete and utter bollocks," had come the reply, "just like the last time I did it, in the nineties." She sat down and stared upwards towards the ceiling. Was there anyone who enjoyed their job? No, she didn't think so.

CHAPTER 36

Friday 18th December, Early Evening

A season of peace and goodwill to all men was surely doomed in a place where people couldn't even keep their bags off the few available seats left on a train. The thought had kept Wendy busy as she walked back to her house, trying to get inside the mind of someone who had probably spent hours during the previous weeks writing out cards to offer all and sundry Seasons Greetings, but who then placed a small suitcase on the seat next to them, imagining that a fixed stare in front would somehow make both themselves and their case invisible. Yes, you may be old and weak, but surely you can pluck up the courage to ask someone else to put your case up on the shelf for you? It was supposed to be the future, public transport, but it would never be a success. It wasn't necessarily the lack of cleanliness, infrequency of the voyages, or even the inability to respect the few departure times that were communicated that were the main problems. No, the problem was entirely down to the other people who used the so-called transport, the rest of the general public with their hot food, bikes blocking doorways, seats filled with hob nailed boots and shopping bags. It would never catch on.

The journey through Harshton had been as painless as could be hoped on what was now endearingly known as Mad Friday. Greg Lake had been moaning yet again about the lack of peace on earth, and finding instead just a downpour of tears as she had rushed through the busy streets, completely transformed by the addition of some cheap, colourful lighting and a few happy people. The sound of her suitcase wheels had been drowned out by the coughs of the smokers and the coarse jokes and laughter of those around them as they huddled together around each pub doorway, with office workers in festive jumpers besides workmen, still dirty from their morning shifts. Amongst them, like tinsel on that barren tree, were the ladies, already dressed up for an evening of dancing despite the rain and falling temperatures. A quick look at her watch had told her that she still had thirty minutes to wait before her train and so she had spent them in the Railwaymen's, squeezing both herself and her case into the last seat available in the bar and staring blankly at her faceless reflection in the condensation covered window.

Now though, she was home and the entrance hall erupted into light as she flicked the switch, accompanied by a sigh of relief. The wooden floor on which she left her suitcase was easy to clean and the simple bookcase was home to all sorts of keys and other articles that needed to be taken immediately from warm pockets and stored in safety. Above the bookcase was a large mirror, reflecting the pastel colour of the facing wall and making the space look bigger than it actually was. At the end of the hallway stood a coat stand, empty and inviting her to fill it up, whilst next to that was a small door leading to the area beneath the stairway, the home to many pairs of shoes and the final resting place to be for the case. The coat was dutifully placed on its stand and her shoes were replaced with warm slippers. The case, not yet emptied, glided

HE'S MAKING A LIST

behind her into the living room. Wendy was home.

"Musico, play some musicals." The familiar command was quickly responded to, almost as if Musico had been expecting it.

A banal duet from Carousel accompanied her movement through to the kitchen, a soon to be married couple warbling on about what they would get up to when their children were asleep. Even Musico could get it wrong sometimes.

The fridge had been the only thing on Wendy's mind and in a matter of seconds her glass was full with a nice crisp Chablis to celebrate her homecoming. She had chosen ironically, as her small giggle testified, as the first mouthful was dispatched. A week of New World Chardonnay could only be forgotten with the help of a glass full of the same from the Old World. She placed the glass carefully on a protective coaster on top of her coffee table and then quickly got to work returning the contents of her case to their correct locations. Once empty the said case was finally rolled into its corner in the cupboard under the stairs, which she gently closed with a small, final click.

She lay back, sat sideways on her sofa, eyes closed and glass in hand. The sound of the deep breaths, in and out through her nose, were clearly audible above the sound of the song from the Phantom of the Opera that sang to her of darkness, and fears and protection. Love me, that's all I ask of you. It was the soundtrack of her life.

The walk to the kitchen for another glass was quick, the crispness of her own wine giving her a new energy as the rubbish that she had been drinking all week became a distant inconvenience. During her absence the postman had delivered two Christmas cards, both from far away relatives, five bargain packed advertisements from local supermarkets and a copy of the local newspaper. For people like Wendy who refused to buy things off the internet the postal service would soon be about as useful as a landline telephone. She sat back down again, quickly scanning through the local announcements of births, deaths, marriages and court appearances.

Wendy had often wondered when it was that people became evil and turned into monsters. Newspapers and television screens would often show the photographs of those who had been convicted of the most horrendous crimes, and every time it would be obvious, just by looking at the faces that stared stupidly back at her, that those people were bad. She guessed that these people must have all been born with badness inside them, and if it wasn't corrected on their path through life it was inevitable that it would come out when given the opportunity. Nobody was ever going to see her face staring out stupidly from some newspaper, as firstly she wasn't evil and secondly she wasn't planning on getting caught. She relaxed again, eyes closed and neck arching back in search of the warmth on her face from the lights in the centre of the ceiling. She was calm now, in the almost trance like state she was used to experiencing in that short period between the last-minute nerves of rehearsal and the exhilaration of finally taking the stage. She was more ready than ever for her first time playing the leading lady, and she concentrated intensely on the breath as it passed the end of her nose, in and out, in and out, in and out. Her feet planted firmly against the floor as her body rocked forward and she stood in one smooth movement, opening her eyes instinctively just as she reached her maximum height and a good old Wendy smile formed across her face.

CHAPTER 37

Friday 18th December, Early Evening

It was never a good night for trolling, Mad Friday. ITK had seen them all out in the pubs on the way back from the hotel. On any other evening they'd all be up for an argument or ready to swallow some more bullshit, but tonight all they wanted to do was drink beer and drag up some old memories of Christmas from days gone by. Never mind, perhaps the lightweights would be home early, ready for ITK to manipulate whilst patiently waiting for Wendy's final downfall.

Moving around the small flat was not a problem, there not being too much furniture to get in the way. The wet coat was hung up to dry over the radiator and the few Christmas treats that had been bought on the way home were neatly stored away for later. ITK had seen Wendy waddling towards the station, her suitcase an uneven accompaniment for Greg Lake as he looked to the sky with excited eyes, according to the music that had been piped out through the town centre sound system.

A small sideboard, half hidden behind the open door,

contained a handful of Christmas cards, a plate of clementines and a bowl of nuts. ITK had fond memories from childhood when there had been enough cards to cover whole doors, all neatly attached to ribbons that passed from top to bottom, but the senders of cards were now few and far between. On a small table in the corner a set of coloured bulbs did their best to hide the nakedness of an old plastic tree. The ritual was automatic, the installation of the tree and the preparation of the sideboard, and even though there was no love for a Christian Christmas the tradition continued to be respected once a year. ITK sat down in a small, threadbare armchair and looked around, already fidgeting through nervous boredom. Arriving home after the pub all week had been easy, with the rush to enter the flat and to get online, but being home so early on this maddest of Fridays just gave ITK more time to do what ITK hated doing the most, thinking about life and how it seemed to always cruelly pass by. A loud click in the kitchen announced that the kettle had boiled, giving a welcome release from the less than positive thoughts.

Scanning through the internet feeds confirmed that it had been a quiet day, the period before Christmas rarely being one for big news stories. It was not so much a case of Peace on Earth but just a time when people decided to do less, and as a result less got done. A dozen Christians being beheaded in Nigeria, plus another stabbing in London involving the usual suspects, gave ITK a couple of opportunities to antagonise, and appropriate pictures were quickly found and posted. Wearily leaning back in the seat, ITK blew gently across the top of the mug of tea, waiting for the first responses to come back, determined to make the most of this quiet time while Wendy was still travelling home.

'Of course they don't want you to know about it, that's what the

MSM does!'

'Well, you better get used to it. Can't you see that we're sleepwalking into the same thing ourselves?'

'A true patriot wouldn't even need to ask'

'God bless Trump'

'I'll pray for you too'

Prayers, that was all they offered the religious fanatics of America, prayers for your freedom, prayers for your families, prayers for your guns. They somehow failed to see the mutual exclusivity between their own bigoted views and the good Lord's favour, but in any case they were all good patriots and always brilliant for a wind up. The ones that ITK knew well would certainly never be coming to visit soon, all of them too scared of all of the exaggerated stories from Europe that they saw and believed every day.

The fingers were now warmed up so it was time to focus on the mind, as ITKs thoughts went back to Wendy. Prayer was most probably not going to do much for her, but there was a definite fear that she was far too vain and lacking in confidence to get through the task on her own. There would be no difficulty in motivating her, getting Wendy drunk wasn't going to be a problem, but once she was outside in the real world, ITK feared that a physical presence may well be needed to provide a more practical support once the moment of truth came along. Wendy had spent hours that week telling them all about the importance of decisions and actions, as without action nothing ever changed. ITK saw every day the people who talked a good game, but who never made it further than their bedroom door when it came to actually doing things, and in fact it was this concept that made the whole experiment with Wendy so exciting. ITKs fingertips joined together in some sort of Millenium Prayer, and the eyes closed tight as plans whirred around. If Wendy was going to be supported right to the death it was going to involve ITK literally stepping outside of the comfort zone, so perhaps the lessons from the week wouldn't be wasted after all.

CHAPTER 38

Friday 18th December, Early Evening

Smiler had followed Wendy through the dark, drizzly streets of Harshton, determined to stop her and talk to her again but never finding the right moment to do so. Now back home the clenched fist fell down hard on the work surface causing the plate and fork to clang together. Of course there had been right moments, it was the right words that had been missing.

'Hi Wendy, I know that you don't really know me at all, except for the four nights we spent drinking in the bar, but I'm really worried that you might be going off the rails and be ready to do something stupid. Do you want to have a chat about it?'

Yes, there had been moments, but the words weren't there. That she was in danger was not in doubt, the question was how? Smiler had seen it many times before, and even though Wendy was a stranger there was something that could be done, and Smiler was determined to do it. It was a strange view of the world and one that the majority of others didn't seem to share, one where you could help out your fellow citizens simply because you were able to. Perhaps one day it would start to catch on.

The few last-minute purchases for the festive period were tidied away and the few steps to the bedroom were taken. Christmas had never been a big event but had always been kept, all be it within the means available for each particular year. As with everything in life that was the best way to avoid disappointment. Smiler pulled on a bright blue Christmas jumper, a throwback to a long past party, and delayed paying for the heating by another hour.

As the computer spluttered into life Smiler looked again at the written notes from the night before, a sorry collection of information scribbled out in a messy handwriting that any outsider would surely mistake as being in code. That previous evening had been spent searching the internet in some vain attempt to solve the whole puzzle in one go, but nothing had been found and so the puzzle remained. The latest information, hastily written down on hotel headed notepaper during the lunch break was added to the rest of the papers, but no magical transformation occurred before Smiler's eyes, confirming that plan B would in fact be necessary.

A fresh sheet of hotel paper was pulled out from the worn cardboard folder that had accompanied Smiler through the week, and a pen was taken from the mug on the edge of the desk and left hovering in anticipation. Writing, or more often drawing, helped with the thought process.

The word 'MOTIVE' was written out in large, uneven capitals. Underneath was added a matchstick cartoon figure of Wendy and a large question mark. It was clear that she believed that her already easy life should have somehow been better than it was, and she obviously blamed others for the comfortable position she found herself in, but during the week something in Wendy had changed. Smiler added what could just about pass as a

HE'S MAKING A LIST

wine bottle and a wine glass. She was undoubtedly a drunkard, but had been at the beginning of the week too, so though it obviously didn't help the situation it wasn't the main cause. There were the other members of the drinking club who had both had the same opportunity as Smiler to influence her, but why on earth would either of them want to do Wendy any harm? No, Smiler was sure that it was the old friend that she had rediscovered during the week. From that point on she had become a smartphone junkie, just about respecting the groundrules during the sessions but addicted to her screen during every other moment. Next to the picture Smiler wrote down carefully the two words that may between them hold the key, 'SHAZ' and 'RON'. Wendy had often mentioned the name of the friend, but her hushed slurring had been impossible to decipher when accompanied by Shakin' Stevens.

Next came the word 'TARGET', below which Smiler started on a masterpiece of cartoon characters, again annotated with names. 'FOLKS', 'STEW', 'TEACHER', 'SHANDY', 'GARETH', each one accompanied by their own, very large question mark. Snippets of information were available for every one of them, but for each there was a complete blank when it came to thinking of what stupid thing Wendy could be planning. A last figure was quickly added, 'WENDY' herself completing the set. Smiler's first instinct had been that she was planning to hurt herself, and even though she appeared far too self-centred to actually do that she needed to stay on the list anyway.

The page was turned and the word 'WHAT' was written and underlined. Whoever it was they were going to 'get what they deserved', that much had come directly from the horse's mouth, though what exactly 'they deserved' was still unclear. There was no denying that

Wendy had a venomous, unforgiving tongue that sometimes revealed a disturbed deeper being. Left on her own things would probably be alright, but the combination of Chardonnay and her tormentor made Smiler feel most uncomfortable.

Last, but not least, was written 'WHEN'. Through now fading letters Smiler added 'TOMOROW'. That much Wendy had made clear as she had walked away from tormenting the three poor lads at the end of the Christmas party. People always revealed their secrets when they were on a high, believing themselves invincible, and Wendy had proved no different.

So, the jigsaw was immense and Smiler held just three pieces of information of any real use. It was clear that Wendy was going to do something that she regretted, and that she was going to do it the following day. On top of that her address was known, the one successful result from hours of internet searches. It was certain that she had to be stopped, and so with no other information of real use available plan B became the only realistic option. The next morning Smiler had to be there, near her house. Her every step had to be followed, and when she started to make her move, Smiler had to be quicker and stronger than her in order to prevent whatever catastrophe she had planned. The splash of sherry going into the bottom of the now empty tea cup completed the plan. Smiler was surely outgunned, but would prevail.

CHAPTER 39

Friday 18th December, Late Evening

Wendy pushed through the door with a combination of left elbow and left thigh, a half full wine glass in one hand and a half empty wine bottle in the other. The bottle was carried in an ice filled bucket, a rare Christmas present from her parents that she had found a use for. A press on the light switch from her right elbow brought the bright lights to life and the glass and the bucket were carefully placed on the table. Her telephone was then extracted from the pocket of her jeans, not an easy task given the size of the phone and the tightness of her jeans, and a few touches of the screen sprang the speaker in the corner of the room into life.

There was a relief to see that the crime room in real life looked exactly as it had done in her head during the week, though to be honest there was no reason why it shouldn't. It hadn't changed for a few years now, the photographs and other evidence would surely have left marks on the wall behind had any light ever been let into the room. Her glass became fuller as the bottle became emptier and she looked to the far end of the wall. There were now just two suspects left, but neither could realistically have been the true cause of her suffering. She had revisited all of the evidence again that week and her target had already been chosen, but Wendy needed to close the cycle and that meant reviewing one more time those two remaining characters.

Top right was a photograph of a teenage girl smiling eagerly into the camera, her mud-spattered face framed between a hard riding helmet and a bright silk shirt in bold yellow and green quarters. Looming large behind her were the toothy grin and pointy ears of Pippin, the horse that Wendy had borrowed over several years when she was younger. Her thoughts went back to 1982.

***

There were five of them, mud spattered young girls in brightly coloured silks, preparing to receive their rosettes. It would be a special day for Wendy as receiving a rosette didn't happen every show. Mind you, there weren't often only five competitors. Whilst the three girls who had won the main prizes giggled amongst themselves Wendy stomped around, hoping that somehow the energetic movements would reduce her anger levels. The girl beside her was called Jane, and Wendy had come across her at other shows. She was about four years younger than Wendy and hadn't yet learned to shut up when people were clearly pissed off.

"He's crazy your horse is, what's his name again, Pippin isn't it. Mind you, with horses like that you have to be alert all the time, that's what my Dad says."

Wendy continued to stomp.

"You shouldn't let him get away with stuff like that in the dressage, else he'll never learn, and it's no wonder he's so undisciplined in the show jumping, the way he charges around the cross country."

HE'S MAKING A LIST

One of the downsides of a small field of competitors was the fact that they all saw you and that they all remembered you.

"Discipline and practice, practice and discipline, that's what my Dad says. The last time I got a horse like that we had to change him for a different one. We're lucky like that, because we've got quite a few to choose from."

Wendy's fist tightened around her riding crop as her eyes squeezed shut. The really young girls often cried when they didn't do well, but at her age it just wasn't done.

"Mind you, you'll get some lovely pink ribbons for fifth. I like those much better than all of the other colours. In a few weeks' time nobody will remember that there were only five people who turned up, and you won't have to tell them. You can just add them in with all of the rest and nobody will even notice."

Wendy didn't have that many others to add to. She had been sure that today was going to be her day. They were better prepared than ever, and with only four others up against them she could surely get one of the top prizes? She hadn't factored in the bloody horse though. Her stomping calmed down as her legs stopped trembling. She looked down at the worn surface beneath her feet.

"Come on, it's time for the medals and the photos. You're on first. Are your parents here, mine are? And my sisters, but they're not riding today, they're waiting for the big show next week. Will you be going there too?"

Wendy was glad that she didn't have any sisters. Or brothers for that matter, and especially not younger ones. Her name was announced in fifth place and she put on her best false smile as the camera clicked and she was handed her rosette.

***

Wendy didn't need to remember the day to know that the smile was forced, she could tell a false smile just by looking. She had almost devoted her life to that borrowed horse. Day after day she had woken up at dawn to go and muck out, rushed around after school to brush and feed and ride, and how had she been rewarded? With nothing but nervous disdain. She struggled to believe how a horse could be so prone to nerves, rarely understanding the urgency in her commands as her legs squeezed and her hands pulled on the reins. She flashed a glare at her parents, wishing for them to take their share of the blame too. She had told them that Pippin wasn't good enough for her and pleaded with them to buy her a better horse, but they had always said no, told her to wait and see if it was what she really wanted to do. She shook her head slowly from side to side, disgust in her eyes as once again the stupid equine smile taunted her. Blinking away a tear the uncanny randomness of the musical shuffle brought her back to the brightly lit room and the dulcet tones of Billy Bragg's Milkman of Human Kindness as he promised to leave her an extra pint.

There he was before her in the last picture, the singer of the song, surrounded by old concert tickets and press cuttings from her younger days. His looks were handsome and boyish, somehow ruined by a protruding top lip and a great big nose, but Billy Bragg had been a breath of fresh air for a young Wendy, trapped in a world of show tunes and the bland pop music of the early 80s. The raw energy of his lone guitar, plus the searing beauty as he sang of love and a life on estates that Wendy could never even imagine, had captivated her from the first chords she had ever heard. Closing her eyes she listened on, enthralled by the raw passion, the pleading in the voice as it sang of a love of the type that she had never known herself. Most artists change, developing as they grow, but Billy's crossroads arrived far too early in his career. Would he carry on singing his songs of love and life or would he succumb to his political rubbish, songs about ship workers in Leningrad and all of the rest? He made his choice and Wendy, like many others, was cast aside, forced in an age without selective streaming to listen through entire albums just in order to find the nugget of a love song that was occasionally thrown in amongst the socialist songbook.

Billy was lucky, his face had filled out reducing the impact of the nose and a beard had grown that now hid the top lip. Wendy had just drifted, the temporary anchor that had held the teenage girl in position had disappeared, leaving her to face the merciless waves of the eighties and nineties alone.

That was it, she had once again passed over all of the evidence that she had. Her eyes moved across the wall, picture to picture, suspect to suspect as her elbows on the table steadied her in her seat. There was Stuart Palmer, the first love who had broken her innocent dreams of marriage and a simple life, and there was Mr Denzil, the teacher who had humiliated her for her lack of intelligence. There was Shanny Easter, the best friend who had failed to return the compliment, and Gavin Bright, who had proposed marriage and then jilted her. There was Elizabeth Trout, who had let her go at the first sign of power, and Hassan Ahmed, who had loved her, but not enough for him to abandon his family to be with her. Finally, there were Pippin and Billy Bragg, and above them all her parents, the ones that the psychiatrists would have her blame but which no living memory could ever accuse.

A vibration on her phone startled her back to the present. She had known that the message would arrive but none the less it frightened her. Swiping away she saw that Sharon was back and that it was time to finally make her choice. Taking the ice bucket in her left hand she stood and turned towards the door, it was time to get some more supplies.

CHAPTER 40

Friday 18th December, Late evening

The moment had arrived and ITK hit the send button on the latest message that Sharon was sending to her long-lost friend.

'Well, come on then Wendy, you must have made your mind up by now. I'm so excited, who's it going to be?'

It still looked strange, like Wendy was expected to choose the person who had won first prize in a poetry competition or something, not to choose the person who between them they were going to kill. ITK used 'they' because it would be both of them carrying out the deed. ITK wouldn't necessarily be there, or at least that was how it was supposed to work, but there was still a long way to go before Wendy would be ready to fulfil her quest, and ITK would need to stay close to her every step of the way.

Switching from the messages to another session the screen went dark, revealing for a fraction of a second a distorted reflection of ITK's face in the half light of the room. It wasn't easy to piece together the transformation, the moment when ITK had turned into a mentor of murderers, but it had happened all the same. Anyone who had known ITK, and experienced the same life destroying effects of greed and the search for profit, wouldn't be too surprised at the changes anyway. Did they honestly expect to be able to destroy the fabric of a whole society, to abandon the millions of people who had made their wealth possible, and for there to be no consequences? This would just be the start and it was happening everywhere. Whilst intelligent people like ITK could provide the brains, and dumb bitches like Wendy could be persuaded to carry out the deeds, there would always be a way for the common man to fight back. ITK checked again the complex series of routings for the messages that Sharon was sending to Wendy, making sure one last time that there would be no way of tracing anything back to this flat in Harshton. The chiming of an incoming message broke the concentration, leaving just the low whir of a cooling unit as the only sound in the room.

There was no surprise with the name. From the very first time that ITK had heard the sob stories, spat out angrily with an alcohol sodden breath, this had been the life that was most in danger. The rapid tap of fingers communicated Sharon's joy at the news.

'Well done Wendy, you're the greatest!'

Now was the time to be silent again, to wait and see how Wendy wanted to play it. Pushing too hard could break the spell.

ITK checked the carefully taken notes from earlier in the week. The address was in a great location, having few properties overlooking it and being far enough out of town to be quiet in the evening. The internet gave a 360-degree view from outside the main driveway and the online map showed at least three ways to access the property using back alleys and a passage via the local cricket pitch. There were no CCTV cameras in the immediate vicinity, the closest being outside the local Co-Op store almost half a mile away. There was a yellow alarm box attached to the wall on the outside of the front porch, but even if that was real it was doubtful that it would be set when somebody was at home. Wendy would need to visit the property the next day to make sure that the target was at home and double check for any obvious signs of extra security, but it looked perfect for a short, sharp, violent hit and run. The message indicator rang again.

ITK should have expected it, an excited Wendy fretting because she had no clue what to do next. She easily found the time to wallow in self-pity at the bottom of a wine bottle but never to do anything practical in order to change things. The internet links were carefully copied and added to the message, meaning that Wendy could now spend the next few minutes looking at what ITK had just seen, whilst hopefully coming to the same conclusions herself.

'Look at these links that I found. It looks just wonderful! A quick visit to do some final checks tomorrow and everything looks made for what we have in mind!'

The use of the word 'we' was important, the stupid cow mustn't feel alone at any moment as, at least until it came to actually doing the act, they were in this together. During the day Wendy's smile was clearly her armour, as its gentle curve protected her from people she underestimated as being idiots and fools, but with a drink or two inside her the smile lost its power and her anger poured out. Given the time to commit the act, ITK couldn't imagine anything more sophisticated than one of the classics, either strangulation, piercing or bludgeoning, but the choice of weapon would be left entirely to Wendy.

The very thought of Wendy committing the act brought a wave of excitement all over ITKs body. There had been moments when there had been doubt, when talk of taking a life had seemed absurd as a reaction to nothing more than the progress of a world in motion. That had been the problem though, for year after year since the progress had started people had just sat back and accepted that their lives should be destroyed, sacrificed for some greater good that never seemed to arrive. They were guilty by association all of them, the ones that hid and did nothing, the ones that collaborated and jumped on the bandwagon, the ones who lamely played along and blamed others. Tomorrow night would be the first blow, the start of the fightback and a moment when two birds could be killed with one stone.

CHAPTER 41

Friday 18th December, Late Evening

The moment had seemed as empty as Wendy's glass, as if writing the name and hitting the send button on her telephone had taken her to a point of no return. Until she had sent that last message she had done nothing other than share stories with an old friend, and shared words could never be punishable on their own. But the moment now felt important, a pivotal passage in her life. After years of searching and trawling through her mind, she now knew who was to blame and tomorrow she would finally do something about it, to banish the curse on her life for ever.

Her glass had been filled, but the emptiness in her feelings remained as she looked over the information in the message from Sharon. Everything did look ideal, the location being both easy to get to and also to get away from without being noticed. She would do as Sharon suggested and go and visit the next morning, to get a better feel for the lie of the land and to make sure that her target was there. She deleted the message, making a mental note to delete all of the other messages that they had exchanged, leaving nothing behind to incriminate her.

HE'S MAKING A LIST

Back in the crime room she had at first just sat there, staring almost blindly at the face of the person that she had chosen. Bit by bit her body had warmed, until the mixture of apprehension and new found excitement gave her a glowing feeling all over. It was now time for the details, and despite her slow start Wendy was soon fully absorbed in the task at hand. The board game makers had left her little choice for her character, she would have to be Miss Scarlett, the young, cunning femme fatale that she obviously was. It was unlikely that there would be a library, billiard room or a ballroom at the house she would be visiting, so for the location her money was firmly on the hall or the lounge. She imagined a quick and brutal ending, a knock on the door with a rapid, surprise entry followed by a savage onslaught. Finally, the thoughts passed to the weapon and Wendy tutted disapprovingly, disappointed that she didn't have the real cards there in the room to pin against the wall and create a proper crime scene. There was a candlestick, a dagger, some lead piping, a gun, some rope and a monkey wrench as she recalled. The gun and rope were out of the frame straight away, there being no time to get hold of a gun and the rope being a weapon that would require her to sneak up from behind. In any case, keeping the rope tight long enough for the kill might rely too much on a strength that she wasn't sure that she had. The knife was also discarded quickly, all of that blood being surely a pain to clean up when she got home and one more potential giveaway clue to worry about. There were just three left to choose from then, all weapons for clubbing or bludgeoning someone to death. For the moment she had none, so it would need to be added to the shopping list for the next morning. Wendy made another mental note to not get caught on CCTV buying the bloody thing. Last but not least would be the disguise. For tomorrow evening it could only be one thing and Wendy was sure that she had most of what would be required. She would go downstairs later and double check, just to make sure.

The sound of the music rose above her thoughts. It was from Follies, the female character fearing that she was losing her mind, and small tears started to run down Wendy's flushed cheeks as the demons in her head did battle. Quickly she sprang to her feet, her left foot catching against the chair leg and forcing her to lurch forward and spill a large portion of demon drink over the table in front of her. Steadied by her left hand she pushed backwards, the chair now falling against the wall behind her with a loud bang. Unperturbed the singer carried on and a reinvigorated Wendy strode forward, the sound of her stamping feet cushioned by her slippers. There she stood, rocking slowly backwards and forwards, her tear stained face just centimetres away from the photograph covered wall.

It was explosive once it arrived, and with a brutality that Wendy couldn't explain. The empty glass was thrown behind her, rolling along the floor and thudding, unbroken into the skirting board. Before it was even half way there her hands had ripped away the first photograph, accompanied by chunks of plaster that were now nestled beneath Wendy's finger nails. The torn pieces of heavy photographic paper were still floating down to the floor when the next document, some invitation to a party or an old school report, was dispatched in the same manner. It was a violence that exhilarated Wendy as much as it frightened her. Yes, she would be able to do the deed the next night and yes, what she was doing was right.

Her breathing was almost back to normal as she looked at her handy work with a smile of satisfaction, not a Wendy smile but a real one. She was perched carefully on the table, very conscious that the weight in her backside, combined with the wine and the quality of the table, could be a painful combination. Along the bottom of the wall was a snowstorm of torn paper, leaving just one solitary photograph looking back at her. Any question she may have had about the rights and wrongs of what she was doing disappeared immediately as years of hate focussed on that one, lonely picture. The face in it may be smiling unknowingly back at her now, but come that time tomorrow it would be a different story.

CHAPTER 42

Saturday 19th December, Early Morning

It was a cold, cloudy Saturday morning as Smiler walked quickly towards the town centre and the bus station, every second step being accompanied by a slurping sound as trapped air was released from between the heel of the foot and the heel of an oversized wellington boot. There had already been a few good-natured jibes shouted out, but in just a few hours time the red costume would make Smiler almost invisible. In an old canvas bag a flask and a sandwich box clattered together, an offbeat accompaniment to the slurping. The weather forecast was for snow and looking up at the sky there was no reason to doubt that this time the forecasters might get it right. Determined not to be late, Smiler upped the pace a little, a misty breath coming out through lips that were busy telling everyone to be good for goodness sake, as Santa Claus was coming to town.

The buses from Harshton to Webledon were every two hours and at this time of day were thankfully empty. Later it would be different, with the festival that night tempting other pleasure seekers who had no car or couldn't afford the train to also make the journey by bus. Smiler actually preferred the long, winding trek through moor and mountain, and especially liked the fact that it was much cheaper. Settling into a seat near the back, Smiler placed the bag with the flask and sandwiches between the rubber boots making sure that the adjoining seat was free to be taken by anyone getting on at one of the villages along the way. A hissing sound announced the closing of the doors, meaning that the bus would soon be moving and that the heating system would soon be able to do its job. Smiler looked eagerly out of the window as the bus wound its way out of the town centre and on to the road to Webledon, the streets still empty as most people seemed to be sleeping off the effects of Mad Friday. Secrecy may be important later, hence the disguise, but nobody looking on would recognise Smiler through the window of the passing bus, never mind recall it as an important fact at some later date. The bus moved slowly at first, passing through the outskirts of town where the broken-down remnants of a proud industrial past had been 'regenerated' through conversion into offices for small design companies, and fancy apartment blocks for the people who couldn't yet afford a house. It was ridiculous of course, like a sticking plaster placed on an amputated leg, but it gave some sort of comfort to the people of Harshton to cling to. It was far too late to bring the old times back, with all of the work having already moved too far away to make relocating it a reasonable proposition. However, so long as the few companies that had found a way to survive and prosper in this environment continued to light up dark days like this with Christmas lights it would continue to give Smiler and the rest of the town the impression that there was hope for them after all.

The last lights of the town passed by and the flask and sandwich box clanked again as the bus ran through another series of potholes. Smiler was now mumbling about jingling bells, and perhaps a sleigh ride would be smoother and better for the bones. The countryside had never ceased to amaze Smiler, always beautiful no matter what the season or the weather. The villages along the route had mainly been farming villages, with their pollution stained houses just a small pavement away from the main road. Light shone out from behind condensation filled windows, feebly forcing itself into the darkness of the day, whilst barren winter trees and dark clouds played hide and seek with each other, joined from time to time by looming barns in varying states of disrepair. Amongst this darkness the only concessions to lightness and pleasure were the occasional pubs, where signs adorned with Kings Heads, Blue Bells and Horseshoes swung freely in the wind, though Smiler knew that most of these were fighting the same desperate battles for survival as the farms, in these places that the world seemed to have forgotten. Every now and then it would appear, nestled between the villages and breaks in the trees, a sweeping view over winter green pastureland where hedgerows and stone walls kept cows and sheep from different tribes apart, though whether it was to prevent fights or intertribal mixing Smiler wasn't sure. The green of England had always been impressive, if not pleasant, and even in the darkness of Winter it still felt like home. Smiler sat back, eyes closing, and started to think again of the day's main problem; what to do with Wendy.

***

The sound of kids laughing brought Smiler out of a slumber caused by the gentle rocking of the bus. There was something about children laughing, even dirty adolescent teenage ones, that just made things seem good. There was enough evil in the world for them to discover later in life, so best to make the most of laughing while they could. Wendy was not in the evil category, or at least

HE'S MAKING A LIST

she shouldn't be, but she was certainly in the worrying category. The extra time on the bus hadn't shed any more light on what was going on so Smiler was back on plan B, the only plan that there had ever really been. The bus was now on the outskirts of Webledon, a town that was just like Harshton but posher, its situation where the river was much narrower on a plateau between the hills making it for some reason that Smiler couldn't understand more suited to agriculture than industry. Now, whilst Harshton fought its rear-guard action against industrial decline, Webledon was a fat, lazy town, full of fat, lazy farmers, accountants and solicitors. Everything just seemed more spacious, cleaner and more authentic, with far fewer older buildings requiring conversion to something that they were never intended to be.

It was time to dig deep into the bag on the floor, ignoring the flask, the sandwiches, the gloves and the mobile phone and searching for the old book. Not quite as rare as rocking horse shit, there must be other copies around somewhere, the A to Z of Webledon was a full twenty pages long, with ten giving details of the streets that had been there in the 70s when the guide had been published, whilst the other ten advertised the wares of various pubs, ironmongers, butchers and grocery stores that in all likelihood no longer existed. A quick look the night before had found Wendy's address and the hope was that not too many changes had happened in the previous forty years to complicate the journey too much. An application on a smartphone would probably have given the exact journey duration as eight minutes and fifty seven seconds, but Smiler reckoned it would take at least ten. The route was quickly memorised and the book was carefully placed back in the bag just as the bus came to a gentle halt at one of the three stands in what passed in Webledon for the bus station.

A glance at the clock above the café showed that it was already ten to nine. Smiler hadn't imagined that Wendy was an early bird at weekends, a gamble that could prove disastrous if she was. As soon as the feet touched the floor the cold hit, a sign that either Webledon enjoyed its own little micro climate or that the duration of the bus ride had been long enough for the temperature to drop four or five degrees. The wind was bitter and the air was filled with the sound of plastic covers jingling against the metal frames of the market stalls that they protected. Amongst the swirl of wind and clanking of metal the far-off strains of a brass band playing God Rest Ye Merry, Gentlemen, could just be heard.

Smiler hummed along, tightening the coat hood and placing gloves on already cold hands, realising already the challenge that would be faced later when the over coat would need to be stored away. Two policemen, young and clearly happy to be posted in such a quiet market town, gave an accusing glance.

"Hey up Santa, you're a bit early, aren't you? Don't you go drinking all day and causing any trouble." Unsurprisingly the accent wasn't local, there being little to encourage anyone young to want to stay in the area. His colleague joined in.

"Yes, you stay out of trouble today. You'll have enough time for fun later on, especially in this weather." The two coppers laughed together.

Smiler nodded and offered a large good-natured smile.

"Of course, officers. You both have a Merry Christmas now."

If they had replied, it was lost in the sound of flapping material, swirling wind and the slurping wellington boot. Smiler went straight through the market place, past the Post Office and off up the hill towards the town's old, abandoned hospital and the road where Wendy's house was to be found. It was game on.

CHAPTER 43

Saturday 19th December, Morning

It was impossible to believe that just one week before Wendy had woken up worrying about marker pens. Thanks to super Sharon her whole view of life had changed, and she was taking as much advantage of her new found energy and confidence as she could. As she and Sharon knew well, it was going to be a momentous day. The one thing that worried her somewhat was that, despite this new confidence and a pair of dark glasses, she still looked a right old state. The purpose of Lycra was to stretch and then retake its original shape afterwards, and Wendy's current garment had done its stretching all right but it remained to be seen if it would ever return to the form it had enjoyed at the moment she had first taken it out of the packet. The music had probably been playing all night, Wendy couldn't remember switching it off, and there could have been nothing more motivational than Eye of the Tiger blaring out in order to get her into a Rocky mood. The long mirror on the inside of her wardrobe door was the only full length one in the house and she looked again at the sight before her, the room dimmed by the grey winters cloud outside as well as the sunglasses that were needed in order to stop her head throbbing. She had been clever keeping hold of all of those old Christmas presents, from when would it have been, five, ten years ago? She could see the look on her Dad's face now, smiling into a glass of red wine as her Mum explained to her how she should look after herself better. It had been the last time they had spent Christmas Day together.

The leggings were a mixture of black and grey, the differing angles and sheens of material doing their best to make it look as though she was actually looking into some fun fair mirror. It had been a bit of a battle pulling them on, a struggle worthy of a sit down on the corner of her bed, but in the end she had managed it. Hopefully she wouldn't need to pee again before she went out. On top she wore a bright fluorescent yellow sweatshirt which, despite a small zip below the chin, constricted her breathing so much that she wondered how anybody could ever actually run whilst wearing it. The effect of this top on her breasts was extraordinary, clamping them to her torso at angles that gave them such a strange look that no manoeuvring, of either the top or the breasts, seemed able to return them to their natural form. To overcome this a waterproof jacket had been chosen to cover everything up as much as possible. On her head she had placed a grey woolly hat, useful for both keeping out the cold and for keeping her glasses and hair in place. Yes, she might be seen and remembered, but it was certain that nobody would know that it was her beneath. The plan was to leave the house under the cover of her long winter coat, revealing her athletic alter ego secretly once she got to the sports ground. All that she needed now were some socks and a pair of sports shoes and her disguise would be complete, and as Bon Scott screamed out about his Highway to Hell, Wendy set off to have a good rustle around her drawers. The smell of a pot of hot coffee greeted her on the landing, to which she would add some wholemeal toast with butter, some organic yoghurt and blueberries and a large glass of Pinot Gris from Alsace, for the most important meal of the day.

Twenty minutes later and her bag was filled with pink socks, ear muffs and a few other bits and bobs that she thought might come in handy. The moment had arrived and now was the time to act. Her finger moved slowly and deliberately on her smartphone keyboard as she typed her first message of the day to Sharon.

'D-Day is here!'

Rocking back on to her feet she uttered a small curse under her breath, she would need the toilet again before she left after all.

CHAPTER 44

Saturday 19th December, Morning

The clank of the spoon in the tea cup was the only sound in the small kitchen. It was still very early, before the normal hustle and bustle would break out on this last Saturday before Christmas. The town would be full of people desperate to spend the last of their hard-earned cash on any old tat that they could get their hands on, preferring to waste their money rather than being the parent who didn't leave fifty presents per kid under the tree. It was how things were these days, the only problem on Christmas day being to find enough storage space to hide away all of the god-awful presents that had been shaken once and then left to rot with all the rest. At least they would have rotted, if it weren't for the fact that they were all made of plastic.

It had been a long night for ITK, baiting oversensitive snowflakes. Yes, it had to be said that in years to come people would wonder why Bing Crosby had ever imagined that a White Christmas could be possible in these parts. And yes, there was a possibility that some sort of change in the climate might be playing its part. And yes again, it might be possible that mankind had somehow had a helping hand in all of it happening, even though it was a long time since any smoke had come out of any chimneys round Harshton, but why did the young kids get so wound up about it all? The student types were the easiest targets for late sessions, they being never asleep, always logged in and so full of ideals that there was no room left for any common sense. ITK switched the radio on and sat down as some old crooner sang all about how Frosty the snowman had been brought to life by an old silk hat.

ITK was alive at last too. It shouldn't have been like that after a hard week in training and a long night stirring up trouble on the internet. It shouldn't have been like that after years of disappointment and decline. Just give me a job that I like and let me do it had been the only wish, but nothing was made to last in this town and ITK had suffered like thousands of others. Today would be different though, and it was as exhilarating a feeling as ITK could remember. A bottle of Cava was chilling away in the fridge, an unnecessary expense but who cared? ITK stood and took the few steps to the work surface, carefully washing and drying the cup and spoon and placing them neatly in the cupboard above the sink. Reunited with the two others that remained intact, the cups provided suitable company for the two saucers, four dinner plates, five dessert plates and one solitary soup bowl. There were rarely guests for dinner and ITK hated soup.

ITK unplugged the smartphone from its charger, wondering yet again at the power of the small device that allowed you to do so much without needing to move. It sometimes seemed to ITK that nothing had fundamentally changed since the 80s, it was just that smartphones kept people occupied so that they didn't notice that everything was falling down around them. In fact the phone played a double role, in one sense accelerating the decline whilst at the same time hiding it from view. Thatcher could probably be reborn and nobody would notice. In any case, as Wendy had said, change needed to be embraced and ITK had been an early adopter, using the handheld encyclopaedia now for the final checking of train timetables and locations, as Wendy had also told them perfect planning prevented piss poor performance or something like that. Talking of Wendy, the stupid cow seemed in fine form, with the content of her few messages suggesting that she was coherent, determined and only slightly pissed. Would she go through with it? It was a risk that ITK didn't want to take, hence the decision to be there, present for the entertainment that night. The idea was to remain unseen, an uninvited observer to the tragic events. That was the idea anyway, but if the silly cow needed any help, ITK would be there, ready to step out of the shadows and provide it.

'Sharon here, all ready for the big day I hope?'

ITK couldn't resist a short message, oiling the wheels of disaster. The planning reviewed and the message sent it was time for a long bath and then a quick trip into town to pick up the costume. That would be fun, even if it might turn out quite cold. Yes, ITK was alive at last.

CHAPTER 45

Saturday 19th December, Late Morning

Wendy had sent the message and waited eagerly for a reply but ten minutes had passed and there was still no news. She had been silly expecting one so quickly, she knew. In the five days since she had received that first message from Sharon on Tuesday morning their contacts had been regular but respectful, with neither one putting pressure on the other to participate any more than they had wanted to. It had been exactly because of this that Wendy had found Sharon such a wonderful discovery. Not only did they share a distant past but they also had very similar views on what the future should hold. In any case she hadn't replied and so Wendy closed the door behind her and walked purposefully down her driveway, holdall in hand and her long coat wrapped round her and providing protection from a drizzle that became more glacial with every drop. Trying to look normal was difficult but armed with her magic smile and with her running hat pulled down over her ears nobody should notice that she was even there.

"Hi Wendy, I thought you were home last night. We're off to the daughters, so if we don't see you, have a Merry Christmas!" It was Mr Jones, from number twelve.

A quick exchange of pleasantries followed and Wendy carried on, past the last house and up the hill. Her street was tasteful with large detached houses with bay fronted windows, mainly neat lawns, driveways for most of the cars and thankfully few outdoor Christmas lights. The road up the hill was on another level, real countryside now alternating with larger gardens full of trees, driveways equipped with automatic gates and half wall and hedge combinations hiding luxurious houses from prying eyes. Perfect, she thought, all the better to give her cover. Finally, she arrived at the sports ground, a place where football in winter and cricket in summer had been common sights during the later years of the last century but where nowadays a handful of hunched dogwalkers and brightly coloured joggers was all you could ever expect to see. She spotted a clump of bushes next to a plastic bin that overflowed with bags of dog shit and walked past it before quickly removing her coat, placing it in her bag and then hiding everything in the bushes.

She now needed a route to take her to the far side of the field, from where she could discretely climb over the wall at the far end. From there she would circle round the back of two houses before finally arriving behind the target's house, giving her a good enough view to make sure that someone was home and also allowing her to plan her entrance for the show that night. Moving slowly she started her walk around the field doing mock stretching exercises as she went, timing her arrival to perfection as her fellow runners were all towards the gate end of the park, and she quickly located a footpath behind some trees. The wall was not high, perhaps five feet at most, but still she needed to find an easy way of getting over it. Moving carefully to her right Wendy stumbled along, her hands holding the wall for support until finally she came to a gap, surely created over the years by various dog walkers seeking a quick passage from the top road into the sports

HE'S MAKING A LIST

ground. She removed her sunglasses to take a closer look.

The noise was unmistakeable and in a fraction of a second Wendy stopped as still as a statue, her limbs frozen and her mouth filled with a thick liquid that seemed to have appeared from nowhere. It had come from her left as if someone was following down the path and she turned slowly, straining to make sense of the sounds over the booming of her heart. There it was again but louder this time, forcing her into a crouch as the half-light stimulated her ears into overdrive. Seconds passed in silence before the next and loudest, but this time she could tell that the source of the noise was moving further away. Quickly she passed through the gap, accelerating silently round the pathway on the other side, and once around the corner she came to an abrupt halt, again dropping to her knees and listening. There was nothing but silence. Could it just have been the sound of the wind through what remained of the hedges and trees? Her breathing returned to normal, and she turned again, taking the last few steps until she came to the house.

The wall and hedge around the house were in a bad state of repair with many parts of the wall crumbling and parts of the hedge being non-existent. Wendy continued round until she had a good side on view of the house front. A snort of laughter came out of her nose and she quickly put her hand to her face to quieten it down. In the garden there were even Christmas lights, some on the trees and others wound around low bushes planted in the lawn. Who'd have thought that? Wendy had seen on the internet that there were just four houses in the cul-de-sac and that none of the three others overlooked the entrance that she could now see to her right. Next to an empty, gated driveway was a smaller iron gate at the head of a footpath that lead straight to a front door that was itself part of a small porchway. On either side were neatly kept lawns with their smattering of bushes and exterior Christmas decorations. The porch had a small outside light, one of the old-fashioned types with a small box at the bottom that Wendy guessed was some sort of movement detector. On the outside wall, just underneath one of the windows, was the bright yellow box of a burglar alarm. Wendy took out a pair of binoculars and examined it more closely. As she hoped there were no signs of cables either in or out, a clear dummy box to frighten off the unknowing or stupid and Wendy was neither. She was more than happy with her performance so far, caging out the joint was pretty impressive.

A quick walk around confirmed that there was no one else about, and just to make certain she stood still for a good five minutes facing the direction of the earlier noises but hearing nothing other than the sound of wind and branches dancing together. It was time to get back to work and to find out if there was anybody home. She moved now to get a closer look at the back of the house, standing on tiptoe to peer over the hedge. There were two upstairs windows, both with drawn curtains, and downstairs were three ground level windows plus a double patio door. None of these had curtains drawn but all had net curtains in place, surely designed to stop the bright summer sun shining through but serving no purpose during the winter apart from blocking Wendy's view. She was sure that she saw a light shining inside but couldn't be certain. Carefully she moved back once more towards the front of the house. Here the hedge seemed to get taller, either that or the pathway dropped, and it was impossible for her to see over the top. Unperturbed she carried on.

Her patience was rewarded as she found what she was looking for, a tree just before the pathway met the road. The wall had clearly been built around the tree and over the years its growth had caused parts of the wall to crumble away. Even Wendy would be able to get her feet in those gaps and climb up to see over the other side. Third time lucky and she made it, her admiration for sporty people getting bigger with every climbing movement. As she had hoped there were no net curtains at the front and both the upstairs and downstairs windows had flashing Christmas lights around them. From the front room a main light shone brightly out into the Winters day; someone was home. Her reconnaissance done Wendy slowly started her descent, stopping briefly as her foot got caught between the wall and the tree. She pushed herself upwards in an attempt to free the foot and just as she reached her full height she heard the unmistakeable sound of a door opening, a door in the house that was now before her. Panic set in followed by an unmistakeable vibration in her pocket that was quickly followed by the peace shattering sound of the finale from Bizet's Carmen ringing loud and proud on her phone. Nobody ever called her, especially on a Saturday.

"Who's that there?"

CHAPTER 46

Saturday 19th December, Late Morning

When it wasn't your day, it wasn't your day. Never active at the best of times, Smiler had arrived later than expected at the end of Wendy's road, the walk up from town having morphed from a ten minute stroll to a thirty minute route march. Roundabouts, supermarkets, and in particular the fences surrounding supermarkets, had all sprung up during the previous decades and the A to Z had turned out to be a bit less useful than had been hoped. When a final detour had ended up on a new road that didn't exist on the map, Smiler had asked a dog walker for directions and the somewhat bemused old lady had offered some relief by simply pointing down the road towards the next turn off.

In desperate need of a cup of coffee and a bite to eat, Smiler headed straight for a wooden bench just opposite the turning, where in olden days people would have presumably sat whilst watching the world pass by. Nowadays they were usually overrun by stinging nettles and surrounded by cider bottles, fag packets and bags of dog mess, all items that the owners didn't have the energy to take with them the extra twenty or so yards to the nearest litter bin. Smiler placed the bag on the seat, breathed deeply and stretched out, the aching back making the most of the small pause in the action. The wind had not calmed down and the sleet that was falling was becoming heavier and heavier. Smiler gave a small sigh of satisfaction seeing the flask in the open bag, and bum made firm contact with wood, only to immediately separate again as a first look into the street opposite showed a familiar figure moving determinedly towards the main road. In an instant the bag was up and over the shoulder, and the hood was pulled tight as Smiler shuffled towards the bus stop.

Despite the obvious attempt at a disguise the person on the other side of the road was clearly Wendy, the lack of heels and the presence of a long cream overcoat failing to hide either the waddle or her chest, and the tell-tale hair flowing from beneath a grey bobble hat confirmed it beyond reasonable doubt. She'd need more than a pair of sunglasses to disguise herself in that manner. Smiler feigned injury, or a handicap, foolishly believing that an injured person wearing a dark overcoat and red trousers would somehow be less noticeable than an able-bodied person dressed in the same outfit. Everything was easier in hindsight, and in any case, Wendy didn't seem to take any notice, carrying on unperturbed in the opposite direction to where Smiler had just come from.

Following people wasn't quite as easy as it looked. After a few seconds waiting for Wendy to move away, Smiler hurriedly crossed the road, taking advantage of its curve to remain unseen. Twenty or so paces later Wendy was now out of sight and a fear that after all of this effort she would get away forced another quick crossing in search of a better view. In just those few seconds Wendy had almost doubled the distance between them, moving surprisingly fast for a big lass, so an already out of breath

Smiler was forced to make extra effort to catch up. Eventually a pattern emerged with ten very quick steps for speed, a quick look over the hedgerow feigning some interest in ornithology, and then another ten quick steps. If Wendy looked behind her she'd either see a dedicated birdwatcher or someone who was late for an important meeting, though with the determined way that she had set off up the hill she didn't look like a lady who was up for too much turning. The road soon levelled off revealing an old sports ground and as Wendy went through the main entrance Smiler accelerated, passing the entrance and cutting quickly into a medium sized car park that contained a couple of small cars, a hundred pot holes and a few handfuls of gravel. The surface was already taking on a white coating as the sleet became heavier and the ground became colder. Smiler forced a last few quick steps towards the shelter of an old changing room, and then took a deep breath before looking around the corner and out over the field.

A quick scan revealed a small number of brightly dressed joggers, plus a couple of people in normal clothing, with the accompanying sound of barking suggesting that the latter were there walking dogs. For the moment there was no sign of Wendy, though her cream coat should be easy to pick out even against the cover of barren trees and hedges in the background. With an increasing panic Smiler took a couple of steps forward, trying to get a better view of the entrance to the park. Yes, she was there, hovering at first around an overfull litter bin before finally disappearing into the bushes behind it. Through the branches came bright flashes of colour, reds and yellows with hints of pink, and seconds later Wendy resurfaced, minus her bag and magically transformed into a jogger herself. Smiler turned quickly towards the car park.

"Come here Scooby, come on boy." An imaginary call was shouted out for a dog that had always been wanted.

HE'S MAKING A LIST

Wendy was now walking with determination around the edge of the field, her arms and legs moving in some strange directions that seemed to be testing the already overworked Lycra to its physical limits. Smiler started moving around the opposite side of the field in a never-ending search for an imaginary pooch, hoping above hope that Wendy wasn't about to spring into a surprise thirty laps round the park.

As suspected, Wendy wasn't there in order to exercise and having glanced quickly behind her she passed behind a group of bushes. With no time to lose Smiler left Scooby all alone and hurried towards the place from where Wendy had disappeared, slowing down as a hidden passage became clear. There was no sound other than the howling of the wind and the tapping of the sleet on the branches, so the odds were that Wendy had already passed through to the other side. A decision had to be taken, and after a first aborted attempt, Smiler pushed through the first layer of branches, slowing to a halt whilst eyes adjusted to the reduced levels of light. There was a narrow path between the bushes and a reasonably high wall and Smiler moved instinctively forward, stopping almost immediately as the backpack snagged in the branches. It was hopeless, moving without making a noise would be impossible and in any case a meeting with Wendy any time soon along the narrow path would be disastrous. In the end the decision was easy and Smiler backed gently away, soon regaining the sports field and surprising a passing jogger in the process before looking around frantically to find some other way to see what was going on behind the wall.

It wasn't a really tall tree but it was one that seemed to be made for climbing, with decent sized branches close to the floor and a continued good coverage of branches right up to the top. In saying that it was obviously a tree made for being climbed by small, lithe children on warm summers days, not Smiler in wet wellies and a thick overcoat. A pair of binoculars were quickly taken from the bag and the ascent began, with the first steps unsurprisingly being the hardest. The solid branches that seemed so close to the floor were found to be just a little bit thinner and a little bit higher than they had first appeared, but a good dose of determination meant that by the fifth attempt Smiler was upright and standing at base camp. From there it was easy to reach the higher branches from where a hesitant glance downwards showed very clearly the outer path that Wendy had taken, plus an inner wall complete with a breach. Inside that was a further pathway snaking between the initial wall and the external garden wall of a house. Holding very tightly to the trunk of the tree a search was launched for the red or yellow colours that would give away Wendy's location. Starting at the outside of the house and working methodically outwards the garden was ticked off as clear. A flash of colour to the right gave her away, Wendy now also climbing in the space between a tree and the wall that protected the house. Enthused with confidence, Smiler leaned out to the left for a better view, taking the trunk in one hand and the binoculars in the other.

"Who's that there?"

The shout was loud and came from nowhere. The surprise caused quick nervous movements and as the feet moved too far and too quickly the smooth rubber soles of the old boots were useless as Smiler began to lose balance.

CHAPTER 47

Saturday 19th December, Late Morning

There was nothing like the feeling of being clean, something that people took perhaps for granted but which was a basic right that everyone should have. It only made ITK wonder more so why the great horde of unwashed students and eco warriors could be so against such a fine institution, especially when it was available to most of them on a daily basis. The shower had been hot and quick and the only water falling down in ITK's direction currently was the rain tapping on the small window over the sink, which in a few minutes would turn to sleet and in a few hours would be snow. It was perfect weather for the evening to come.

Wendy hadn't sent any more messages, clearly preferring a quiet morning in advance of the excitement to come later that day. She may have taken a quick drive out to have a look at the location, innocently turning around outside the house as lost travellers do, though to be honest ITK wasn't even sure if she had a car or not. In any case she'd been quiet, so all must be well. Saturday mornings were poor timing for trolling, most of the youngsters being asleep whilst a very large part of ITK's followers started to focus on the afternoon football, having little time for politics whilst there was a match to argue about. It was slow news time too, the Americans struggling even now to get over Thanksgiving, whilst the storms in the south of England were all blown out and finished. Breaking the habit of the last few years the BBC News got a looking at, just to make a change.

As the song said, Santa Claus was making a list and checking it twice before he came to town, and ITK would need to do the same to make sure that everything was in place for that evening. The costume had been reserved earlier that week just in case, and would be taken back on Monday morning, along with an apologetic smile and a story about it being too big. It would need to be big though with a few extra layers surely being necessary beneath it in order to fight off the expected cold later that day. Glad of a reason to move, ITK went into the hallway taking first a packet of Post Its from the top of the book case, the ones where the stupid cow had moaned that the glue wasn't strong enough when they had started falling to the floor, and then a Grand Hotel pen from the inside pocket of the coat that sat all lonely on the set of four hangers unevenly fastened to the wall. Back in the relative warmth of the kitchen ITK sat down and started making a list of what needed to be bought later on.

A quick vibration on the smartphone broke the silence.

'All done. Target in place. Wendy.'

A large smile broke out over a face unused to the sensation. Perhaps Wendy's little car had been out for a spin after all. She was showing good character and initiative, for an idiot, but the decision had been long made and ITK would be there to offer a helping hand if needed.

HE'S MAKING A LIST

In any case it was going to be a spectacle that just couldn't be missed. Inspired by the sandwiches during the week, and supported by the meagre end of weak contents inside a very small fridge, salmon and cucumber sandwiches were made, the vinegary salmon and end of life cucumber juice somehow softening the stale bread just enough to make it feel normal in the mouth. Cut neatly into quarters they were eagerly dispatched and two reusable shopping bags were recovered from the cupboard under the sink. Armed with an overcoat and hat, ITK went out to brave the cold under a heavy sleet that was just starting to turn into snow.

CHAPTER 48

Saturday 19th December, Late Morning

Wendy had never given much thought to Sports bras, but now, as she sprinted over what remained of a cricket square in the middle of the field, the subject did spring momentarily to mind. The Lycra that had just a few moments before appeared rigidly unmovable was now proving to be helpless against the swinging, bouncing movements of her two best assets. Considering how slippy the grass was underfoot, her ability to keep her balance in such conditions was the highlight of her day so far.

Fortunately, her fall had been straightforward and pain free. Rather than twisting her ankle and rendering her helpless the old wall had simply crumbled, leaving her to fall cat like to the floor. Fight or flight had fallen firmly on the side of flight and instinct had kicked in, the sunglasses taken in hand and the legs powering her around the corner, all the time accompanied by the still ringing Bizet on her telephone. Bursting back onto the sports field had brought her into close contact with a jogger, a dog walker and a small ugly looking mongrel of a breed that she wasn't familiar. Looking left and right she had instantly decided to ignore the cover offered by the joggers' normal circular path and to favour instead the speed offered by the more direct route that she now found herself taking. In, out, in, out, her breathing stabilised, Wendy finding that pursed lips were best for reducing the volume of her gasping breaths. Her phone finally stopped ringing, giving Carmen a respite, and she could hear no obvious shouting from behind her. A Wendy smile started to spread across her sleet drenched face as her running motion became more theatrical and more exaggerated. She had done it, and the increased adrenalin levels were almost as good as a nice glass of fine white wine.

Approaching the litter bin Wendy slowed down, sliding gently to a halt on the by now almost white surface. A quick one eighty turn allowed her to pretend to be performing a long-practiced end of run muscle shakedown exercise whilst at the same time double checking that no one was in pursuit. There was nobody there, just as she expected, with the chasing of strangers being a dangerous business in these times. Warmed by the success of her mission, Wendy stretched her arms upwards, shoulders back and chest out, forcing the Lycra into one last physical exertion. A brief wait for a particularly slow dog walker to move on followed, then in the flick of an eye she was back in the undergrowth, quickly covering herself up with her coat before passing again through the gates and heading towards home.

It was exhilaration, an excitement that Wendy had never imagined possible. Her steps were light and she felt none of the cold that the wind and sleet should have been inflicting upon her. Any mirror placed in front of her would now be reflecting nothing but rosy cheeks and bright eyes on her effortless return towards the warmth of her house. Her eyes had served her well, showing her the best ways to approach the property and giving her the layout of the house and garden. How she could have ever imagined 'just turning up and doing it' she didn't know. It was her ears though of which she was proudest. Whoever had come out of the door had not been seen, but had been well and truly heard. It had only been three words, 'Who's that there', but they had been enough. It had been a while since she had last heard that voice and as she had been accelerating away after her fall from the wall she hadn't even given it any consideration. Speeding across the field it had started to register in her mind for the first time, and the processors that were her brain had whirred into action. In the bushes behind the litter bin she had doubted, questioning her memories and disbelieving her own senses but now, marching towards home and surrounded by a downfall of dancing, fluttering snowflakes she was certain. People may change visibly with age but the voice in shouted excitement stayed true. Wendy was a singer, all be it a long time ago and not an exceptionally good one, but singers had ears for things like this and she was sure. A few hours ago, she had woken up undecided, once again a victim of her old worries and insecurity. Now she was the leading lady, ready to take to the stage in her own show, to bring the tragedy that had been her life up to that point to an inevitable end. With each step she was more certain that what had to be done would be done, that later that day she would close this chapter and open the next.

CHAPTER 49

Saturday 19th December, Late Morning

Smiler's eyes squeezed tightly together, desperately trying to force away the pain. The head throbbed and the back and left leg were numb from the impact with the floor.

"Are you all right there?" The elderly gentleman had a kind voice, even though he was probably laughing beneath his bulbous nose and large, bushy moustache.

Smiler's head nodded slowly.

"Yes, all's good thanks. Just a new yoga move that needs a bit more work." A wide grin was more difficult to produce than it appeared.

The man moved away, closely followed by a small, docile spaniel and Smiler stood slowly, leaning against the base of the trunk for support. The fingers still moved but the palms stung from the many scratches they had received whilst grasping at branches. The left leg had clearly been in contact with something a bit more substantial, leaving a thick red scratch line on the underside of a thigh which was clearly visible through a hole in the red tracksuit bottoms that was also letting the cold wind blow around the newly exposed nether regions. The back was in shock from a landing which had thankfully avoided the head and been made on a backside that was now both sore and sodden. It had been a fall of three yards, nothing more, but a fall none the less, and one that despite the pain had undeniably been lucky.

Turning now towards the field a passing jogger shook Smiler back into action and the search for Wendy. The short distance between the tree and the field was quickly crossed despite a small limp and wet cloth clinging to the backside. How long had it taken to fall down and get up? Perhaps no more than a minute, but anything could have happened in that time. The sleet was now transformed into large flakes of snow that were falling heavily. The nearest half of the field was just about visible, with the far side now nothing but a blur of snowflakes dancing in the swirling wind. Was Wendy still behind the wall, or perhaps somewhere in the field? The decision was quickly taken, and with all caution thrown to the wind the wellington boots were soon crossing an old cricket square in the centre of the field and moving towards the gate. There was still no sign of the prey though and a panicking Smiler was soon knee deep in the long grass where Wendy had been seen getting changed earlier. Smiler passed rapidly around the area, looking for signs of hidden bags or human movement, but found nothing there and so moved on towards the gate.

A moment of forced concentration followed and was rewarded almost immediately as the merest hints of footprints were spotted, just visible in the snowy slush. Smiler set off with a double caution to neither slip nor be seen. The clouds above had turned a deep grey, giving the impression that it was almost night time already, and the few cars on the road passed at walking pace, their lights revealing them at the very last moment as they crept by, windscreen wipers frantically swatting away at the snowflakes as their tyres faithfully followed in the tracks left by the cars that they had followed. Staying as close as possible to the hedge at the side, Smiler accelerated, desperate not to lose the woman whose now clear footprints were carefully being followed.

Nervously, Smiler started to sing, the words to Jingle Bells being forced through half open lips, just about audible at close range but certainly not carrying above the patter of the fluttering snow. Another car approached and there she was, her shadow unmistakeable against the glaring headlights. Breathing calmer now, Smiler slowed a little, trying hard to identify exactly where on the route back they were but abandoning the mental search as Wendy turned off the main road. Smiler held back, despite the cover of the snow, suspecting that this would be a place where a backwards glance could be expected but Wendy just marched onwards, seemingly oblivious to everything around her. Just a minute later she had found her house, mounted the drive and was inside, a light jumping into life in the living room as Smiler took refuge behind a large four by four parked across the road.

It had all happened so quickly, one thing leading to another with no time at all to take stock. Crouched there, shivering and wet, just one thing came to Smiler's mind; it had been brilliant. Despite the aches and pains and the cuts and bruises, despite the cold and the wet and the runny nose, Smiler was actually doing something, something that would have been unimaginable earlier that week. Yes, Wendy had her faults, but if Smiler could prevent her from doing whatever it was that she had planned, then how great would that be? Having a mission, a purpose, even if only for the day, felt good.

Wendy's house was a big house, with large bay windows upstairs and down. It was most likely built in the 20s or 30s and as such was more functional than beautiful, and it was certainly too big for one person to live in on their own. Smiler wouldn't have known what to do with all of the space. The road was a circular one, having just the one way in and out. A quick, shuffled tour showed that the only ways to exit the close were by either passing through a stranger's garden and climbing over a fence into the fields behind, or by passing along the road that they had just taken. Wendy had already demonstrated her climbing abilities that day, but Smiler was certain that the next time she left her house she would do it using the road. In the absence of any other places to wait, Smiler made for the old wooden bus shelter on the other side of the main road and as the snow continued to fall a flask of coffee was removed from the bag, with praise given to the inventor of ones that didn't break when falling out of trees. With the two hands half thawed against the outside of the cup the sandwiches followed, the cheese and pickle on offer being a far cry from the freshly grated cheddar of the Grand Hotel, with the waxy slices barely keeping the two pieces of bread apart, but it still did its job. Anyone passing would have simply seen another innocent person desperately waiting for the bus to take them back to the warmth of their home, but Smiler was there for a different reason. Almost hypnotised by the darting snow, Smiler was there to save Wendy.

CHAPTER 50

Saturday 19th December, Early Afternoon

By the time ITK got back from shopping it was blowing a real blizzard outside. Lunchtime was normally the best time to shop if you wanted to avoid the queues but that day it had been overly quiet in town, especially so considering that it was the last Saturday before Christmas. The many people who were normally obliged to use the poor selection of shops that remained in the town centre had been noticeable only by their absence. The weather had obviously played a part, with those not waking up early enough to avoid the blizzard clearly deciding to stay at home whilst hoping that the forecast for a calmer afternoon might for once be right. Anyhow, ITK had done the necessary shopping and collected the costume and everything was now ready to go.

Putting the shopping away was no trouble, the kitchen having a place for everything and everything being in its place. Some of the items would be needed that evening, so a small head lamp fastened on a red strap, a large hand torch and a nine-inch kitchen knife were carefully placed in the middle of the table. The trembling of the hand as the knife was put down shocked ITK a little, though it obviously wasn't nerves, and even if it had been it was just a nervous excitement, not fear. ITK sat down, clenched fists resting gently on the table, with sharp, deliberate breaths being forced through the nose. The ticking of the kitchen clock was comforting, the second hand making yet another pointless journey around the face, as if people these days cared about seconds, when even minutes no longer seemed to have a purpose. Gradually the shaking disappeared, the palms opening out to reveal the now steady hands that would be needed later that day, once the fun really started.

Waiting had never been a problem for ITK. There had been the waiting for an ill mother to waste away and die as a teenager, the waiting for a father to implode under the pressure of trying to raise three children on his own, the waiting for the love of your life to realise that you should be together, and then the waiting for that doomed relationship to end. Finally there had been the waiting for the job that had somehow held you together and given you purpose through all of the rest of your challenges to disappear, as the industries of bygone ages had withered and died. It had been a world that had owed ITK nothing and had seemingly relished in giving just that. Yes, waiting had never been a problem. A cup of tea would have helped, but the night would be long and there was nothing worse than needing a toilet when none were around, so just a biscuit would have to do instead. Still the second hand ran around, encouraging the smaller, more important hands to catch it up. Perhaps there might just be some time to do some trolling after all.

***

An hour of abusing and ridiculing people on line would normally have calmed ITK down, but today was different.

HE'S MAKING A LIST

Agitated and unable to concentrate there had been opportunities missed and mistakes made. The bedroom window gave panoramic views over the car park in front of the block of flats next door, and the sight of a smooth covering of freshly fallen snow finally started to bring calm. The flurry was now over, with the darkest clouds having been blown away whilst the remaining lighter clouds spread out in a vain attempt to cover up the hints of blue sky that were already starting to peek through. A long line of unneeded cars were still in place, almost invisible under the thick layer of snow that covered everything in view. It was the most beautiful of sights, pure and fresh, a bright white snow with its perfect, unbroken surface. It wouldn't last though, it never did. First would come the birds, hopping around and leaving their tiny marks on the surface, and then the humans would follow, leaving crater like footprints everywhere they went. Car owners would finally find the courage to use their vehicles, with the large tyres wreaking devastation on what was left. Already unrecognisable, the surface colour would change, the warmth and the passage of people turning it grey and yellow and every colour in between. Finally, it would start to disappear, leaving behind just slush and all of the rubbish that had been hidden beneath it, the memories of its initial beauty already distant and forgotten. That was what Bing Crosby had dreamed of, the freshness of new snow, not the mess it left behind. It was a calming sight, beautiful, and ITK decided that now it was time, that the waiting was over.

The costume had been placed on the side of a large double bed that hadn't been shared for quite some time. Shining bright from inside its see-through protective covering it calmed ITK even further, the deep red lure of a super-hero uniform. It was a good one and it would need to be, with the temperatures due to drop considerably under a night sky that was forecast to be clear. The package was opened and its contents laid out for inspection. There was a poor quality pair of black plastic over boots that wouldn't be needed at all, as ITK had a good pair of walking boots that would be perfect that evening in the snow. As there was no intention of winning a prize in the fancy dress the lack of detail wouldn't be a problem. The trousers were large and baggy, the material thick and grainy between the fingers, but even then an extra layer would be needed underneath in order to avoid death by freezing. The large white bag with long ties attached was a false belly, something surely not very often needed in England these days, but which might be worn later for warmth if nothing else. The red jacket, complete with furry white cuffs and collar, had a proper opening with proper button holes and all, giving a true idea of the costume's quality as did the large black belt, designed to keep the belly, false or otherwise, firmly in its place. To top it off was an elasticated beard, a fur trimmed hat and even a sack for the presents. Yes, it was a fine costume, and one that would do its job that night. ITKs fingers stroked the material again, all signs of nervousness now gone, calmed at first by the snow and finally by the beauty of the costume. The mind was now firmly focussed on what would need to be done that evening. There would be no more waiting, it was time to go.

CHAPTER 51

Saturday 19th December, Early Afternoon

Could it really be a feeling of happiness that Wendy was experiencing as she changed out of her wet running clothes to the accompaniment of Leroy Anderson's Sleigh Ride? She was even singing along, just like the Spice Girls had when Girlpower had still been a thing. Perhaps it would be coming back in fashion for a few hours that night.

There were just so many reasons for Wendy to be feeling so happy. Her sports bra had been replaced by something drier and more comfortable and as a result her breathing was almost back to normal. She was also still taking full advantage of the adrenalin that seemed to be making a last defiant turn around her body before finally allowing her to calm down. She would never become a full-time jogger, but boy hadn't she shown all of the others a clean set of heels as she'd slid past them in her escape from staking out the joint. If only she'd realised that she could run when she had been at school. Her mystery caller had not wanted to reveal their number and hadn't left a message and was, as such, probably yet another scammer or insurance claims manager, much like most of the other people who had Wendy's number to hand. It had been an important lesson though and Bizet would surely forgive Wendy as she switched her phone on to vibrate mode, thus avoiding any problems later should the person decide to call back. With a sigh she sat at the kitchen table, a small thing that was barely big enough for a few friends to sit and play a game of Monopoly around, with a cup of tea for warmth and a glass of Pinot Gris to celebrate her expedition. She clutched the now silent telephone to her chest, eager to let Sharon know what she had discovered that morning whilst at the same time uncomfortable at how much she now relied on her old friend. It was a strange situation that she was still trying to work out. Getting in touch with old friends was common enough, Wendy had even signed up to a website once where you could see what everyone from school was getting up to, but the traditional roles from before seemed to have been forgotten. Wendy had nothing against Sharon, after all they were better friends now than they had ever been before, but as far as she could remember Sharon had always been a follower, not a leader. As Wendy carefully constructed her next message in her head, she could almost believe that the old roles had been reversed.

***

The door clicked shut behind her once again as Wendy left the house and walked into the tail end of the blizzard that had been anticipated throughout the week. The snow was already slowing down and a clearer, brighter end to the day looked a distinct possibility which would make moving around much easier. She was refreshed and as eager as ever for the day, and for her torment, to come to a close, and her quickly exchanged messages with Sharon had put her already saturated senses into overdrive. Snow was always at its worst when it was fresh, its distorted form under foot making it more slippy and difficult to walk in and its dazzling reflection of light making it difficult to pick out detail and see what was really going on. Even though they called it the main road the few tyre tracks suggested that not many vehicles had passed, and Wendy had nothing but pity for the poor soul waiting at the bus stop in such treacherous conditions. For Wendy however, kitted out in old riding boots and a warm ski jacket, the walk into town would be straightforward. Say what you would, the old town still had some character, the smell of smoke from woodfires up and down the road giving her that warm feeling you get from imagining being snuggled up in front of a roaring fire. The houses nearest to her own were all high walls, spike topped gates and security cameras, keeping the solicitors and accountants of the town safe and sound inside. Next came the larger buildings, now divided into apartments, where young couples and professional people spent the years between having a bedroom at their parents and owning their first house. The final hundred yards to the centre of town was all takeaways and mobile phone shops, with the students and low wage workers living in first floor bedsits above, thankful for the heat that rose through the floor but forever inconvenienced by the smells from the kitchens and the late-night noise. Everyone had their place and Wendy's house was far enough away from the centre of the town for her to be happy. She finally arrived at the market place and stopped, admiring the scene before her as her mumbling lips encouraged the Christians to wake and salute the happy morn.

Wendy didn't need the help of other people singing along in order to know the words, she had sung all of the carols often enough when she was younger. The brass band was cooped up in the corner nearest the Blue Bell, which she was sure was a relationship from which they were both profiting. She called it a band but there were fewer than a dozen players, just enough to get all of the harmonies out whilst allowing the band to split up and play in more places at once. On the back row was a young girl, almost drowning in a woollen hat and scarf, and Wendy sighed at memories of Christmas past. The main market square was full of metal framed stalls, their roofs now benefitting from a deep covering of snow on top of the green and yellow striped plastic covers that were just visible beneath. In the short time since Wendy had left her house the weather had continued to improve and the last of the snow had stopped falling as the wind had blown itself out. From behind the church tower the low, late sun of the day was shining out over the festive scene before her, causing the baubles on the town Christmas tree to glow as if they were lit by a powerful current. It was a beautiful sight. On the other side of the market place everything was set up and ready for the festival that night with some families already there in costume, no doubt hoping to get everything out of the way and the kids in bed nice and early so as to cause minimum disruption to the Saturday night television schedule. Having taken in all of the sights Wendy set off again, moving slowly around the outside of the square so as to minimise the possibility of contact with the locals.

Modern town centres were an embarrassment, put to the sword by high costs and competition from the online giants. In order to survive the main stores had been drawn to larger centres on the outskirts of towns, leaving the smaller traders to fight amongst themselves over the few people left with real money to spend. To be fair, Webledon had survived better than most, through the combined impact of a large, regular market and a group of traders that were willing to fight. Wendy was now amongst the best of those shops, away from the market place and the pedestrianised zone and in amongst the maze of smaller streets around the old church. There were no opticians or travel agents here, and the mobile phone and pound shops were also far away. Wendy was seeing clothes shops that deserved to be called boutiques, real butchers, proper jewellers and bookshops that didn't have any shades of grey. Each one was decorated for Christmas and lit with imitation gaslights, not the awful flashing, multi coloured rubbish that she had seen in Harshton the night before. The last defiant flakes of snow and the fading, end of afternoon light just added to the wintery landscape. These were shops where you could get to know the name of the owners without having to read it off their badge.

Wendy worked quickly, her trips to the butcher, the green grocer and the delicatessen providing the meat, fruit, vegetables and wine that would help her survive until the twenty seventh of December. Next on the imaginary list was a visit to her favourite clothes shop, a glance through the already frosted window showing that the item that Wendy had come for was still available. Just ten minutes later, very quick by Wendy's standards, she was walking out with a new red coat neatly packed inside a stylish bag. Slowly she continued towards the church, a collection of haberdashers and tea shops, scented candles and ironmongers almost tempting her away from the person that she had become and the deed that she was preparing to do. Then she saw it and everything came back into focus. Perhaps it had been the wine wearing off, or the cold and the festive sights and sounds, but her heart beat increased as she pushed into the warmth of the old antiques shop.

As a candlestick it was magnificent, everything that it should be. The base was round and solid, thick layers of silver giving it a weight that was perfect for keeping it steady and for smashing in a skull. Of course, it would need a sack or something around it, not so much to keep it clean but more to prevent tell-tale traces of silver being left inside the wound and giving the weapon away. The expertly curved surface would keep the impact blunt, with no sharp edges to tear away at the flesh and cause excessive bleeding. The stem was thick and strong resembling the pillars that were often seen in churches, and here providing the strength needed to wield it as a weapon. At a good twelve to fifteen inches it was also the perfect length to bypass any flailing arms that might desperately claw out in protection. The actual holder for the candle itself literally topped off the piece, its circular, flower shaped head would prevent it from slipping out of gloved hands and there were no pieces delicate enough to become detached and left behind as unwanted clues. Yes, it was magnificent and perfect, an ideal addition to the sideboard in the living room, a perfect home for one of the old candles that Wendy had bought from the last Church sale, and above all a perfect murder weapon for the night to come. She took it in her hands marvelling at the weight and balance, and once again at the beauty of the piece. She had known that the weapon would find her, a bit like Harry Potter and his wand, but she had never expected it to be so perfect, instead imagining buying some uninspiring piece off the market, head bowed in shame as she hid her face to avoid being recognised. In wilder dreams she had even seen herself stealing it, slipping it quietly into her bag as a distracted shop assistant or stall holder looked elsewhere. No, this was different, something that she would buy with her head held high, that she would keep in pride of place as the tool of her liberation from the shackles of her past. She added a lace doily to protect the sideboard from scratches, paid and then left.

The shopping was completed and Wendy pushed out into what was now a clear, cold evening. As her foot touched the pavement a small bell rang out behind her announcing that someone had passed through the door, that Rudolph was coming and that round one had started.

CHAPTER 52

Saturday 19th December, Late Afternoon

During their short acquaintance Smiler had never been so glad to see Wendy as she walked briskly out of her road and turned towards town. Efforts had been made to look inconspicuous in the bus shelter, but they were hardly necessary, the few flutters of residual snow and Wendy's determined look in front of her ensuring that Smiler wasn't going to be discovered this time around. Waiting briefly for her to open up a gap the eventual walk behind her was heaven, with tired muscles coming back to life as the blood was pumped faster around the near freezing body. The picnic had been fun at first, with even a few snorts of laughter as Smiler had imagined the best way to recount the 'falling out of a tree' story to friends the next time there was an invitation for dinner. But gradually the reality of the situation had sunk in, as the bones had grown colder the arse started to freeze against the wooden bench and the bladder started to swell, whilst all the time Wendy was luxuriating inside her warm house. There had followed a sort of catch 22 situation, where movement for warmth had agitated the bladder and being still had brought on the cold. In the end a quick trip over the gate and behind a hedge had brought relief, and would surely be added to the list of dinner party stories. In fact, should any such invitations ever arrive, the whole day would probably entertain friends for years to come. Anyhow, there was now motion and warmth and an empty bladder that no longer complained, and whilst keeping a discrete distance behind the quarry the hunter advanced.

The route taken by Wendy was very different to the one that Smiler had taken that morning, the walk along the main road only serving to confirm that Webledon was just posh, full of lah di dahs and farmers driving around in their big four by fours. It had never had any character, not real character like Harshton, because all it had to offer were nice houses and quaint little shops. Real character came from people and it was they who determined if a town was great or not. The people of Harshton may have lost a lot over the last fifty years but it was that fact in itself that made the place so special, the shared sorrow of yet another disappointment. The people of Webledon had never known that loss, and probably went about their business not caring about the suffering of their near neighbours. Following Wendy into town confirmed it all, with the high walls and spiked fences just there to keep neighbours apart, and it was only once they approached the town centre and its fast food shops and pubs that Smiler started to feel more at ease. Approaching the market square Wendy stopped, looking around as if lost and forcing Smiler to take shelter behind an old telephone box. The box was clearly no longer in use, the days when people needed to pump ten pence pieces into old-fashioned phones was long gone, and this one had been kept on as a sort of book sharing centre, its sign announcing that if you took a book could you please leave another in exchange. As always the project was well intentioned, though even in Webledon it had generated nothing more than an empty kebab box, a Dick Francis novel and a corner full of piss. Behind Wendy, far in the distance, the first Santa Claus costumes were visible, with tiny herds of small children wandering around in front of a stage, their red costumes standing out against the snowy ground like cherries on a Bakewell tart.

The word tradition was often used to describe things such as Christmas crackers, wigs on judges and the chasing of foxes by people on horses. Then there were other types of tradition, mostly recent additions that had piggy backed onto more classic events, like some sort of lopsided Siamese twin. The Webledon Santa Claus festival was one of the latter types. Smiler had never actually been but had often seen photos and posts on the internet, sanitised highlights of dogs with shiny antlers, horses with big red noses and families in matching costumes standing beside the town Christmas tree were common place. For most people however it appeared that going out for a few pints on a Saturday evening had been replaced with going out for a few pints on a Saturday evening dressed as Santa Claus. Yes, there was always music and dancing, the collection of presents for charity and carols besides the late-night market, so perhaps one day it would become a tradition that deserved to be remembered. For tonight it would just serve to make Smiler as anonymous as possible, just in case a discrete exit was required, and the still wet and sticky Santa costume beneath the coat was all ready to be revealed once the time was right. Smiler stared back at where Wendy had stood, eyes blinking towards a sunlight that dazzled from behind the old church tower, the realisation coming that something was missing from the wintery scene of a short daydream before. The forward motion, initially stuttering and slow, accelerated towards the market square. Wendy had disappeared.

The brass band from the morning was still there and the people with far more stamina than Smiler would ever have were now playing Away in a Manger. There would be no time to stay by my side until morning is nigh as Smiler took a hurried right turn into the first aisle of market stalls, coming up immediately against the first obstacle, a group of older ladies admiring some handmade scarves. The sun was already fading away, leaving behind a now almost clear sky overhead. Each stall had its own lighting beneath the snow-covered roofs and sharp rays of light from the tens of stalls in the aisle were crisscrossing above the heads of the group of shoppers and the steam rising from their wintery breaths. Smiler pushed past the group, hoping to find a large enough break in people to get a good view. The mind whirred, updating the profile of the person that was being searched; medium height, a cream overcoat and auburn hair. Had there been a hat? No, that was that morning, it was just auburn hair, long and bouncy. There was no one like that in the aisle so Smiler moved into the next one, the heartbeat increasing with every step. This passage way was even more crowded with a cheese stall attracting an even larger group of people than the scarves, and as Smiler pushed through a sort of panic set in. What if Wendy had seen and guessed? Perhaps it had been a trick, waiting at the entrance before dashing off into the bustle of the market. What a stupid idea it had been, thinking that hiding in the cover of a bus shelter, in plain view of the road, would fool anyone. Wendy had been clever, but Smiler would be cleverer.

There it was at the side of the square, the cross that served as a tribute to the fallen of the Great War. Three steps went up to a square limestone base, the sides engraved with the names of the fallen, many whose families surely still lived in the town. From this base the stone rose high and was topped by a Celtic cross. It was much shorter than the large Christmas tree on the other side, and it wouldn't give the best view of the market, but it was surely the safest way to get some additional height, especially after the climbing escapades of that morning. Smiler took a quick look around, the last rays of light giving no sign of high visibility jackets or police helmets. All it took was a quick step over a small protective fence and then the short distance to the plinth was easily negotiated. Clinging to the central column, Smiler looked around, the higher position now giving a clear view of the far side of the square. Instinctively the arms tightened and the rubber boots pushed, inching further and further up the cross. Sweat started to run down into the eyes, a strange feeling on such a cold evening, and the arm muscles started to hurt once again as Smiler's head turned urgently from side to side.

"Oi, you. What are you doing, get down from there!" It was a loud voice, but a faraway voice, coming from the market entrance. The non-stop noise from all around seemed to get quieter. Smiler needed to concentrate.

Yes, there she was, just next to the tree on the far side of the market. Smiler slid down to the bottom of the cross, the arm muscles relieved after their second climb of the day. Two police officers were approaching, walking urgently down the side of the market, so an escape through the throng of cheesebuyers seemed the best option. Ignoring the shouts and insults from the people that were pushed to the side, Smiler decided that it was time for a pitstop. A disinterested seller of scented candles looked on as the overcoat was whipped off and stored quickly in the bag, being replaced just as urgently by a cheap fur lined hat and an elasticated beard. Without the protection of the coat the cold struck immediately, and Smiler was already shivering as the last yards were completed towards the exit from the aisle, where any onlooker would have seen nothing other than a bulk standard Santa sauntering out towards the Christmas tree.

The band had given way to carol singers, not the type who come knocking on your door but proper ones, all bucking the Santa trend and wearing Christmas jumpers as they sang of the Little Town of Bethlehem and the hopes and fears that would be met there that night. Wendy was stood just to their right, her back to Smiler as she admired the tree, and Smiler edged around towards her, expertly avoiding the people with the collection buckets and finally settling next to a stall that was selling leatherware. Wendy was clearly waiting for someone and Smiler was soon rummaging through expensive gloves whilst throwing regular sideways glances towards her back. The pretence lasted just one or two minutes when finally there was movement, a raised hand of acknowledgement as she turned towards someone coming from the direction of the church.

Bugger, it wasn't her. It was the same height, same hair and same overcoat, but the wrong person. The panic was absolute as the realisation dawned that Wendy had managed to get away, whether she knew she was being followed or not. A quick look at the Christmas tree was enough to realise that climbing it was out of the question and Smiler's options were quickly running out.

"There he is, Santa." The cry was urgent, an almost high-pitched scream.

There was no time to see if the shout was a warning to the police or an alert from a child to their put-upon parents, because Smiler was off again at full speed towards the church. There would be less people there as well as more nooks and crannies to hide in. In any case, Wendy was surely not still in the market and so she must be somewhere else.

The streets behind the church were like another world, all fine window displays and tinkling door bells to announce yet another visitor to a high-quality boutique. They were proper shops too, selling good old-fashioned products in a good old-fashioned way. Unlike in the market place, where hundreds of feet had squashed and spread the snow almost as it had fallen, here it had been left to rest longer, making it treacherous underfoot, especially for people wearing old rubber boots. At that moment Smiler was simply moving without real purpose, yet again thankful for the warmth that it gave the tired body. Quick glances were cast in shop windows as well as back towards the square, searching eagerly for either Wendy or an irate follower. There was nothing in the bookshop, nor the record store, and the toyshop and the hardware shop were equally as empty. Sensing no commotion from behind, Smiler finally slowed, now taking more time to look around. One minute the eyes were fixed on a vintage toaster, a bargain for someone at forty nine ninety nine, then the next there she was, directly in front, head down and walking at a determined pace. In panic, Smiler forgot the presence of the false beard and its powers of invisibility and turned quickly in search of cover. The speed of the turn was too much for the worn soles on the boots, and for the briefest of moments the legs moved all on their own whilst the body remained still and upright. A slight contact between the left boot and a curb stone gave a forward impetus that the body was unable to take advantage of, and when the final fall came it was swift and graceless. The soft surface of the snow cushioned the fall but Smiler was down and out, face in the snow and with the gaping gash in the tracksuit bottoms now facing the star lit sky. Through the corner of a half-clenched eye Smiler followed Wendy as she walked briskly past, just before the arrival of two pairs of regulation issue boots.

CHAPTER 53

Saturday 19th December, Late Afternoon

The decision had been taken even before it snowed, the snow simply confirming that ITK would be taking the train to Webledon. The difference in quality of customers made the extra four quid that it cost for an off-peak day return on the train a far better option than taking the bus, and no doubt a quicker and more comfortable one too. Walking through the town early doors the atmosphere was a little subdued, perhaps no surprise considering that it was the day after Mad Friday and also the day of the Webledon Santa Claus festival. There was nothing really festival like about it, it was just a run of the mill event that had been made up twenty years earlier to try and encourage some late-night shopping, but the good drinkers of Webledon still kept it going, almost religiously you could say. In Harshton the shops were starting to wind down, with a handful of customers still being served and cash tills already being checked, the shopkeepers hoping above all that the takings on the last Saturday before Christmas would help them to keep trading just a little bit longer. ITK took a quick look around, and seeing that nobody was particularly interested took off the long overcoat and stored it along with the other goodies in Santa's sack. Next came the beard, followed by a practice ho-ho-ho as ITK fondled the false belly that was more for warmth than effect.

Pretending to be someone else had become normal for ITK, from the profile photograph of the pretty girl that encouraged followers on the internet to manipulative Sharon, the old schoolfriend. Between the two had passed tens of similar characters, each one having been invented in order to fool the fools. Sometimes ITK struggled to remember which parts of life were real and which were made up, but then again perhaps in the end there was not so much difference between them after all. Could pretending to be evil really make you evil? It would be a question to think about on the way home, but for now there was work to be done. ITK purchased a ticket and then found a quiet part of the platform, avoiding the snowballs that were being exchanged between the dozen or so other Santas that were also waiting to make the trip. The laughter and insults faded into background noise and the night became calm and bright, the calmness being the biggest surprise. There had been many moments during the day when the self-doubt had been there, a regular companion that was often reinforced by the behaviour of others, of family, friends and colleagues, each one adding their own doubt to the mountain that already existed. ITK's hand brushed the side of the sack, briefly touching the handle of the knife that had been hidden within. Well, the others could doubt whatever they wanted, but tonight was going to be the night. The daft cow was going to do all of the work whilst ITK sat back and revelled in the mayhem it caused, though if the bitch did look like bottling it, ITK would be ready and willing to finish things off as required. The power that derived from doing was one thing, the power now being experienced from controlling the thoughts and actions of someone else was the ultimate victory. A small hipflask was pulled out of one of Santa's side pockets, a never before used second prize from a long-forgotten raffle, and the thick spirit burned the lips and throat before finally forcing a small cough. To the left a bright light announced the arrival of the five eighteen.

During the week the train would have been packed full of commuters, taking the townsfolk to the city and then bringing them dutifully back home again. Weekends were different and there was no problem finding a space amongst the struggle of returning shoppers and the eclectic collection of Clauses. ITK walked through the carriage in search of a clean seat, finally settling for one where the pattern was partially recognisable and the floor showed no obvious sign of vomit, spilled drink or discarded food. The rest of the Santas seemed to have settled into the next carriage, the sound of their laughter and of rattling beer cans a perfect accompaniment to the sound of the advancing train.

Five Gold Rings rang out in reasonable harmony, they were even having a sing song bless them, Christmas being the time of year when even the roughest of the rough could manage to string a few long-remembered words onto their lips. It was clear from the rest of the song that the lyrics had been updated to give them more of a Webledon Santa Festival feel. Perhaps there was a choir competition that ITK had missed?

The train at night was not the most interesting journey, the rare lights from houses and passing roads providing the only distraction from the shadows of hill and valley. The snow clouds that had been all around earlier had at first completely disappeared, leaving a beautiful clear sky with the stars already in position and shining brightly, but newer clouds were already darkening the horizon. The singers were continuing their impromptu concert with songs of ladies' underwear. How fantastic, no elastic, not very safe to wear. The lightness of the song was at odds with ITK's thoughts and the poker face that hid beneath the false beard, as whatever ITK might feel about the world and the people in it, that night bad things were going to happen. Virgin births were out of the window, as were three wise men, because it was the other end of the cycle of life that would soon be in the spotlight, death. The smartphone was brought out from its slumber and the stiff thumbs did all of the swishing and swiping necessary to access the afternoon's messages. Arthritic thumbs would be the next health crisis to arrive, as in about twenty years time the first set of smartphone junkies would find the use of their hands completely restricted. Unable to hold a knife and fork they would not manage to feed themselves, thus causing a great strain on the NHS whilst at the same time drastically increasing the need for single use straws. Just like the first effects of smoking cigarettes and vaping, it was lying there, bubbling away in the first generation. ITK switched to the index finger to scroll back through the messages, keener than ever to avoid being in that first wave of sufferers.

Wendy had been busy and eager to share her progress with Sharon. The poor cow must have been very low on real friends to have fallen like she had for a contact from someone that she hadn't seen for thirty years. In any case, she had done her reconnaissance mission in the morning, positively beaming about her voice identification of the target, and afterwards she had rested at home before preparing most of the equipment that would be needed that night. She'd been out shopping, finding the perfect murder weapon on the way, and was now putting the finishing touches to her costume as the train trundled on its way towards her. All of this had been accompanied by copious amounts of wine and a hardening resolve that she could do it, that she was a real killer. ITK sniggered at her last message, as she had thanked Sharon for all of her help, telling her how she was looking forward to waking up on Sunday morning 'free from the sad chains of my ruined past'. What a clown she was. If she was lucky enough to wake up having not been chained up in a police cell, she was going to find herself with the same shit life as before and a bloody great hangover. That was the price Wendy would have to pay for being stupid.

The phone vibrated as a new message arrived, it was Wendy again. Beneath the beard a disapproving pout spread across ITKs face. As expected last minute doubts seemed to be creeping in. Perhaps it wasn't such a great idea after all, what if there was a struggle, what if someone saw her? Wouldn't it be best to wait until later when there were fewer people around or to just do something to frighten, not kill? Not for the first time the situation was delicate, and with eyes closed and raised towards the above seat lighting, ITK thought about the best way to reply. Get the response right and Wendy would be back in the land of everything being rosy, get it wrong and she might be lost for good.

CHAPTER 54

Saturday 19th December, Late Afternoon

Just the day before, Wendy had spent the afternoon listening to yet another group of ungrateful underachievers telling her what had worked and what hadn't, as if any of them had a clue about how she should do her job. It was one of the modern-day curses, where Google turned everyone into an expert in everything, whilst all of the time still knowing nothing. For today though, the plan was different, with Wendy being back where she felt most comfortable, on her own. She had done her reconnaissance trip and purchased the perfect murder weapon and now it was time for her to slump down into her armchair, stretch her legs and toes in front of her and slowly rotate her neck in a vain attempt to loosen the tightened muscles. It was the mid-afternoon lull, the moment when tiredness risked catching up with you and transporting you away from the action. How many plans had she made in the past only to change her mind mid-afternoon and decide on something else? The shopping trip had been great and she had managed to get everything that she needed in order to carry out her mission, though even as she had been stepping over the already drunken

Santa she had sensed that her old friend, uncertainty, was close by. Sitting there now in the half-light she wasn't at all sure that she really wanted to go through with her quest after all. She scrolled through her messages, the small hand held screen lighting up her face in a haunting white light. There was nothing from Sharon, further deflating her just at the crucial moment. She leaned forwards, squinting into the dark, her thumb caressing the smartphone screen as she aimlessly searched for a sign to help her forward.

"Musico, play some music." She sought comfort where she always did in times of trouble and was rewarded with a song about a Lady in Red.

She carefully composed the message, choosing her words very carefully. She didn't want to show weakness, especially not to Sharon, but she urgently needed someone to tell her that everything would be okay.

"No, I think you'll find I'm on my own, there's no you and me. And it's not red, it's scarlet. Miss Scarlett, with the candlestick. Haven't you been listening?" Wendy muttered to herself, her eyes adapting gradually to the darkness whilst her thumb continued to wear away the glass front on her phone. If in doubt, there was only one thing for it.

Her current corkscrew had been a Christmas present the previous year, from herself of course as nobody else seemed to know her well enough to buy her things that she actually liked. It was a large, automated thing and could actually open a bottle of Muscadet in under two seconds, releasing the fruity aroma into the air around her. As far as inventions went it was the best. The first glass was soon poured out and Wendy switched the main lights on as she went back into the living room, found a coaster and carefully placed the already half empty glass on top of it. She was starting to feel better already. Next, she took out her new red coat and the candlestick, carefully removing all of the labels from the clothing and any fingerprints from the silverware. It was time to get the rest of the costume ready.

Wendy had never really been to the Santa Festival, or whatever it was called, only occasionally having the misfortune to be going out or coming home when it was in full swing. Already the sight of the drunk that afternoon, with flesh sticking out from a split pair of trousers whilst wallowing in the snow, had reminded her exactly why. Most of the families would already be going home, desperate to escape the debauchery that was yet to come. Years before a kind old lady at the toy and games shop had made a few pounds hiring out half decent costumes, but nowadays cheap, throw away outfits arrived in the post by the dozen during the entire month of December and the lady's shop had since closed down. It was the perfect cover though and so off she went to gather the rest of the items that she would need.

It had taken her fifteen minutes to collect everything and she poured another glass as she revelled in the treasures before her. It was the same, excited feeling that she had always felt on the night the costumes arrived before a show, only this time it was her who had chosen what to wear. There were her old riding boots, an old pair of red skiing trousers, her newly acquired coat to which would soon be added a temporary white trim around the hood, a pair of tight-fitting leather gloves, a large belt, and an old bobble hat that would also be getting a quick upgrade with some white trimming to match the white pompom. Finally, she had an old coal sack that would be tied shut with a leather shoe lace, giving her the perfect, authentic Santa look. Laid out before her it looked great, but once she was wearing it, it would be magnificent. As a final touch there would be no false beard, slipping off her face as the overstretched elastic failed to hold on to the back of her head. Instead, she would use the last of her supplies of real stage make-up, and white hairs would be carefully gummed into place to make it look like the real thing. There was time for one more glass, and then she would get ready.

Wendy had worked quickly and expertly, the light just above her head and the small portable mirror on the table in front giving the perfect conditions to judge the results. She'd done the same before, when old Tony Riff had played Fagin in Oliver. Helping with the make-up had always been fun, and even though gumming the beard on at the start hadn't been without teething problems everything had turned out fine. Muscadet through a straw wasn't the classiest option but would have to be the norm now as the beard and moustache made drinking out of a glass impossible. Quick sideways glances confirmed that the eye make-up and the added face hair were exactly as they should be, and she sat back forcing fake smiles to test the beard as she waited for the gum to finish drying. From the speakers in the corner she heard, not for the first time that week, the rhythmic accompaniment to Another Opening, Another Show from Kiss me Kate.

Her phone was clutched tightly in her hand, desperate not to miss a small vibration that would say that Sharon was still with her, that Sharon had read her message and understood her worries and that everything would be all right. Getting ready had been fun and combined with the wine had lifted her spirits, but the doubts were still there and her messages to Sharon throughout the afternoon had been unanswered. She estimated her feelings as being the same as for the last full rehearsal, or dress rehearsal at best, the time when you still believed anything and everything could go wrong. The feeling of opening night was always different, and that was what she was searching for. For opening night the worries were still there, along with a fair share of mishaps too, but you were committed one hundred percent. The paying public were in place and there was no going back, you just had to go out and give it your best shot. Wendy hadn't managed to get there on her own and there was only one other person who could help her.

As she knew it must do eventually the vibration came, there was no brass fanfare just a small sensation of movement and noise that a person as far away as her kitchen would never have even noticed. There was no need for her to check who had sent it, she received few enough messages as it was and this one had been hoped for and expected. With a feeling of almost trepidation she opened the message, desperate to hear the director's final instructions before the curtain went up.

CHAPTER 55

Saturday 19th December, Early Evening

Smiler often asked questions, and wanting to know how on earth this situation had ever happened seemed just as valid as any of the others that had been asked in the past. Huddled in the corner of the now famous bus shelter, arms tightly crossed over the still wet Santa costume, there was plenty of time to think about the answer.

Worrying about Wendy made no real sense. They barely knew each other and had shared no moments of real intimacy during their four evenings together in the hotel bar. It had been obvious that she had problems, and far too many to name, but it was equally obvious that beneath it all she was someone that was worth looking out for. Her clear decline throughout the week had been alarming, and following the events of that morning it was obvious that something strange was going on. The possibility that Smiler could prevent this happening, or could at least minimise the impact, seemed a reasonable justification for getting up early on a day when nothing else had been planned anyway and making the short trip over to Webledon. Okay, Wendy probably wouldn't have done the same for Smiler, but someone else would have, surely?

The two police constables had been alright in the end, helping Smiler up from the snow and telling the story of the bag snatcher at the market. One look at Smiler's face had been enough to confirm that they hadn't got their man and they'd left with good wishes and sound advice to prevent any more falling over. That advice had been too late of course, as a mildly damp arse end of the tracksuit bottoms was now joined by a front that was soaked from head to toe. The image of Wendy waddling away in the distance, the lights from the market place giving her and her two arms full of bags a Loony Tunes looking silhouette, confirmed that she was still oblivious to the presence of her secret protector, so with a certainty that she would be going back home and staying inside for a while yet, Smiler had been persuaded to stop off at Ye Olde Coffee Shoppe for a bit of warmth and a cup of tea. From the market place the sound of Cliff Richard echoed around the closed streets, the fingers numb and the faces aglow that preceded the Mistletoe and Wine.

Smiler knew all about numb fingers and was sure that removing the false beard, kept in place for warmth despite the itches that it caused, would reveal no glowing face. The sight of the cakes in the coffee shop had been tempting, but with half a packet of biscuits in the backpack still available they had been ignored, and the beard was now lifted up an inch or two to allow another palm full of crumbs from the broken packet to be sucked into the mouth. Yes, being there that morning had seemed to make sense, but still being there now, cold, miserable and hungry? Smiler had seen it many times before, with people becoming involved with a cause for reasons that were very unclear or incomplete, but then doggedly remaining on a path that they had never even really wanted to be on.

Brexit had been a fine example, with people being asked to vote on a subject that most of them had never even thought about before. The almost apathetic vote was then followed by a delayed implementation, which bought out an extraordinary level of rage and anger. The anger wasn't because they were missing out on any material benefits that they expected as a result of the decision, but because the result wasn't being implemented, something completely different. Smiler now saw exactly the same that night, realising that the decision to save Wendy from an unknown fate had been almost throw away, built on a whim and an old-fashioned sense of decency. Sitting in the bus shelter, shivering in the cold as the temperature plummeted, was a defiant determination to see through what had been started, even if it was painful to do so and that the final result could end up being pretty shit. There must be a scientific term for it somewhere but Smiler didn't know what it was. As a token reward for the logic of the thought process a round of applause was self-offered, the beating together of the sodden woollen gloves providing a feeling of much-needed warmth.

Smiler stood, stamping feet and freeing up the circulation of blood to bring further warmth back to the lower part of the body. The clothing was now just damp and the darting wind that had been present all day seemed to have disappeared. All around were the tell-tale signs of small ice crystals, their sparkling tips reflecting the light of the moon. The temperature was dropping quickly.

"Hey up, you're going the wrong way there. All the fun's in town tonight."

Crikey, Smiler hadn't been paying attention. A young Santa coming out from Wendy's street had shouted the greeting cheerfully, and two others had already passed and were on their way into town. Smiler raised a cold hand in a ho ho ho sort of wave, realising now how strange someone cowering away in a bus shelter must look when all of the action was in the opposite direction. A better place to wait was needed, somewhere with more cover that looked less out of place. Smiler thought quickly, would Wendy really go back down into town when it seemed like her final destination was up the hill?

The route from that morning was much darker now, with the streetlight above the bus shelter and the frequently cloud covered moon being very poor sources of light. Smiler crossed the road, urgently examining the hedge that ran up towards the first of the larger houses. It was a typically threadbare Winter hedge that had a drainage ditch separating it from the pavement. Underfoot there was now the crunch of the gradually freezing wintery surface, with just one solitary set of footprints leading up towards the sports field. An approaching car lit up a fence post at the point where the last house joined with a farmer's field behind it, the light passing quickly but clearly showing a proper gap that could give access to the field behind. Smiler carefully straddled the drainage ditch, gloved hands feeling the top of a fence post as the rubber boots searched for a good contact on the far side of the ditch. With the moon now covered it was completely dark and the left hand started to fumble around in the bag for the torch as Jona Lewie sang silently about how cold it was in the snow and of some need to stop the cavalry.

The voice was clearly Wendy's and Smiler duly panicked. Looking back down the hill there was a shadow approaching, picked out by a newly uncovered moon. Smiler's left hand, complete with torch, went towards the bag as the right hand grasped for more purchase on the post. The left leg swung towards the fence side of the ditch, just as the right foot started to slip and slide in the untouched snow. The result was inevitable and seconds later Smiler was lying horizontal at the bottom of a snow-filled drainage ditch, eyes fixed firmly on the stars above as a singing Wendy strode past, wishing she was at home for Christmas. Dub a dub a dumb dumb, Dub a dub a dumb, Dub a dumb dumb dub a dub, Dub a dub a dumb.

CHAPTER 56

Saturday 19th December, Early Evening

As ITK walked out of the station the combined band and choir were in full O Little Town of Bethlehem swing, hiding like plainly wrapped toys beneath the large Christmas tree. Around them thirty or forty people were joining in, the token religious offering at an event where the streets would definitely not be filled with an everlasting light later that evening. It seemed a small price to pay for absolution, singing a few songs once every year, but perhaps the ones singing weren't the biggest sinners. The market was still attracting a fair number of shoppers, and as far as could be made out almost everyone was dressed as Father Christmas. Not many people would be arranging to meet around the tree that night saying 'you'll find me easy enough, I'll be the one with the red hat'. A little snigger forced itself out at the witticism and another drink was taken from the hip flask. It was always nice to be back home.

ITK pulled the beard back into place, becoming instantaneously invisible, the only distinguishing factors now being the height and waist size. The lack of decent lighting and tape measures would ensure that those features remained meaningless for someone who was nothing but average all round. Moving on into the market square a confidence returned, ITK thankful to be covered again by the anonymity normally reserved for the time that was spent on the internet. In the sky above a low, long cloud was starting to drift overhead, obscuring one by one the bright stars, a seemingly late arrival for the snow storm that had earlier filled the sky with dancing snowflakes. Underfoot the remains of the afternoon's snow now crunched. It was perfect weather for a Christmas mystery.

ITK had been raised in Webledon, the youngest child of a shopkeeper, always struggling to fit in with the offspring of the professional and farming classes. There had always been the view that because you sold things you had money, but nobody ever understood the other side of the coin and the periods of uncertainty that the family had to endure. By the time the end had come to the local green grocers, hidden away on the big estate, ITK had been long gone, taken away from Webledon by an often-unhappy relationship and a job in another town. Tonight that upbringing would come in handy as the memories of alleyways and shortcuts came flooding back. The last message to Wendy had been a success and now ITK had to rush to be in place in order to witness the entertainment to come. For that, a quick, discrete route was needed, one that would avoid tell-tale signs like footprints as well as ensuring that there was no chance of bumping into the star of the show herself.

Most of the Santas were congregated around the church, showing no desire to venture too far from the pubs and hot dog stalls. Around them was a fairy like fluttering of lights, each one giving away the recording of yet another video or photo on a smartphone. Gone were the days of a photo album being produced each year, the fashion now being for a full feature length movie recorded every night. The stupid bastards. On the off chance that any cameras dared to come close enough to ITK all they would see was yet another unremarkable Santa. Avoiding the throng, ITK went left, away from the market square and towards the cattle market buildings. Built to be used just once a week they were large and dark, dominating an ever-darkening skyline as the increasingly large cloud continued its lonely path across the sky. At the back of those buildings was a now overgrown train line, unused in decades but once a way to bring cattle in from the north. Gradually the housing estate had built up around it, before eventually the long, looping road that wrapped around Webledon had cut it off completely. Fortunately, enough of a pathway remained, hidden and unloved amongst the 1960s ex council houses and it would cut the journey time in half, as well as providing perfect cover for someone who didn't wish to be seen. Approaching the entrance a group of teenage Santas ran merrily past, bottles of cider and beer clutched tightly in their gloved hands. A pang of panic quickly passed as ITK located the overgrown gap between the bushes and pushed on through. Yes, there was always a risk of someone coming in the other direction, and they would surely remember another Santa moving away from the action, but that risk would have to be run in order to get there in time to take that front row seat for the show.

A rejuvenated wind was starting to build, pushing the ever-larger cloud further over an almost full moon. Gently touching the bag to make sure that the knife was still there, ITK carried on forwards. Fifty yards passed, then another fifty, moving unseen amongst the houses. Now at the edge of the estate there was one more road to pass, a lane in everything but name, and then it would be on to the last section of track, out amongst the fields. Suddenly the last of the moonlight disappeared and ITK stopped dead, the breathing deepening and the ears taking over whilst the eyes adjusted to the newly arrived darkness. There was a sound, over to the left, ITK was sure. More seconds of silence were spent trying to make out the source of the sound that appeared to be merging with the noise of the barren hedgerows moving in the wind. A few spots of liquid splashed on the face just as the piece of cloud responsible for the pause finally moved on. The changing rooms at the sports field were now clearly visible to the right and a glance behind showed a trail of tell-tale footprints that would fortunately soon be covered over by the fresh snow that was once more starting to fall.

ITK moved on towards the group of houses now visible ahead, glad to be leaving the claustrophobic feelings from the enclosed part of the path but suddenly feeling naked and exposed to the snow and any prying eyes. It was typical of life, with the things that you wanted to get rid of suddenly becoming the things that you craved. Hidden by the darkness and the flurry of snow, ITK finally arrived at the outer wall of the house. Again there were sounds, but this time much clearer; someone else was coming. A quick investigation found a gap between the wall and an old garden shed and ITK was soon through and sheltered from the falling snow and cold wind. All there was to do now was to wait for the curtain to open and the show to begin.

CHAPTER 57

Saturday 19th December, Early Evening

The door banged loudly this time as Wendy walked briskly out into the middle of the road. The snow had only just started to fall again but she was taking no chances on stray footprints giving her away. Following in the direction of the few cars that had braved the winter weather she slid her feet along in the tracks left by their tyres, making it impossible for even Davy Crocket to track her movements. A gentle clanking came from the sack on her back, the wrapped candlestick making regular contact with a recently added two foot long piece of copper tubing, which in the absence of lead piping would make a respectable second choice should there be any problems later. Her eyes still stung, the cold of the wind not helping after the tears that she had been shedding just a few minutes earlier.

'Go and look at the photograph that's still stuck on the wall, and then ask me again.' Sharon's response had been simple.

There had been no need to ask again, the object of her hatred and loathing had looked back at her, smiling in contempt just as it had always done. She had believed herself to be stronger than that, but the tears had come as a release and with every sob she had become more and more determined in her challenge. She had toasted the evening with her last glass of wine and then, in a rare moment with no control, she had thrown the glass towards the photo, looking on in surprise as it had fallen down onto the carpet unbroken. They didn't make them like they used to. It had answered all of her questions though and there she was sliding step by step in the middle of the main road, on towards her destiny, the combination of wine and tears having seen off any doubt she may have had left.

Onwards she went, oblivious to the movements all around her, each one a shadow amplified by the darting snow and the copious amounts of wine, and in no time she arrived beside her favourite litter bin at the gateway to the sports field. Looking out over the snow-covered field she planned her next steps as the lonely cloud continued its journey across the sky, releasing a burst of moonlight that was momentarily reflected in a thousand small crystals of ice. The walk from her house had been one through the disfigured ridges of twice frozen slush but before her now the snow was white and pure, deep and crisp and even. It was perfect, far too perfect to walk over, and Wendy swayed a little in the breeze as she evaluated her options, deciding in the end to once again go round the field's edge with her new, footprintless sliding action. Passing once more over the wall would surely be a less risky option than walking into the street and up the driveway. Picking out where the grass got longer under the snow she started to edge round towards the back of the field.

For the first time that day Wendy started to feel a physical weakness creeping over her. The sliding movement of the legs was unnatural, she must have looked like a tin soldier on skates, and her thigh muscles were starting to ache. Dancing white flecks of snow fluttered before her eyes, combining with the wine to add further confusion to an already overcrowded brain. In the mid distance there was nothing but an empty, white expanse, glowing in dull splendour, an apparently endless blanket over the higher ground. With every sliding step she took her heart beat faster and her head felt lighter as the shadows and noises of the dark night closed in all around.

Wendy made it at last to the back of the field and the cover provided by the hedgerow. Her hand rested firmly against a large trunk as she closed her eyes and steadied her breathing, regretting now the decision not to use a false beard that could have been removed for a few seconds of respite, as the tickly hairs from the stage beard stuck to her face. The realisation that it would all soon be over drove her forward and a quick check over the wall showed the tell-tale sign of a warm light escaping through the gaps between drawn curtains: her tormentor was home. The plans that she had made in the bath that afternoon came back to her and without more thought she moved around to the gap next to the tree from where she had so nearly fallen that morning. From this gap she should have comfortable access to the garden and from the garden to the porch and her destiny.

What had at first seemed strange that morning now seemed bizarre. Scattered around the garden were a number of small bushes, each one covered in multicoloured Christmas lights, flashing away as the ones nearest the top swayed gently along with the wind. Nearer to the house, and on what would be her direct route, stood a reindeer, its red nose shining brightly and its thin, tube-like body and antlers lit up at regular intervals by small, white lights. Next to that, the centrepiece if that was the right word, was a full-size snowman held upright by the low thrumming of an air blower, its white body lit from within by a piercing bright light. The weightless body was at the full mercy of the weather, performing a rhythmless Christmas dance to the rapidly changing demands of the wind. Wendy rested, her back against the wall, and opened the coal sack as the howl of the wind accompanied the drone of the air blower in the overture to the night's show. From the bag she carefully took out the copper tubing and the candlestick, surprised by both the apparent flimsiness of the tube and the heavy weight of the candle holder. It would be impossible to carry both so the tube was placed back into the sack that was then slung again onto her back.

Wendy's face felt rigid and fixed, a look without emotion similar to that on the face of a Barbie doll, and her heart was the same with all sign of feeling now long gone as she stood motionless for a number of minutes, thoughts swirling in her mind just as the snow swirled around her head. Now it was show time though and she had walked out on enough non-descript first nights to know that she would be able to get through this one. Her body started moving to an unheard musical beat and her hand moved to pull back a handful of barren branches as she fixed her stare on the snowman's hat. With an instinctive flick of her hair, her left foot moved urgently towards the gap in the wall.

She hadn't even taken her first full pace before the world seemed to stop, as a hundred voices in unison cried out into the night, We Wish You a Merry Christmas.

CHAPTER 58

Saturday 19th December, Evening

Smiler struggled out of the ditch, the back of the costume dripping wet from head to foot whilst a large piece of compressed snow slid gently down the back of the leg, from the split in the tracksuit bottoms to the top of the rubber boot. Smiler stood still and rearranged the false beard over a face that was wet from both snow and tears before then searching for Wendy up the hill, being relieved to find her clearly visible and sliding on into the distance. The reaction was then as instinctive and generous as usual as the wet and the cold were instantly forgotten and Smiler, realising that this was now the real thing, set off in pursuit of a Wendy who was already taking a turn at the top of the rise.

The first tentative steps had allowed Smiler to regain some composure but there was now something else that didn't feel quite right. It was difficult to identify exactly what, but from behind there came a noise, a murmuring and stamping like a herd of small, quiet cattle being carefully moved along. Straining to look behind through the mini blizzard there could just be made out a number of bodies surrounded by a ball of rising mist, no doubt the result of the breath and chattering of a large group of people. Through the falling snow odd pieces of bright clothing were coming in and out of focus, a hat here, a scarf there, a shiny coat in the middle, but making sense of it seemed impossible, and having no time to lose, Smiler decided it would have to wait for later. Ignoring Wendy's method of using the car tracks for cover, Smiler set off up the hill at a jog with the old worn boots slipping and sliding with every step. Any tracks would surely be covered by the crowd that followed on behind and the most important things at that time were firstly making sure that Wendy didn't get up to anything stupid, and secondly making sure that neither of them were seen.

The noise from behind got quieter as Smiler advanced, the following crowd seemingly out for a stroll and not a race. In front there was no sign of Wendy but the entrance to the sports field was close by. At the gate there was nothing to suggest that anyone had been through, the surface as crisp and even as when it had fallen. A series of slide marks were there though, just visible before the gate post, confirming that she must have gone into the field. Smiler quickly decided that following would be useless, with the risks of being seen far too high. The image of the old A to Z flashed quickly in front of Smiler's eyes revealing that the main entry to the road was just a little further up the hill, around the corner. A glance backwards confirmed that the followers were still following so Smiler set off again as fast as the flat soled boot would allow.

An extra heavy flurry of snowflakes accompanied the arrival in the road, and worried by the possibility of somehow being seen by Wendy, Smiler took a path next to a hedge that ran adjacent to the rougher ground in which the tree from earlier that morning was to be found. Squatting down against one of the green boxes that held the electrical and telecommunications cables, Smiler took in the scene. The term road was incorrect, it was more like a square, with a large, round piece of land in the middle, if that made any sense. Around this piece of land was the roadway itself, serving the four large houses that were all so different as to make them feel the same, if that made any sense too. Around each house was a garden, split in every case by a driveway that entered past gates of varying heights and styles. Strangely for a road these days, there were no cars parked outside and from what could be made out there were none visible on driveways either, so either the garages were full or the occupants were not at home. From the target house came shadows and the dull glow associated with outside, festive lighting, whilst the other houses had nothing but an occasionally lit up window to warn off any particularly hardy burglars that were brave enough to venture out burgling in such weather.

Now that the lie of the land was clearer it was time for Smiler to get into position. Whatever it was that Wendy had planned she was going to have to get across the garden in order to do it, if of course she had the courage to put her plan into action. What Smiler needed was a place that had a good view of the garden whilst giving quick access to it, and also providing a good hiding place. Smiler wasn't going to win any running races, and any physical contest with an enraged Wendy would be evens at best, but from a good start point everything could be stopped if needed. Already soaked to the skin there was no problem now crawling between the council hedge that protected the famous tree and the outer fence of the house. Feeling carefully along the hedge bottom, Smiler soon found a loose piece of plastic covered metal fencing, which when rolled back was just high enough to allow a person to pass underneath. Just to the right-hand side of this entry point was a nicely protected cubby hole in the corner of the garden. Finding just enough space to sit upright, Smiler observed the garden, the falling snow now backlit by the flashing lights on various bushes, Rudolph the red nosed reindeer and Frosty the snowman.

Smiler breathed a sigh of relief, at last in place and apparently so before Wendy got up to any mischief, but the calm lasted for only a second or two before the neck muscles became taught again as a half-detected movement somewhere behind Rudolph raised the alert level to maximum. There had been frightening, dancing shadows since the light had first started to fade but far away, towards the back of the garden, were movements that appeared man made. Focussing as hard as possible just to the left of Frosty there was a shed, barely visible in the darkness at the rear of the garden. The movement came again, to the left, a dull flash of red that became clearer as Smiler's eyes became accustomed to the combined effects of the Christmas lights and the glare of the snow. There she was, Wendy, hiding discretely against the side of the shed. It was a vital discovery, one that would make the rest of the evening much easier, and with the puzzle now almost complete, Smiler once again started to relax.

And then the singing started.

CHAPTER 59

Saturday 19th December, Evening

Wendy jolted backwards, forced that way by the invisible soundwaves from four sopranos, three altos, two tenors and seven basses. Her foot caught on a patch of tree root and she stumbled, eventually coming to rest sitting on a pile of snow that was prevented from getting too close to her bum by the thankfully long red coat. What on earth was going on?

Regaining her senses she slowly adopted a crouching position, looking urgently through the gap in the wall in a vain hope for some indication of what was happening. Yes, of course, how could she have forgotten? Every year after the main carols in town parts of the choir would spread out focussing on the older, wealthier householders and spreading even more Christmas joy, whilst hoping to get a few drinks for their efforts. In a few minutes time they would be outside Wendy's house and old Mr Phillips from across the road would be sliding through the snow with a tray of sherry and mince pies. Some people were always the same, insisting on being the goody goodies, looking like they were doing something for nothing whilst all the time basking in their supposed superiority. Now that she understood the situation the initial panic was over but the problem was just beginning as everyone in the close would now be on alert for activity outside. At home she would have sat down silently, taking another glass of wine and waiting patiently for them to move on, but here they would probably be like Phillips, coming out and getting all excited and talking to each other. What she would have done for another glass of wine.

Two carols? Did some people's goodness know no limits? Wendy became agitated as a glorious song of old was sung to the midnight clear. She had been all ready to start the show but the curtains hadn't opened and now she was stuck on stage, all made up with nowhere to go. It all served to give her even more of a desire to just get things over and done with, to walk quickly across the lawn, knock loudly on the door, bash in the head and then go home. There would be no time for emotion, for self-redeeming speeches that explained her actions, just the time necessary in order to smash some brains out and then make a quick, discrete get away. She needed to see what was happening but climbing the tree again in the dark was not going to happen so instead she peered forward, craning her neck around the tree in an attempt to get a better view through the gate and out into the close. It was useless though, the horizontal body and stretched neck bringing on another head ache and almost causing her to fall down through the gap. A childlike grimace came over her face as she stepped back, now moving agitatedly from side to side as she contemplated what to do next.

Bloody carol singers, how many were they going to do? Freezing cold, falling snow and they were starting on a third? The poor souls must really have nothing better to do if Good King Wenceslas was making an appearance. Wendy pitied them, she really did, being out and about on a night like this singing unwanted songs for strangers. There were different sounds now, other voices either joining in with the singing or talking in the background, and Wendy guessed that people must have started to come out from their houses, no doubt in order to share a brief moment of Christmas spirit before going back inside for the next episode of Eastenders. She was now fidgety, even keener than before to know what was going on. She gracefully slid around the wall moving towards the street end and hoping to find a place that she could look through that had been missed that morning. The snow was shallower here, the pathway protected by the branches overhead and the wall itself, but sliding was still possible despite the humps and hollows of a frozen country path. As she approached the end of the wall the choir stopped again and the sound of voices and clinking glasses became clearer. She had still found nowhere from where she could take a proper look at what was happening in front of the house, and with Santa costumes being great for anonymity but less useful for peering over walls unseen, raising her head to look over the top was out of the question. With a snort of frustration she retraced her steps back to her start point, taking up once again the candlestick and flexing her fingers with gentle movements that warmed the muscles and brought a calming comfort to her brain. It would soon be time again.

For Christ's sake, four! Wendy's eyes looked to the skies, seeing the last edge of the cloud slowly passing overhead as they all started warbling on about a Silent Night. The moon was now completely uncovered giving the last flurries of snowflakes a theatrical lighting effect as they danced around in the darkness above. The hypnotising feeling from before returned, forcing Wendy to snap her head back down and search for stability by focussing on the tree in front of her. The feelings of weakness returned, the day again catching up with her and reminding her of the helplessness that she had felt in the crime room earlier. At last the heavenly peace passed, followed eventually by the sound of the crowd dispersing, with doors closing on one side and eager conversation and muffled footsteps on the other. As Wendy's breathing evened out the silence fell again. She would give them all five minutes to settle in again in front of their televisions, and then she would get it over and done with.

CHAPTER 60

Saturday 19th December, Evening

Everybody loved a choir at Christmas, but why the fuck had they decided to be there at that time? ITK had been forced to flatten up against the side of the shed, putting even more strain on muscles that were already suffering from the cold, wet conditions. Gradually the muscles had been relaxed and once it had been clear that the singers were outside and wouldn't be coming in to the garden there had been time to loosen up completely and take a closer look around.

The carollers had set up beneath the street light in what looked like a square between the houses, giving a grandiose effect to the falling snow as it gently danced its swirling dance around their heads. The pale, orange lighting, combined with the distance of the singers from the hidey hole, made generalities easy to see but detail impossible to detect, ideal conditions for spreading fake information but not perfect for seeing what was really going on. There must have been a dozen of them, a mixture of dark, practical clothing for keeping out the weather, topped off with bright hats and scarves that were there for show. To believe Dickens, you would think that it was the poor who came around singing songs for small comfort and a few pennies, but by the sound of this lot it was now a rich man's job, the money presumably still finding its way eventually to the poor but taking away the need for the lazy bastards to get off their fat arses and do something for themselves. In any case, the singing was very fine even to someone of ITK's musical talent and Wendy, wherever she was, must be absolutely loving it.

The garden itself was strange, not at all what ITK had expected, the many lights and other decorations seeming somewhat out of place for the person who owned it. The prominent porch would surely be Wendy's entry point, with her moving swiftly across the lawn, drunkenly ringing the bell before finally doing the act and making her escape. At least the passage of the singers would have provided good cover for footprints in the snow. The thinking had somehow warmed ITK and the sound of doors opening and people coming out into the street gave a further call to action, as buttocks and backbones were once more pressed tightly against the shed and the abdominals strained to prevent the false belly from sticking out too far.

It was an instantaneous event, just a flash caught in the corner of a subconscious eye, that alerted the brain to an unknown presence. The first priority was to check if the opening doors had come from the house that belonged to the garden, and once that was discounted the eyes went back to where the slightest of movements had been detected moments before. There it was again in the far corner, where the hedge at the side of the garden met the one next to the road. It was a dark corner, one where hardly any of the rays from the streetlight were strong enough to penetrate, and where the non-stop veil of snowflakes did their most energetic of dances. ITK slowed the breathing, concentrating and focussing on that corner, and as the eyes gradually adapted to the conditions it appeared again, a hint of bright red with a small, but noticeable, movement. It had to be Wendy, cowering under the hedge, and the thought brought a warming grin to the cold face, imagining her sat there, no doubt desperate to join in with the singing but biting her lips to avoid detection. The stupid cow.

Everyone had a favourite carol, or at least they should have. Silent night was ITK's, a sure sign that the choir were giving their blessing and that everything would go as planned. The lips had been moving but no sound had come out, silently encouraging everyone who wanted to believe in Christmas to sleep in heavenly peace. Belief in such things was meaningless next to the injustice in the world and the non-stop fight against the real, dangerous, leftie snowflakes, and that night would be a good tester, a trial for the true power of persuasion. The carol singers were now finished, their harmonious singing replaced by eager chattering as they moved away towards their next location. It was now just a matter of time, with Wendy surely waiting for everyone to get over the excitement of their visitors before launching a devastating attack on her own ghost of Christmas past. ITK sat back, leaning against the shed while focussing fully on Wendy over in the corner in eager anticipation of her taking her next steps.

CHAPTER 61

Saturday 19th December, Evening

The footsteps shuffled past and Smiler let out a huge, but definitely silent, breath. The relief was enormous, as if that breath had been held in since the very first note in a desperate attempt to not be heard, but that was clearly not the case because the choir had been singing for over fifteen minutes. In reality the singers had been more than a few yards away, so the chance of actually being heard had been small, but people's first reactions in times of crisis were often irrational and unrelated to the problem at hand. Fortunately, nobody had been looking out for red cloth at the bottom of the hedge and so nobody had found any, leaving Smiler cold, wet and extremely relieved.

Christmas carols had always been a wonder, how once a year everyone could remember the words and sing along. Almost everyone anyway, as for Smiler the tunes had always been good to hum along to but the words had remained a mystery. There had been no humming along that night though, and now that the danger had passed it was back to observation duties. Adjusting once again to the light in the garden, Smiler quickly relocated Wendy, still in her hidey-hole next to the hut as she either planned her next steps or, more likely, built up her courage.

Building up her courage for what, that was the question. Something had worried Smiler early in the week, though what it was couldn't be described. In the days since then there had been a definite fear of something happening rather than a fear of something specific happening, and despite spending the entire day hanging around, exactly what that specific thing could be was still a mystery. Could it be sabotage, or vandalism? Graffiti on the wall, a brick thrown through a window, glue in the locks or dog shit through the letterbox. She would struggle to find any dog shit that wasn't frozen, that was for sure. Smiler could think of many ways to annoy the householder, but would Wendy really think the same way? The red covered shape was still motionless, taking her time.

Smiler could do nothing but stay in place, still under the hedge with bones and muscles aching from the unnatural positions they were kept in, whilst the brain continually asked 'what the fuck are you doing here?' about ten times a minute. There was almost a temptation to shout out, 'Come on Wendy, either get on with it, or let's go home, have a brew and get warmed up and talk about it.' Despite all of this, Smiler still had those slightly upcurved lips, content in the knowledge that caring and a willingness to actually do something were still honourable, even in this day and age. It gave out more a sentimental warmth than a physical one, but it was some kind of warmth none the less. Soon the thoughts started to stray with Smiler wondering what all of the online contacts would be getting up to on this last Saturday evening before Christmas. Would they be missing Smiler? Perhaps some of them were even at the festival in Webledon, enjoying themselves and taking photos of all of the misbehaving

Santas.

A bright flicker of movement over to the left stopped the thoughts dead, an initial blur becoming as clear as day. It was no trick of light, a cheating shadow trying to fool a tired brain, this was the real thing, but it didn't make sense. Gliding in from the wall in the middle of the garden was a red coated Santa, but not Wendy from beside the shed, another one.

Now there were two of them.

CHAPTER 62

Saturday 19th December, Evening

The shivering and shaking had taken longer to tame than had been expected. With one hand firmly placed against the tree and her body still swaying gently, Wendy had tried to understand what was going on. She had been there all primed and ready for action when the singers had started so it couldn't be first night nerves, yet now she felt once more almost helpless, surely a combination of the long day, the cold weather and the wine. She would just have to force herself through, take the first steps and get out there knowing that once it was all over she could start to feel normal again. For the second time that night she prepared her candlestick and fastened her coal sack over her shoulders as she waited for the rhythm of the music to return. The tight-fitting leather gloves stretched as her hands flexed and with an energetic snort of hot air she pushed through the gap and started moving across the snow-covered lawn.

The Bach-like theme tune to the Ski Sunday television programme replaced the previous music in her head as one after another her feet slid forward, carefully advancing without leaving a trace that could identify her. Why thousands of English people had sat round their television sets each week as Europe's finest skiers whizzed down dangerous mountain slopes Wendy had never understood, but she would never forget the music that always came back to her whenever it snowed. The sliding movement was more difficult than she had imagined, the combination of wind, snow and fatigue making progress much more difficult than it had been just half an hour before as she had glided around the sports field. Perhaps the excitement was playing its part too as her body weight moved from side to side whilst the candlestick was kept tightly clutched to her chest. Deprived of the shelter of the bushes and the wall the effect of the wind increased with the gummed-on beard rising and falling over her nose and in front of her eyes. Focussing with all of her force she continued on the course that she had set, aiming for the gap between Rudolph and the Snowman. Slip, slide, slip, slide, she was almost there now, a mere ten or so yards from the front door and her destiny.

"Bastard!"

The cry was shrill and was the result of a stabbing pain that had passed like a lightning bolt up through Wendy's right leg. The foot had stopped dead and the rhythm of her movements had taken her body over towards her left whilst her foot stayed exactly where it was, held tightly in place by some sort of cable. Her right hand still held on tightly to the candlestick and her left hand had grasped desperately at Rudolph, only for the cheap Chinese made wooden frame to buckle under her top-heavy momentum, and as her body had fallen through the shattered remains of Rudolph her ankle had twisted, finally releasing itself as she hit the ground with a dull thud and a puff of snow spray. Crawling around on the floor amongst the reindeer remains the uncertainty of a few moments before was gone and Wendy untangled herself from the rapidly flashing light bulbs and was just getting to her feet when

HE'S MAKING A LIST

for the second time that day she heard the door to the house being opened.

"And you can piss off, you little bastards." It was the same voice from the morning. "Get back in town with the other morons, and leave us alone."

Wendy looked up, her stare piercing through the gummed-on moustache and beard combination that was now partly obscuring her view. She saw immediately that something was wrong and that her memories of the voice from earlier that morning had quite clearly been mistaken.

"Who are you?" The shriek was shrill, piercing through the once silent night. The man facing her was not going to be out shouted.

"Who am I? I bloody live here, you piss head, now get up off your arse, get out of my garden and get lost before I call the police."

Rage was rising inside Wendy, the pain in her foot and the unexplainable situation that she found herself in taking away any semblance of control that she may have had left.

"You don't live here, Denzil does. Where is he? Bring him out here, now."

"Denzil? Nobody called Denzil lives here." The response was just as defiant.

"Oh yes he does, Mr Denzil the old maths teacher. He lives here, he must do, it said so on the internet." The last words were spat out in a fanfare of triumph.

Her opponent had clearly not been expecting such a fierce resistance, obviously hoping that a few shouts would quickly clear his garden, but Wendy wasn't going to be giving up now. Faced with opposition but still desperate to protect his property the man ambled forward but then stopped dead in his tracks as a newer look of fear spread across his face. Sensing her moment, Wendy stepped forward, her arms moving upwards as she swung the candlestick behind her head.

CHAPTER 63

Saturday 19th December, Evening

The initial shock at discovering an additional Santa quickly passed and ITK could tell from the profile of the upper body that the latest arrival was the real Wendy, currently performing a sort of slidey goosestep across the garden. Even in times like this the stupid bitch managed to look ridiculous. In any case she was now in action mode, so the other person dressed in red was instantly forgotten as the excitement mounted and ITK sat back ready to watch the spectacle.

Even though the sliding motion was unorthodox the general effect was familiar. ITK had seen her waddle back to her room from the bar enough times to know that she had been unable to avoid the advice that had been sent in Sharon's messages and as such was completely hammered. It was another small worry to add to the list, but the main concern was that there wouldn't be a good enough view of the real action once it arrived at the front of the porch, so ITK leaned carefully against the shed and got up, shaking with excitement at the prospect of what was to come. ITK had always been cool, dishing out abuse at will and

HE'S MAKING A LIST

ignoring any incoming attacks with ease, but this was different. There was no longer a false identity, a computer screen or a keyboard to hide behind, there were just real people with real flesh and blood.

"This is it, at last." The words were quietly spoken as the fists clenched and ITK looked up to the sky, catching glimpses of the bright stars now visible between the cloud and the last of the snowflakes. "Follow the stars!"

Wendy's movements were awkward and slow as she made her way across the garden. The silently spoken encouragement seemed to work, as Wendy accelerated but then fell with a shriek of pain. The stupid cow wasn't even capable of making her way across the garden in one piece. Shocked by the scream ITK looked around, catching a glimpse of a moving curtain and then froze as the door opened and a man of about forty rushed outside. He looked like new money, not someone who had a right to live in such a fine house, dressed smartly in jeans and jumper and sliding around in pair of overly large slippers that were clearly not made for outside wear. Who he was it was difficult to say, but ITK would have bet a fair few pounds that he wasn't related at all to Mr Denzil. Could something have gone wrong? ITK had checked it all out on the internet and Wendy had even checked it out in person that morning, so it had to be Denzil's place. Back in the garden Wendy and the man were now shouting at each other, their exact words unclear in the wind.

"Come on Wendy, do him, he'll do."

A sudden frustration hit hard, ITK becoming rapidly agitated and hopping quickly from foot to foot. Wendy looked like she was doubting, which wasn't supposed to happen.

"Go on Wendy, he'll have to do. He looks just like Denzil would have done, surely?"

Despite the increase in volume it was clear that neither Wendy nor the man in front of the house had heard, and the lack of activity just served to increase ITKs levels of anger. Making people take the final step had not been as easy as had been imagined, but there was one last chance. Reaching quickly into the back pack, ITK carefully took hold of the knife handle, pulling the blade out and brandishing it in the air. Seeing it there before the eyes the anger rose further, finally turning to an uncontrollable rage as ITK started accelerating forward towards the two others. It was there in the man's eyes as he now realised that a second Santa was moving towards him, and that this one had a bright, shiny blade that glittered in the night. With a deliberate action ITK raised the blade high above the head.

"Kill the fucker!"

The final scream broke the air and must have been heard by everyone. With that scream ITK had disappeared, as had Sharon, the no longer needed go between. The deep, female voice may have been recognised by some, and no one was capable of seeing the twisted face through the false beard, but beneath it all, Dot had at long last found her real identity and come alive.

CHAPTER 64

Saturday 19th December, Evening

Hiding under the hedge had made the bones cold and the muscles slow. Sensing that there may soon be work to do, Smiler moved first into a crouching position and followed that by adopting a hunched lean forward. The now drenched woollen gloves provided support and kept Smiler firmly in place, like a one hundred metre runner waiting for the sound of a pistol before snapping into action. Hopefully there wouldn't be the sound of any real pistols.

The awkward, sliding movements of the newly arrived Santa quickly confirmed that this one was indeed the real Wendy. The identity of the other red costumed person next to the shed was neither known nor important, as preventing Wendy from doing anything stupid was now the only concern. Since the morning, Smiler had truly believed that, if the time came, sorting Wendy out would be no problem, but several hours later, cold, wet and tired, things felt a bit different. Strange thoughts were whirring around the brain with all of the options that existed. She could be stopped now, undoubtedly creating a scene and risking that they would be found out anyway. Smiler could wait until the last minute when it was clearer what she was going to do, but that risked Smiler reacting too late and not managing to prevent the disaster. There was also the option of just crawling out under the hedge and letting her get on with it and hoping that the mystery person by the shed was also a guardian angel. The choices were many but the time to decide was running out fast.

When it all happened it was comical in its simplicity. The sliding Wendy had been making steady progress across the lawn when her leading foot became blocked, at which point she had shouted out a very uncharacteristic profanity and then lost her balance. Smiler instinctively stood, arms out stretched, but too far away to be able to offer any physical help. There then followed a slow-motion fall as one of Wendy's hands clenched tightly to a strange object, whilst the other waved around in thin air, searching for a support from something that clearly didn't exist. The thin frame of the reindeer stood no chance as Wendy's flailing arm destroyed its supports, scattering the smaller lights all around and extinguishing the red nose on the snow-covered floor in one final act of destruction. Wendy soon followed it downwards, her landing accompanied by a large thud in a final sight that gave Smiler a momentary boost of courage. In that instant the true person beneath the disguise was finally forced out. Smiler spent happy hours looking at the photos of friends and acquaintances on the internet, but this situation called for a real person, and so it was that Sachin took two large steps forward. His confidence lasted the half a second it took for the front door to open and for the person who lived in the house to come outside, at which point Sachin panicked, diving quickly behind a small, light covered bush over towards the main gate, and it was from there that he watched and listened as Wendy and the man argued between them.

HE'S MAKING A LIST

In spite of the closeness to the action, Sachin struggled to follow a conversation that he had obviously joined way too late to truly understand. The inflatable snowman was still in place, preventing a direct view of exactly what was going on, but from behind its bobbing movements it was clear that Wendy was now on her feet again, agitatedly moving from side to side as if being directed by the still swirling wind. Her hand still clung tightly to the cloth covered, metal object, which was now waved in front of her as she continued to exchange shouted phrases. A glint in the dark night then caught Sachin's attention, as he picked up on a bright shining star that had started out behind Wendy but was now moving towards her. Frantically trying to focus past the bobbing snowman Sachin finally got a good view of the source of the light.

His mouth dropped, the look on the face hidden behind the false beard now a petrified stare. Whoever the other person was they were now moving slowly towards Wendy, and in their hands they had a fucking great big knife. The intention was clear, they were going to kill her, but Sachin wasn't going to let that happen, not on his watch. A warning shout would have done no good, simply sowing more confusion, so there was no other choice. The first steps were slow and hesitant but soon replaced by quicker ones as momentum was finally built, and Sachin accelerated towards the new attacker, his shoulder dropped and ready for combat.

CHAPTER 65

Saturday 19th December, Evening

The speed with which promise can turn to disaster had always impressed Wendy. She had seen it before, a confident stage during final dress rehearsal turned into an undisciplined mess as a poorly installed book flat fell backwards into the wings and a leading man consequently forgot his lines. This was now her own disaster; one she had owned from start to finish.

Mr Denzil, the tormentor of her youth, the destroyer of any small confidence she had ever had, may have lived here once but clearly didn't anymore, and in front of her the new owner of the house was cowering away from Wendy's anger and the swinging rhythm of her candlestick. Her natural instinct was to carry on forward and finish him off anyway, the man guilty simply of being there and being in her way on a night when old debts were due to be repaid. The decision was taken in a split second, in the absence of Denzil this bloke would have to do. Moving to the side in an attempt to avoid the snowman Wendy swung the candlestick back over her shoulder ready to strike.

HE'S MAKING A LIST

First she heard the shout, an Alison Moyet like war cry of encouragement that had the exact opposite effect, as whoever it was that had shouted out was an unwanted witness, a person who shouldn't have been there. Then there was the movement from the other side of the snowman, a large red shape moving quickly towards her. In front of her was the victim, which in the absence of his real name seemed the politest thing to call him, now looking scared out of his wits and back peddling as fast as his slippers would take him, in conditions that could only be described as far from favourable for back peddling in slippers. The danger to her right needed to be sorted first so the candlestick had to be swung the other way before her bulky attacker arrived.

Just as the candlestick reached its zenith Wendy's arm jolted as it made an unexpected contact with something behind her. She half turned to see what had happened and then screamed in terror as she saw a long, sharp, pointy knife hurtling towards her; she was being attacked from both sides. Alison Moyet, or whoever it was hidden behind the false beard, had very fortunately been stopped in her tracks by the back swing of the candlestick. Lunging forwards the attacker slipped, and the knife came down stabbing Frosty the snowman fatally in the side. Wendy was now in a state of utter panic with the sight of the knife rapidly evaporating any courage that she might have had left, and she quickly stepped to the side, the remaining pieces of the reindeer crunching beneath her feet. Just at that moment her other attacker dived towards the place where she had just recently been standing with some sort of school boy rugby tackle. With Wendy no longer being there the momentum took the second Santa into the dying dance of the rapidly deflating snowman, whilst also knocking her first attacker backwards and to the floor. No doubt sensing an opportunity the householder lunged forwards, his hands reaching out towards the now stationary candlestick but the sudden change of direction was ill judged and the smooth soles of his slippers failed to make a decent contact with the snow that had recently been trampled underfoot. The movements of the householder's legs became quicker and more desperate as he lost his balance and fell backwards, kicking Wendy's legs away from beneath her at the same time as his head cracked against the wall of the house.

CHAPTER 66

Saturday 19th December, Late Evening

Her body was cold, her head hurt and all around it was dark. Wendy guessed that the darkness was due to her eyes being squeezed tight shut, hoping above hope that the person now crunching through the snow around her wouldn't notice that she was still alive and would go away and leave her alone. The buzzing noise next to her head disappeared following a small click and the next sound was the noise of a dead body being dragged through the snow. The half-attached moustache blew about in the wind and Wendy sneezed. Damn.

Squinting through her left eye she saw a blurred red body move towards her, kneel down next to her and then she felt a hand carefully scoop the back of her neck before gently lifting her head up.

"Wendy, Wendy, are you all right?" The voice was gentle and quiet, but urgent.

Wendy gradually opened her eyes, her rapidly adapting vision revealing a person disguised as Santa Claus in front of her.

"Who are…."

Santa took the bottom of a soaked beard in his hands and pulled downwards, revealing a broad smile.

"Sachin? What on earth are you doing here, and why were you attacking me?"

The smile got even larger as the elastic pulled the beard back in place. He didn't reply, simply making her sit upright whilst looking deeply into her eyes. Behind him the man from the house was sitting unconscious, his back against the wall and with a bandage made out of an inflatable snowman wrapped around his head. Blood stains were clearly visible next to his ear, just as they were on the snow at the foot of the wall.

"Don't worry, he'll be okay. It's just a small cut, all blood and no damage. He'll have a bit of a headache when he wakes up, but he'll live."

Wendy closed her eyes again and started crying. What on earth had she been thinking.

"He seems to be here on his own at the moment, but by the looks of things he doesn't live alone. The others are probably down at the festival, so we need to get things cleared up and get out of here." Wendy had never heard the kindness in Sachin's voice before. It must have been one of hundreds of things that she had missed that week.

Composing herself she tried to stand but gave up half way as her head started spinning. She sat down again, and it was then that she noticed the other person sitting against the wall further along.

"Dot?" Her voice was a mixture of surprise and exasperation.

Dot had her false beard pulled down under her chin. Her right hand was tightly bandaged in yet more snowman and was also stained with blood. She didn't acknowledge Wendy, preferring to sit staring vacantly in front of her. What on earth had been happening that night? Wendy didn't remember making any plans when they had all been together with Brian drinking in the bar. Yes, she had been a little drunk once or twice, but not that drunk surely?

"Don't worry, Dot's alright. Not that she perhaps deserves to be, but we'll cross that bridge when we get to it. Now then Wendy, are you going to be able to get up this time?" It wasn't really a question, Sachin had already taken her hand and pulled hard.

A steadying hand supported her waist for a couple of seconds and then he left her on her own. She had felt better, but she could stand. The head and the ankle still hurt but deep down she was a tough old boot.

Leaving her and Dot to stare at each other, Sachin took the unconscious man by his arms and pulled him towards the open porch, returning alone a few grunts later.

"Right, he should survive the cold in there, at least until his wife, or whoever, comes home. In any case, we can give the ambulance service a ring when we get out of here and into the warm. So, how can we get back to your place from here Wendy, without giving ourselves away any more than we already have done?"

Wendy wanted to protest but it was inevitable that they would end up back at her house, knowing that the other two didn't even live in Webledon. In any case it was snowing again and she urgently needed warmth and wine.

"We could follow in the carol singers' tracks, our footprints would just be some more boots amongst all of the others? Or we could go back around the sports field, if you slide your feet, you don't really leave any prints." Wendy was always enthusiastic when it came to ideas. Sachin looked to be weighing them up when the deep voice of Dot cut in.

"Too dangerous. Either way we'll end up on the road into town with the risk of bumping into people coming back home, and then we'll have to walk past all of the houses on your road too. It'll be best to take the old train track, and then cut through Wendy's back garden."

The speaking appeared to have given Dot a bit more confidence, though she hadn't been particularly lacking in it when she had been screaming her battle cry whilst trying to stab Wendy in the head just a few minutes before. Wendy gave Sachin a questioning look, but his lack of concern was reassuring.

"Just follow me, it's out through the back." Dot was already getting to her feet.

Two minutes later the ladies were waiting at the top of the entrance to the old track, each carrying a packed bag. Sachin was just coming back from the house, using the coal sack in his hand to carefully clear away the footprints as he backed out towards them.

"They'll obviously know that something's been happening, and matey boy will surely remember everything, but this is the best we can do. I've left two sets of footprints out to where the carol singers were, and two more in to the sports field. Let's hope that with the snow that's falling now everything else will be covered." Sachin sounded confident, even if Wendy wasn't.

The sound of a car made Wendy look up as a set of headlights came into the close.

"Come on, let's get going. We should have at least ten minutes, by the time they find him and make him comfortable."

The ladies walked on in silence beneath a now dark sky, a mass of passing clouds covering any stars that could have guided them whilst bringing more flurries of heavy snow. Behind them walked Sachin, coal sack in hand, doing his best to disguise any tracks that they might leave behind as clues.

A scream rang out in the darkness, suggesting that the body in the porch had been found.

CHAPTER 67

Saturday 19th December, Late Evening

Wendy had heard the phrase 'walking around aimlessly' a hundred times before, but now she knew what it truly meant. She had a house full of guests that had never been invited, with nothing in common at all and who had just, hopefully, got away with the most stupid thing she had ever been involved with. There they were, the most perfect real-life triangle of victim, persecutor and saviour that she had ever seen. Or at least two of them were as Sachin was still in the back garden carefully trying to disguise their tracks in the snow. The initial euphoria of arriving back safely had been short lived, very soon being replaced by panic as the wailing siren and flashing blue lights of an emergency vehicle had sped past. At least the man wouldn't freeze to death.

"Do you take sugar?"

Wendy's voice was uncertain, the exact role in the evening's entertainment of the knife wielding granny was still unsure, as was the fact that she was an actual granny, with Dot probably only being a few years older than Wendy herself but having suffered from a larger paper round.

"Yes please, two."

Dot's voice, not often used, was still nervous and uncertain. On arriving at the house they had immediately disinfected the cut and put on a proper bandage and the hand in question was now laying still on the table next to her smartphone. Gone were the false beard, floppy hat and bright red jacket, replaced by a black sweater proudly displaying the words Yo-Ho-Ho. Wendy placed a fine porcelain sugar bowl and a spoon in the middle of the table taking her own cup in her hands and leaning back against the work surface.

The warmth of the cup was welcome, adding to the constant feeling of a great unknown being gradually lifted from her. She had been overtaken by a madness and the feeling of recovery was gradually, but surely, creeping over her. There was a long way to go yet but at that moment she felt good. It had been difficult to turn down a glass of wine, but in the end she felt better for it, as though it was the first step on a Sachin inspired healing process. The door opened and Sachin came in from outside, shaking his head and spreading snowflakes across the kitchen floor as he took off his coat and gloves to reveal frozen hands and an extremely large smile in the middle of a raw face. Wendy poured another cup, ignoring the fact that she didn't even know if he drank tea. Sachin sat down and started taking off his boots, forcing Wendy to look away as he revealed an unfortunately placed large split in a pair of old tracksuit trousers.

"Well that's that then. I've hidden our tracks as much as I can, and made some false tracks up from the corner, just as if we'd all walked back from town. All of the weapons and stuff I've pushed under the neighbours shed for now, just in case, and we'll need to find a way to get rid of those properly later. All we need to do is pretend that we're just finishing off a night out amongst friends. Have you got any board games?"

HE'S MAKING A LIST

Wendy and Dot shared confused stares, unsure how they could ever be passed off as friends finishing off an evening at the Santa festival.

"And the siren, do you know what it was?" Dot asked the question.

"I've seen an ambulance and two police cars. On the way back there were no sirens, just lights, which is normally a good sign. The snow is falling so fast now that nearly all of the tracks from earlier are covered up, so I guess that if they're out looking for three people dressed as Santa Claus tonight, the costumes have served us well."

The coats and hats were all hanging over a clothes horse in the hallway, steam rising as the warmth of the radiator started to dry them out.

"All we can do now is wait and see what happens. Dot, can you see if there is any news on the internet?"

Sachin sat down at the table and seeing an opportunity to be freed from guarding the psycho granny, Wendy wandered into the living room.

"Musico, music."

She walked in the dark towards the bay window expertly moving around the furniture and opened the curtains. The light from the street lamp lit up a road that was now a few inches deep in snow with all tracks covered. The snow buzzed around the lights and Wendy felt tired as Send in the Clowns filled the room. Was she losing her timing, late in her career?

"Come on Wendy, we're waiting for you!" Sachin's voice was as cheerful as ever.

Wendy had been lost in the music, her backside gradually drying out as she sat on the window sill whilst Musico gave her the 21st century equivalent of a mix tape. She forced herself back to the kitchen, every step bringing discomfort to bones and muscles that had already done too much that day. The bright light of the kitchen forced her to squint as she entered, finding Dot on her smartphone and Sachin seated at the head of the table with two boxes in front of him.

"I hope you don't mind, but I found these out in the garage. What do you fancy, Monopoly or Cluedo?"

Dot and Wendy sighed in unison.

"Monopoly for me, and I'll be the dog." Dot spoke freely for the first time since they had got back.

"Oh no you won't," Wendy was surprised at how eagerly she had joined in. "I threw the dog away years ago, the little feet kept making small dents in the board. Perhaps you should be the battleship, Dot?" Their eyes fixed, locked like some anti-aircraft missile on an incoming plane. A hint of a smile spread across both faces.

"Okay, I'll be the battleship. Come on Sachin, dish the money out. You must be used to all of those notes needing sorting out at the end of each day." Wendy could see that despite the bravado there was still uncertainty behind the older lady. "Oh, and I've just had a look on the internet. There are already rumours spreading around. It looks like he's been taken to hospital and they're blaming everything on a group of young lads who got thrown out of the White Hart for chucking beer around. There's already names and photos flying around, so the local vigilantes should be out looking for them already, the poor sods."

Wendy shuffled the Community Chest cards, looking directly in front of her so as to avoid meeting Dot's eyes. The game was soon set up and after a wonderful double six to decide who went first Dot got the game underway. A couple of turns of the board passed, with Dot landing on Mayfair, Wendy going to jail and Sachin getting both of the utility companies on his first round. Through the kitchen window it was clear that the snow had stopped, and there had been no knocks on the door.

"Anyway ladies, whilst we're here, exactly what have you two been up to this last week?"

CHAPTER 68

Saturday 19th December, Late Evening

Sometimes you just heard things that you wish you never had, and Sachin put the tale that had caused the three of them to be there that night firmly in that bracket. The conspiracy between a bitter old woman, a stupid younger woman and an imaginary old schoolfriend had made him shiver with fear. Could it really all be that easy? Anyway, the game of Monopoly had never been finished, the tears and cups of tea giving them little time to buy and sell houses or hotels. Do not pass go.

The ladies were now both asleep with Wendy in her big feather bed whilst Dot's small frame was cuddled up on the sofa. It would have been pointless risking the attention of the police by travelling that night so the decision to sleep over had been an easy one. Sachin moved silently around the strange, black walled room near the top of the stairs, an open bin liner wrapped over the back of the solitary chair as he went to collect another pile of paper from the floor. He knew that he shouldn't, but he couldn't help looking in detail at what was left of the assortment of photos and documents, each one ripped apart in anger. A careful anger though, almost as if the person who had done it had wanted to piece them back together again later, so preferring to shred away corners of sky rather than to destroy the happy, carefree faces. The story that was told was standard, shared by thousands of young girls all over the country, as they struggled to discover themselves whilst growing up and to find the love that they craved. He supposed that some took it better than others.

It might be considered heartless but he knew what had to be done. As silently as possible he completed the job that the initial destroyer had failed to do, each document now reduced to thin strips of unhappy memories. From the brilliant, shining eyes of the girl who had appeared in all of them it was difficult to believe that she could be so unhappy now, but some people just struggled to let things go and move on. It was something for Wendy to add to her development tree, or whatever it was called. In any case, a few hours from now the sack and its contents would be carefully hidden away in a rubbish bin somewhere in Harshton, gone forever.

The wall was pockmarked where the pins that had held the documents in place had been violently pulled out, and a bit of filler and a touch of brighter paint would do it no harm. In its centre, still attached by a bright green topped drawing pin, was the only photo that was still in one piece. A young school master looked out, proud in his cape, a look on his face proclaiming that he would change the world. It was a very old photo, a copy of a cutting from an old newspaper, a reminder no doubt of how the teacher's dreams must have also faded. His name was Denzil, Mr Frederick Denzil, and he had once lived in the house where the broken pieces of Reindeer now lay. How long ago he had moved on they didn't know. They didn't even know if he was still alive. The only thing they could agree on was that he had once been a great shot with a board rubber and that his entry in the town council almanac of 2007 had given his address as being the one that they had visited earlier that evening. It was just another reminder that you shouldn't believe everything that you read on the internet.

Sachin carefully placed the bin bag in his back pack, washed up the last of the cups and spoons and blew out the candle. He double checked that his alarm was set for the morning and gently lowered himself into the armchair, his bones relaxed and finally back to room temperature. In the background the shallow, rhythmic sound of breathing reminded him how tired he was, and he placed his hands on the arm rests.

It was impossible to have lived in this country all his life without falling in love with the time of year, even if the virgin birth wasn't really his thing, and his imagined sound of Chris Rea Driving Home for Christmas raised his spirits. There would be no driving for Sachin, though he did still have the return ticket from his bus journey to use. He wasn't even going anywhere, because this year he would be receiving guests, and having his daughter come to stay with him would surely make it the best Christmas he would ever remember. His lips formed a smile as his dreams finally took him to sleep.

CHAPTER 69

Sunday 20th December, Morning

A burning sunlight had woken Wendy, streaming through a gap in the curtains and highlighting the dust around the room as she got out of bed and wrapped herself in her thick dressing gown. She was sure her visitors were gone, avoiding the need for embarrassed looks and pointless small talk. If everything went to plan she would never see either of them again, and the last seven days would soon fade away in the memory as some sort of bad dream. At least that was what she hoped. The door to the spare room was open, a first for as long as she could remember and she strode in, heading straight for the window and tugging hard as she detached the dark black drapes that had for so long kept the light outside. A dazzling sunshine forced its way inside, its very brightness pushing Wendy backwards. The room was clean, emptied of all of its bad memories, and judging by the marks on the wall and the window sill it would need redecorating and brightening up a little bit. Outside, the blue sky looked down on a ground covered in snow, a perfect setting for a lazy Sunday morning.

Downstairs was also tidy, the cushions ruffled and all

of the stuff from the kitchen washed, dried and neatly put away. That was what Wendy had spent all night doing, tidying away the horrors of the story that Dot had told her and the sad memories that she had been religiously keeping alive from her past. But they were gone now she was sure, packed away at the back of a cupboard certain in the knowledge that they would never be called on again.

In the middle of her kitchen table stood her brand-new candlestick, the smell of the burned wick and the molten wax still heavy in the air. Propped up against the base was a small card with a treasure chest on it above a hand written note.

'Wendy, wishing you a very Merry Christmas. Sachin and Dot.'

She turned the card to find that she had won second prize in a beauty contest and that she should collect ten pounds. Unsure whether to laugh or cry she did neither, preferring instead to put on the kettle and take out her favourite tea pot and one of her best china cups. Seated at the table she felt different. Not in a way that she could describe to anyone, but she knew that the Wendy that had woken the day before didn't exist anymore, and that the one sat at the table was made up of all of the good parts of the old one, having left the bad parts in the snow the night before. The candlestick in front of her would be the testament to that, a permanent reminder to her of the need to keep the darkness out of her life.

She stood and went to the cupboard under the stairs, returning a few minutes later with an old box full of Christmas decorations. Not trusting Musico to meet her mood she sang to herself as she stuck tinsel to doors and stars to windows, as she placed Christmas cards on windowsills and put sprigs of plastic holly on tabletops. Stay by my side, until morning is nigh, she sang, the simplest of songs that meant the most to her. Once it was all done she tidied the box away and then she took her phone and pressed the button.

"Yeah, hi there Mum, it's Wendy. Listen, I don't want to impose on you, but would you have a spare place if I came over for dinner? You would? Great, see you later."

ABOUT THE AUTHOR

Paul Bullimore grew up in Leicestershire and now lives in France with his long-suffering wife and three children. Travelling a lot with his job gives him lots of time for reading and writing.

Having been rarely seen on a musical stage, he did spend some time in orchestra pits, and this helped understand some of Wendy's underlying character, as do the many happy hours he spends beside flipcharts, marker in hand, with his clients today.

Writing about Wendy was fun. Who knows, we may see her again sometime soon…